To' Michelle

⭐

thank you.
I hope you Snjoy ...

I love you Both

Jaye

♡

Burgess Bartlett.

About the Author

Burgess Bartlett

Yes, I understand, this story is literally unbelievable. I've posted on YouTube and JayBirdPartners.com, (the publisher's website), pictures and videos of my journey and even testimonials from those who have witnessed these incredibly implausible events.

Some of you will still choose not to believe, but for those who see truth and follow… your life will never be the same.

If enough of you follow, the world will never be the same.

I'm not a writer. I'm an accountant with a thriving practice, who came upon an incredible, compelling story. I see clearly now, I didn't find this story, this story found me. I'm merely a conduit of Love, Truth, Freedom and Thankfulness.

We all are.

Joyce and her daughter, Elizabeth 'the Kind-Hearted', work together in their accounting practice in south Jersey, while her youngest daughter, 'Brooke', (shown here) continues graduate studies in California near San Francisco.

Dedicated to

Elizabeth the Kind-Hearted

The last 'witch' burned to death in Ireland.
Tipperary County, Thomastown Castle
August 31, 1831

Be still and peace to your kind-hearted soul,
For here-in your untold will unfold.
A beacon for us all to follow
A map to shed values that are hollow
A second prayer, I beg you pray.
Forgive the Mathews curse away.
For all of Wicca, a price has paid.

In loving memory of Bruce, my brother.

Inspiring me, from his 'thinking chair', and beyond.
Urging me every day to 'finish'.

"You Can Do
This, Darlin'"

Finish!

For you, Dad

Edward Sisson Burgess, 'Big Ed' (1914-2007)

As an early pioneer in sophisticated electronics, he worked on top secret radar projects for the U.S. Navy during WWII, later leading the revolution in telecommunication technology in the 40's 50's, 60's and 70's, gracing the cover of science magazines, including FM-TV. His 1959 patented coaxial cable switch design is still used today. While working for Link Radio he invented and held numerous patents for two-way communications inventions. While working for electronics giant ITT Communications, he was in charge of the design, advancements, and maintenance of the giant communication towers. Big Ed was known, throughout his life as an earthy intellectual.

Aside from his brilliant and accomplished career at the cutting edge of electronics engineering, he was an avid and wily tennis player and prolific poet. He is most known for his spontaneous sense of humor, never without an insightful poem or ridiculous pun. He was the kindest, most gentle father, with whom any daughter could be blessed. A True Gentleman.

This is for you, Dad

To: Cheryl,

Thank you,

To the artist who rescued me from calculating my way through life, then securely placed me on a humble path of service.

She enlightened me, then when I was ready, LiFTed me. The muse who told me to think bigger, who graciously forgave my trespasses, and then inspired me more.

A woman who listens ten times more than she's heard.

When, near the end, I didn't know where this tale was going, whispered, 'Walk in their shoes. The end of your novel will present itself'.

Almost impossibly, more beautiful inside than out. Cheryl

To: Colette, my editor

From the Firm, Serial Writer Productions

With your expansive, innocent smile, you so delicately pointed out my errors. For that, I can't thank you enough.

When it rained, your smile was my umbrella.

You are a cherished friend.

To: All Writers.

As a first time author, I thoroughly enjoyed working with Colette and Serial Writer Productions.

From the beginning of this project, Colette came with meticulous editing expertise and tender criticism skills but more valuable was the energy she brought, encouraging me to continue. She developed an affection for my book and the message I wanted to convey.

There is no substitute for an editor who loves the writing process and in love with your project.

Without reservation, I recommend Colette and Serial Writer Productions.

Burgess Bartlett

No man is an island and I'm no exception.

Thank you to everyone. I know I'm not easy.

Dan; Thank you for sharing your family story, your views on Life, and finally for giving me permission to use you and your family history as a backdrop for this novel. Ultimately, it is YOUR story telling gift that inspired me to travel Europe in search of this full, true story. For that alone, I am forever in your debt. This is not just your story, but your message I publish in these pages.

To my Elizabeth, the Kind-Hearted. Thank you for teaching me grace, tolerance, forgiveness... and all the rest of the qualities I would have never learned without you.

To my youngest daughter, Jaimie, C'est quand qu'on va ou? When are we going and where?

To my cherished friend, Robin, who laughed with me through the south of France, patiently listening to me telling this 'story' over and over.

To my 'coach', Karl, who 'took one for the team' and literally saved my life more than once throughout our trip to Ireland and beyond.

Finally, to my blessed friend Patrice, who, not only witnessed that thirty months in my life when dimes were all around me, like necklaces at the Mardi Gras, but who is also a disciple of the universe, and continues to find dimes of her own to this day.

Published by: Jay Bird Partners, LLC
'Because a little birdie told me'
JayBirdPartners.com

ISBN: 978-1-7334813-0-4

Printed in the United States of America, this first printing, September 2019

Most Characters in this account are real, although I have changed their names. Completely true and correct are the facts surrounding historical events and characters, Father Marcilio Ficino, Nostradamus, The history and development of Free Masonry membership, Invisible College, The Thomastown Mathew's Family, especially Father Mathew, the Apostil of Temperance. The story of my adventure and quest for truth is real although I have taken literary license regarding the time line.

Credits:

Photography front cover is a selfie by: Elizabeth Bartlett

Photography front cover and many of the pictures depicted in the 'slideshow' on YouTube: Karl G.

Photography: Many of the photos and videos on YouTube by the author, Burgess Bartlett

Cover design: A special thank you for all your hours of design, (and redesign), expertise and all your years of friendship. Accompanying me through a grueling 12 minutes, 12 laps, forty plus years to present:

Susan Heally V.

My treasured Rutherford High School friend.

Advertising video 'Tommy' Marcinek.

Chapters

This book was written to expose the circumstances surrounding the last 'witch' put to death in Ireland and to show that anything is possible if you hold onto your loving heart.

August 31, 1831

County of Tipperary, Thomastown Castle, the seat of the Mathews Family.

Elizabeth the Kind-Hearted

Be still and peace to your kind-hearted soul,
For here-in your untold will unfold.
A beacon for us all to follow.
A map to shed our values that are hollow.
A second prayer, I beg you pray.
Forgive the Mathews curse away.
For all of Wicca, a price has paid.

Currently, my entire eight-foot dining room wall is corked and pinned with notes, timelines and pictures. My desk no longer has stacks of client files but research books. This is the unbelievable but true story of a once prestigious, titled Irish family; their lavish Irish castle, winter home in the south of France, a tragic accidental death of an innocent toddler, accusations of witchcraft, and murder, all against a backdrop of addiction and deception (which always go together).

It all started in… N.J., Newark Airport Bar.

Chapter 1
Joyous Adventurers have Joyous Adventurers

"Yes, gin and tonic. Thank you," I hate flying. "Make it a double."

Boarding begins in one hour. Plenty of time to medicate myself into a gin coma. I'm praying for sleep through the six-hour flight plus six hour time difference: 9:30 PM Newark to arrive 9:30 AM, London time.

I order another, even before I finish this first. As I drink, my shoulders begin to relax. l think about how proud I am that my daughter is finishing her graduate studies at Oxford, and further blessed, maybe more so, that she wants me to visit. Then alternately, I wonder what it will feel like to crash into the icy November water of the Atlantic.

Struck by fear "Oh help me." I mutter to no one in-particular. To grab the bartender's attention I raise this second empty glass. I need one more. "Double." I say, just in case he's forgotten.

The wall in front of me is a giant rain splattered window. The planes are jockeying around in this stormy night. I pull my focus in, onto the rain drops landing on the window and unexpectedly I see myself. With this dark stormy night behind it, the giant window acts as a mirror. All I see is a middle aged woman, drinking alone in a bar. I really have to change my focus. I'm a traveler waiting for an international flight with three weeks of adventure ahead of me.

Brooke likes to say 'only joyful adventurers have joyful adventures'. My youngest. My perpetually joyful Brooke. Everyone is her friend, attracted to her buoyant energy, 'I can fix it' attitude, fierce protective instincts, and, I'm most proud... of her true ethical compass.

From the second row, life seems so easy for her, but close family knows the one, two, three punch of her middle school years. Beginning with our dog, Samantha, her best buddy, dying of bladder cancer. Then a 'no one saw it coming' divorce. Finally, and maybe most challenging, a diagnosis of severe scoliosis which required her to wear a brace sixteen hours every day for almost three years. Brooke met each with a gracious smile and refocused on academics and athletics. While I was preoccupied with a toxic divorce, she became a self-disciplined, independent force.

I'm her loving mother, but I'm not blind. She's not a one-dimensional 'Hallmark' character. She is brutally honest when 'calling out' the lies we tell ourselves. Brutal and especially embarrassing, is finding out we're all so transparent to such a young analyst. "The other side of Love is Truth, Mom" doesn't help. Her undergrad studies in Psychology were the perfect pairing to her natural talents of seeing the lies we tell ourselves, but makes her criticisms much more lethal. She's just 20. (Yes she graduated High School a year early and undergrad in just three years.) She's not had time to temper her criticisms with the warm affection that I pray will come with maturity. Brooke, like still waters, will reflect the true self of those with whom she engages... at times, brutally.

'Your mission is to hasten your patient's healing.' I warn her often. 'Raw brutal truth may build more walls.'

The crackle of the speaker above me breaks into my thoughts of Brooke. "Boarding for Heathrow."

Before I down this last mouthful of gin, I 'cheer' that middle aged lady in the mirror and mumble to myself, *'I'm NOT going to NOT get on that plane.'* Decision. Made.

While hanging onto my nerve with both hands, I call for the bill and focus on gathering my bags, coat, and purse. I pray for sleep to come quickly. Is it possible to sleep through take off? I have three double gin and tonics working on that question.

There on the floor, under my barstool, I find a dime. Another, in a series of dimes I've found in the last thirty months. One month I accumulated over thirty dimes.

All my life, math has been my aptitude. I see the probability of cause and effect, constantly calculating the trajectory of the 'moving parts' around me. I'm a fifty-five-year-old accountant, dealing in numbers every day. So finding an average of twenty dimes a month for the last thirty months, I know for a fact, is way out of the spectrum of possible. No pennies, no nickels or quarters. Just dimes… Curiouser and Curiouser.

Once I'm tucked into my window seat, blessed sleep begins to take me. I wonder what adventures my daughter has in store for us. I remember her high school graduation cap decorated with the phrase, 'Not all those who wander are lost,' a line from JRR Tolkien, who, coincidentally, is a graduate of Oxford as well. Funny. In the last twinkle of consciousness before deep sleep, I make this connection for the first time.

Heathrow Airport, London, England.

I wake hard. My dreams were disturbing, brought on, no doubt, by mixing alcohol and fear. (Always a bad elixir). I quickly claim my bags, get through customs, and head out to find Brooke.

I spot her instantly. She's tall and beautiful, but that's not what makes her easy to pick out in a crowd. It's her smile; broad, honest and right from a soul that has nothing to hide. Her long, curly blonde hair with honey brown highlights surrounds her, and always looks as if it's in motion.

"Brooke!" I raise my hand "Here."

"Mom!" It's almost a squeal. She hugs me an unusually long time. I get to smell her hair, still a bit wet from this morning's shower. "How was your flight? Did you get to sleep much?" Brooke asks, knowing my fear of flying.

"Flight was good, I slept through it. Thank you, sweetie." As I hand the larger bag to her, "What's on the agenda first? Breakfast in London?" I say, while really wanting to dump these bags. Six hours sleep is not enough for me.

"Let's get rid of these bags at your BNB. We'll come back to London this weekend." Brooke says.

"You read my mind." I say with a nod, showing her my relief, before she leads me to the bus that will take us to Oxford and our fantastic adventure.

The bus lumbers out of London and through the English country side toward Oxford, the heart of English literature, where the best storytellers in history have gone to learn and to teach.

Fitting, this is where I'll hear a story so intoxicating, it will consume me until my only comfort is to publish it here, in these next pages.

Chapter 2

Oxford, England

Beren meets us at the door. "Hello. You must be Joyce."
Surprised by his English accent, my smile gets even bigger. "Yes, hello. I'm so glad to finally meet you. This is my daughter, Brooke." I say, I feel as if I am being welcomed by all of England to the first moments of my adventure.

Beatrix comes into the foyer to extend her hand which is speckled in paint, as is her oversized men's tailored white shirt. She has a loving, crooked smile with wild black hair and her eyes... Green maybe. They seem to be changing as her gaze settles on mine. The entranceway is dark, so it's hard to tell. Behind the color, whatever it is, she has something extra I have seen only rarely. Subconsciously, I tilt my head and furrow my brow as most people do, when trying to figure out a puzzle. I'm feeling silly and wonder if the color changes with her disposition, like a mood ring.

"Beren will take your bags to your room." Beatrix says. I think she misreads my quizzical look as *'What should I do next?'* "Please take your time unpacking. Get settled and when you come down, we'll show you 'round the house and discuss the breakfast routine."

I rented a private room through Airbnb.com from Bea and Beren. Sounds like a little girl's jump rope rhyme and conveniently makes it easy for me to remember their names. I chose, not on the name of the owners, but whichever rental was closest to Brooke's dorm. I had no requirements other than that, and no expectations. But still, Bea and Beren owning a BNB is very cute.

Beren is a tall, sixty-something. He grunts, trying to pick up my giant bag. I apologize and offer to help.

"Nope, this is my job," Beren says, and up the narrow, winding staircase we go.

He is a sculptor. His wife, Beatrix, is forty-something, a painter. The Airbnb website says they currently own and operate this bed and breakfast, but for the last twenty years, they ran a big 'residential artesian center' in the south of France. I wonder why they would leave a life that seemed to me, the perfect 'end game' life choice.

Up on the second floor, I notice all the bedroom doors are open.

"This one is our bedroom. If you have any problems, day or night, don't hesitate to knock." Still struggling with my bag he heads around to the next flight of stairs. Up we go to the third floor, and again, all the bedroom doors are open. Odd.

"Am I the only guest?" I ask.

"Just until the weekend. They start arriving Friday night. We'll have an almost full house next week. We've put you on the fourth floor. It's really the attic. It's the most private, just one room up here and you have your own bath," Beren says, trying politely to hide his huffing and puffing. He opens the door to what will be my room for the next three weeks. With a final huff, (and obviously glad to be free of my bag), Beren says, "Meet Dammie. This is his favorite room. So, if you don't like cats, just keep your door closed."

"Why hello, Donnie." I smile, trying to hide my distaste for cats. I make a mental note, 'Keep door closed.' I've always hated cats. They are usually flea and/or tick-ridden and so unpredictable. Black cats especially are associated with bad luck... Halloween... riding on broomsticks... I'm sure the AirBNB website said nothing about cats. His black hair on this white comforter is particularly distasteful. Yes, I will be keeping my door closed.

"Mom. I think he said, Dommie. Like Dominick, not Donnie." Brooke loves to correct me. She's twenty.

Beren politely corrects us both, "Actually, it's Dammie, short for Nostradamus. My wife's Cat. He's been around for a very long time."

"How old is he?" I pretend to be interested.

"I don't know. Bea and he found each other when he was already an adult."

"How long ago was that?" I'm always trying to calculate and quantify everything. A very annoying quality, I've been told, (by Brooke).

"We stopped counting. Anyway, take your time. Come down when you're ready. We'll show you 'round the kitchen. Out Dammie! Let's leave them to unpack."

Dammie looks uninterested to move.

My irritation that Beren was not demanding enough to require Dammie to get out is interrupted as I move further into the room, turn, and... Breathtaking! There is a large bay window, flanked by two single windows. My new view is down a steep hill, overlooking the city center of Oxford.

"Brilliant!" As they say in England. From atop this attic room I can see rows of brick chimney stacks lining each steep street all the way down the hill. "I need to take a picture of this." But my phone is off to avoid international roaming charges.

"Brooke, please fix my phone so I can use it here," I ask as I hand my phone to Brooke.

"You didn't have to turn it off, Mom." Ahh sweet, Brooke. Condescending as usual.

"Please, just fix it, so I can keep it on to take pictures without getting charged international fees. Also, can you set it to hook up to the internet here automatically?"

"You'll need a Wi-Fi password. Look around. I'm pretty sure they have it listed in each room."

"Yes, I'll look 'round" I say, in a silly English accent. I see an old trunk. It's set like a tea cart, with a white electric hot water pot, a small white porcelain bowl of tea bags and natural sugar sticks. There are snacks of Guinness Thick Cut Chips, Walkers salt and vinegar, and Jaffa Cakes, (whatever they are) and, God bless my landlords, McVitie's Penguin Biscuits which are in the Chocolate food group. Sooo England. I find also a card:

Wi-Fi name; 'Ferguson BNB'

User Name; 'attic'

Password; 'Nostradamus'

There it is again.

Brooke hands me back my phone. I take a picture out my window and make a note into my 'reminders' app to Google Nostradamus, 'when I get back here tonight.'

As I unpack we talk about her dorm mates, where she's traveled with them, where she wants to travel and the adventures she's planning for us.

I love her. Much more than beautiful, her spirit is free, buoyant and seems to find nothing difficult. Yes, she 'wanders but is never lost.' I could stay and catch up for hours more, but I'm sure my new landlords, Beatrix and Beren are waiting for us so they can show me 'round the house.

Even through my exhaustion, Brooke's excitement that I am finally here is contagious. Coupled with the whole 'we're in England!' thing, we can't help but canter down the three flights of twirling stairs. It feels like a ride. A bit breathless and giggling loudly, we land hard in the foyer and make our way to the back of the house, down two steps to meet Beren in the kitchen.

"Ah. You've found us in the kitchen. Brilliant." Beren says.

Again, his accent surprises me. *Yes, Joyce. Everyone here in England will most likely have an English Accent.* Again, I react with a big smile and a bit of a smirk at my own stupidity. My attention is immediately drawn to the back of the kitchen, where extra-wide French doors frame a big, sloping backyard, filled with flowering plants, a vegetable garden and an old shed, which is perfectly decrepit. The roof is a bit moss covered just to top off the picture-perfect effect.

Beatrix enters the kitchen and is speckled with even more paint than earlier. In this bright kitchen her eyes are even more intriguing. They're light blue, but then, dark grey.

"You'll need these to get in tonight." She hands me the keys.

It's awkward to have eye contact too long, so I'm thankful I have elsewhere to direct my attention. I take the keys, "Thank you." And notice the paint on her hands and oversized, white, men's tailored shirt is all light sage green. She's obviously painting the porch, not painting a portrait.

"Now, I think your emails said you usually eat oatmeal for breakfast. I'm not sure what that is. Did you mean porridge?" Beatrix holds up a container that looks like oatmeal.

This is getting even better. I'm in England and have just learned that oatmeal, (my favorite breakfast), is called porridge!

"Perfect," I say, and I mean it. This whole thing is just perfect.

Beren shows me where the coffee is kept and introduces me to the giant, red, antique, coffee-bean grinder. Yes, I will have fresh ground coffee tomorrow morning from a giant, red, antique, coffee-bean grinder! I can't wait to use this thing.

"There are other guests coming this weekend, most of them American, for some reason." Beren said.

"Yes." Brooke takes over. "Next week is the US's Thanksgiving week. The students from the US were told that if our parents were scheduling a visit, this week of Thanksgiving would be best. The University is throwing a party, of sorts, in one of the cafeterias on that Thursday, of Thanksgiving, so we could all meet and mingle. Mom's here a little early." She smiles broadly. "I have a full agenda for us."

And there she is. My youngest child, all grown up. Brooke is more than capable of leading the conversation. I don't have to answer for us or lead for us anymore. I've done no planning because I'm confident she'll have all the details necessary and correctly choose all the rights and the lefts. I feel free of the burden of Mommy responsibility. Sweet freedom.

Now divorced, I truly can focus on me and my future without guilt. Brooke will take care of Brooke. She has always wanted to '…do it myself, Mommy,' since before she could speak. But now she actually can. It's so easy to let her go when I know she's making all the right choices. She always has, but now she can stand on her own as an adult. Yes, I am her mother. I am so proud. That is not surprising. What is surprising me now is the great relief I feel, the feeling that I've been released from the bondage of Mommyhood. Honestly, I hadn't known I felt so 'oppressed' in the first place, until recently feeling the sudden and great relief of being 'unrestricted.'

Liz, my oldest, on the other hand, is very different from Brooke.

Four years older, Liz reacts with all her heart. We dubbed her 'Elizabeth, The Kind-Hearted' when she was just a toddler. Evident even then, that her pure heart would have a hard time trying to understand all us common folk who have egos that tempt us to lie, steal and cheat; Faults that will inevitably lead us to pain and regret. Fear. Anger. Greed. Liz understands nothing of these emotions that darken the hearts of everyone to some extent. She does feel deeply, too deeply, the grief and misery of those around her.

Liz's innocence looks, at first, like a lack of maturity, but you soon realize just the opposite. She's way too advanced for us all. She's a timeless soul from the future and the past. She is so full of love and alternately so full of the pain that all true empaths feel.

It's my knowledge and understanding of Liz that brings me to solve this family's mysterious two-hundred-year-old puzzle as yet unsolved. But this is a discussion for another chapter.

"He likes you." Beatrix says, bringing me out of my thoughts of Liz.

Beren agrees, "He really likes no one, not even me."

They're looking down at Dammie. The Cat is standing on my left foot, staring out the window with me. "It's a beautiful backyard. Are you allowed to go outside, Dammie?"

"Once in a while he goes out with me, if I'm gardening, but not often," Beatrix answers for him.

"When Bea goes into the garden at night, Dammie always goes with her. We have a fire pit way down at the far end of the yard. Dammie never misses a chance for that. All these years, he hasn't taken to me. A real Grimalkin." Beren adds.

"Grimalkin? What's that?" I say.

Beren answers, "Literally a Gray Cat, but alternately can mean a spiteful old woman."

"Beren has taken some literary license. Dammie is obviously neither grey nor female." Bea says, as she answers me but looks directly at Beren. Obviously a conversation they've had before.

Maybe I will not hate this Cat. But, I will keep my door closed.

Looking down and speaking to Dammie, in an apology for moving my foot, "Well, off we go. Brooke wants to show me around campus and through her dorm before dark. Don't wait up." *I hope this cat is going to stay away from me.* Then switching focus to Bea & Beren, "OK, I'll see you at breakfast."

Brooke and I take a while to bundle up; coat, scarf, hat, gloves, and I check to be sure I have my purse, sunglasses, phone, charger, and finally, the key.

Instinctively knowing my new landlords are still there, watching until we get safely out the door, I turn and hold up my key. "I have the key. Don't wait up."

The three of them are standing at the kitchen end of the hall, backlit by the bright light coming from the big French doors. Beren, Beatrix, and Nostradamus are not one big dark blob, but three very separate and distinct figures. I choose to ignore the glint coming from the eyes of Beatrix and Dammie.

Once outside, Brooke walks me ragged, past beautiful, centuries-old stone and ivy academic buildings, dorms, introductions to dormmates then a parade to catch the bus into Oxford Center, for dinner, to the famous Eagle and Child.

The jet lag is catching me but all these twenty-somethings are keeping my adrenaline going. They tell me the Eagle and Child is best known as the 20th-century meeting place for a group of literary artists, which included C.S. Lewis, and J.R.R Tolkien; both prolific writers best known for The Chronicles of Narnia and The Hobbit. Both books in my bookcases at home, and both books I have read more than once.

I hang in there until they're ready to go. While the kids find a cab that is big enough for us all, I duck into a liquor store for a couple bottles of wine for my room.

During the cab ride, Brooke and I make a plan to meet tomorrow, though thankfully, not until lunch. Brooke has morning classes and I need to acclimate to this six-hour time change.

Back in my room, I'm over-tired but find myself lying in bed with eyes wide open. The clock says 11:11 PM. I realize that in New Jersey it's only 5:11 PM. On that note, I get out of bed and go to the desk that's almost as long as the entire window. The cloud cover makes for a very dark night. I look down into the yard. No fire in the fire pit tonight.

Which reminds me... I turn to check the door. Thankfully, I remembered to close the door, blockading myself from the Cat.

I turn my attention back to this enormous desk. If I put the comforter on the desk and a pillow, I bet I could sleep right here, under the stars. Next time there's no cloud cover, I may do that.

Tonight, however, I sit at the desk where my laptop is already open. I turn it on and uncork a bottle of red wine. My reminder pops up, 'Google Nostradamus'.

All I know is he was an astrologer who claimed to see into the future. At the end of his life, he published hundreds of disjunctive four-line prophesies. I have heard that one of his prophecies foretold the rise of Hitler. Nostradamus called him, Hisler. I am sure there is more to this story.

I research for hours until I notice that sleep is just seconds away. When I finally slip into bed, my dreams take me instantly into Nostradamus' world; Deep into sixteenth-century France.

I'm rocking and hugging my five-year-old grandson with the pure love that every grandmother knows. I feel the vulnerability of his innocence. This world can be so unjust.

My grandson, just like my daughter, Liz, has blonde hair and blue eyes.

I move to kiss him on the top of his head and find

...this child has dark hair.

He is crying. Distraught.

I see tears coming from the dark eyes... of... young Michael Nostradamus.

My heart breaks as Michael, calling me Mommy, tells me of his best friend, who's showing early signs of the plague.

I begin to weep as well. I'm afraid for my family. The plague will ultimately take half of his friends in a cruel and ugly death.

My children have seen the fever, coughing, nausea, and then vomiting blood. In the end, like zombies, fingers, toes, and noses blacken and die, falling off while the host body keeps living, weeks longer.

I'm distraught with worry, thinking selfishly of my own family...

..my own children. Even if they escape the plague, what will the sight of all this death do to them? I thank God I have my husband and father to lean on.

As is the custom, my father, a physician with a specialty in pharmacy, is in charge of my children's education. Yes, I'm sure my father will talk to Michael, and make these awful sights better. My father has always known how to comfort me.

I whisper into Michael's ear, "Go to your grandpa. Ask him your questions." I don't want him to know I am even more upset than he.

My shawl, which I've wrapped too tightly around me, and this rocker, are both feeble imitations of comfort. I'm raising my family in a doubly dark time in France, early 1500's. Not only is the plague in full bloom, but also, the quest of Catholic leaders: to seek out and persecute anyone who doesn't agree with the church's beliefs, are both invasive and demeaning.

We are Jews.

Because this is a time of religious intolerance and deep prejudice, my father decided to publically convert to Catholicism to avoid the abuses of the Catholic Church. He insisted on taking Christian names and baptizing all nine of my children, including Michael.

We have seen many of our Jewish friends jailed, publicly abused or worse, hung or burned.

As I watch my father consoling Michael, it's obvious he is my father's favorite, not because Michael is, like him, smart and headstrong, but because of Michael's thirst for knowledge. My father is teaching him Greek, Latin, even Hebrew and of course his specialty, the properties of plants, herbs and teas that are used as medicine. Our home, both inside and out, is filled with hundreds of different varieties of plants. My father, with my children at his side, tend to these plants with much care. My father's lessons in medicine include ideas of the benefit of sunshine, fresh air, healthy eating, washing often, and medicines; all of which go against the Church's beliefs. We have so much to fear.

The Catholics run all the Universities in France to be sure no one teaches anything that conflicts with ideas the Catholic Church believes to be true. I've seen many, here in this town, who dare to practice medicine against the ideals of the Catholic teachings. They are accused of practicing witchcraft, imprisoned, tortured and, at times, even burned to death.

Our friends.

Our neighbors.

Our family.

We are all seething with anger and frustration; fueled by our helplessness.

We have chosen to suffer in silence and practice our beliefs only in the shadows. I pray we all continue to elude both the plague and the Catholic Court of Inquisition.

I'm tenderly aware that my father is encouraging Michael to be curious and take nothing as fact until proven. I'm both proud and heartbroken, for this makes Michael destined for a frustrating and dangerous life ahead. My father assures me that Michael is smart enough to avoid persecution. I am not convinced and therefore, I'm increasingly distraught.

These strong feelings of fear and frustration are still with me as I wake. I'm sweaty. My chest is tight. My head is fuzzy, as is my tongue from the bottle of red wine. My eyes open, but I don't move. The kitchen, and coffee seem so far away.

Note to self: Next adventure, rent at a BNB with a coffee maker in the room.

My teeth need brushing too, but I still don't move.

Something moves next to me and I bolt out of bed. The Cat stares at me from my pillow. My focus jumps to the door. Closed. How?

Still dizzy, my heart starts to ease back into a normal rhythm.

"My pillow? Really?" I know this Cat understands me.

On the way to the bathroom, I open the door that leads to the hall and in a hushed whisper, but still harshly, I demand, "Nostradamus. OUT!"

Dammie slowly stretches one paw out, then the other. Apparently, Dammie is just waking as well. He settles his head back on my pillow while staring me square in the eyes to tell me, this is his bed, not mine and he will move only when he's ready.

Creepy.

I continue to the bathroom.

I really don't like cats.

Chapter 3

The Alphabet Girls

After my teeth, (and tongue) are brushed, I look in the full-length mirror and wonder; *What IS the appropriate dress for breakfast at an English BNB?*

I decide to follow Bea's lead, an oversized, white men's-tailored shirt with black yoga pants.

My head is still a bit fuzzy from the red wine as I begin my slow maneuvers down the winding stairs, holding tightly onto the railing.

Where is that Cat?

I U-turn and go back to shut my door. He's not on the bed. I close the door, shaking the knob hard to be sure it's really closed and latched this time. If Dammie is trapped in there until I get back, maybe he'll hesitate to domicile himself in my room next time.

I hate cats.

Beren is in the kitchen installing new hardware on the cabinets.

"Good morning." I resist the temptation to say 'Top of the morning, Gov'ner,' and head directly to the coffee already brewing and filling the kitchen with delightful java smell.

"How was your first day in Oxford?" Beren has a very easy way about him.

"Wonderful. I'm looking forward to seeing the Botanical Gardens today. Brooke says she held off going, until I got here."

Beatrix comes around the corner from the side porch. She is holding a paint brush. Not the type to paint a portrait, but to paint the porch. I'm guessing they just bought this place and are still putting on the final touches.

"We've got year-round passes for both Botanical Gardens and the Ashmolean Museum if you'd like to use them. Our pictures are on the passes, but no one checks." She hesitates, "You may find that November is not the time of year to see the best of the Botanical Gardens." Beatrix says gingerly not wanting to put a damper on my choices of the day.

"They both sound fun. Yes, I'd love to bring the passes with us, just in case. Thank you. So, do you guys have any boarders coming today?" I say, noticing I'm still their only guest.

"Just my cousin, Dan. He's coming late tonight. He's flying in from Portugal." I'm glad Beren is back in the conversation. Beatrix makes me nervous.

"Cool! Portugal? What does he do there?" I say, wondering how old he is and if he's single.

Beatrix and Beren give each other an uncomfortable glance.

"Well… My cousin," Beren hesitates, searching for the right words, "had a problem." Hesitation again. "He is clean now, and has been for many, many years, but as a teen, he had a heroin addiction. Now he lives in Portugal, on someone else's property, living out of his car. From what I've heard he has a garden and lives off the land. Not my choice but I also hear he has a bloody spectacular view of the sea."

"Interesting." I leave it there.

Great, a single guy coming to the BNB and he's an ex-heroin addict. I change the subject, "How are the two of you related?"

"My mother and Dan's father are brother and sister," Beren said, obviously distracted by painful family issues. "My uncle, Dan's father is having open heart surgery here at Oxford Medical. Dan and the whole family are flying in."

"I'm so sorry about your Uncle. I'm guessing Oxford Medical will be a great place for him. Are they all staying here?"

"Yes, Oxford medical is one of the best in the world. And no," Beren says, obviously pained, "just Dan and his brother will be staying here. My Aunt and Dan's sister will be staying elsewhere."

I look down, stirring my oatmeal, leaving him to his thoughts. I'm not going down that uncomfortable conversational road with these people, who I met only yesterday.

Beatrix fills what is becoming an awkward silence. "Dan is quite an interesting individual. You'll enjoy meeting him. He has some interesting ideas about life and very colorful stories."

Turns out, that may have been the understatement of the last two hundred years...

With only an hour before I need to meet Brooke, I hurry to shower and find clothes appropriate for walking this especially frigid Oxford November.

Beren's coffee was very strong, but clearly not enough to shake this tired feeling. Last night's dreams were not restful, but instead, filled with fear and frustration. Back upstairs, the bed is calling me, but I take a deep breath and head for the bathroom to shower, where I notice there's no shower, just a tub.

All righty, then. I guess I'm taking a bath.

I'm tired and still a bit fuzzy, but I focus on getting ready.

Soon I'm dressed and all packed up, bundling coat, scarf, gloves, purse, sunglasses, phone and key.

As I get to the bus stop, both Brooke and the bus arrive together. We take the short ride into town center, which is just a couple blocks away from the Botanical Gardens. Beatrix was right. Most of the exhibits are… well, they're dead except for this winter's main event which is a beautiful Christmas tree, decorated with ornaments, made entirely from nature. Dried orange slices, decorated with clove, pine cones drizzled with sugar which present as snow, pea pods hung with gold ribbons, tiny wreaths made of thin vines and decorated with dried red cranberries. My favorite, circles of dried, bright silver leaves, with a center of red, heart-shaped blossoms.

I compare this tree and it's graceful, understated natural ornaments, with my annual evergreen, adorned with white lights and a couple dozen red and green balls.

Mine is so obviously, distastefully, commercial.

I make a mental note: Schedule a night for Liz and the boys to come over and make hand-crafted ornaments. I take pictures of each ornament so I can remember how to make them.

Brooke and I explore the greenhouse next, where rare plants and birds are living on display. I walk slowly, stopping at the descriptions and sometimes the medicinal uses of each group of plants, reminding me of my vivid dreams. I wonder why Beatrix became so interested in Nostradamus. Where did Nostradamus live in relation to that art center they ran?

My thoughts are interrupted. Brooke is ready to move onto the next adventure; the Ashmolean Museum.

The walk to the Ashmolean was very short but very cold. As we enter, my attention is not first on the display of items, but on the dozens of patrons sitting and sketching these exhibits. There is one corner where an entire class of students are sitting on the floor, sketching the same bunch of African masks.

Pointing to another group of a dozen or so school kids sketching, I whisper to Brooke, "So cool."

"I'm glad you think so. The Ashmolean is known for some really strange collections." Brooke hands me a sketching pencil and drags from her purse two small pads.

"Brilliant," I whisper in the best English accent I can muster.

Brooke rolls her eyes and leads me to a display of several model sailing ships.

"I'm going to sketch this one. I'll be here for a while."

"Of course." I acknowledge her passion for anything having to do with sailing. Naming her after a sign of water was a last minute inspiration and turns out to be one-hundred-percent on-point.

Stopping in front of a painting of Elias Ashmole I shake my head. I've watched "Hoarders" on TV. This guy is just a hoarder from the 1600's with lots of money who built himself a museum.
I read the inscription. Apparently, Elias has lots of interests including astrology, astronomy, botany, alchemy and other natural sciences. I guess he would have gotten along with Nostradamus except that Elias was born 100 years later. Another plaque says he was a founding member of the Oxford 'Royal Society' and the Freemasons, who both 'believed in experimental science, although his interests spread to the mystical' the plaque says.
Mystical? Cool. Again, I wonder where Nostradamus grew up, and/or went to college in relation to Bea and Beren's art center.
I continue exploring this crazy place. Nothing makes sense. There's no theme to this museum, just hordes of various, disjunctive items. I lose interest quickly and use food to entice Brooke to get out of here and onto the streets, in search of a place to finally sit, eat and relax. My dreams have been disturbing. I'm exhausted.

Finally sitting at lunch, still feeling the effects of the time change and my disquieting dreams, needing desperately a day of sun on my face, I ask Brooke, "Have you seen the weather forecast? What do our next couple of days look like? I'm needing a good solid day of sun."

Brooke informs me in her best, condescending tone, "Mom, this is England, in November. It's cloudy and cold, except when it's cloudy, cold, and raining. The good news is that every town has a Christmas market. We'll go visit Oxford's Market tonight and go to London to see the one in Hyde Park tomorrow if you want!" She knows how to tune into and turn up the positive energy.

I'm on my second wine, Brooke is having her second cup of tea, as we compare Europe's cultural differences with that of our New Jersey experience.

She's a Psychology major with a minor in Cultural Anthropology. I find it impressive, how she defends her positions with interesting facts and observations that demonstrate her points throughout history.

Again, I feel relieved in the knowledge that she'll find a future filled with success and love. Selfishly, again, I could not be more thankful for the freedom her successful independence brings to me.

After lunch, Brooke takes me touring the streets of Oxford. Every turn has another picturesque, poetic scene from literature.

I'm especially struck by the archways from building to building over the streets. Apparently, they were constructed so Oxford University students do not have to weather Oxford's long, raw winter when moving from class to class.

Leaning up against every building are bicycles, sometimes three deep. All unchained, waiting safely for their riders. The lack of locks and chains is a cultural difference contrary to our New Jersey experience, no one has to point out to me.

Daylight is fading and with it comes the bitter, cold, damp, chilling walk uphill to the dorms. Scarf, gloves, and hat are required here during an Oxford November as we head back to Brooke's dorm.

We hang out in the dorm's warm kitchen while the crowd gets ready for the trip to the Oxford Christmas Market. They're all excited about the upcoming Thanksgiving gathering and plan on making Sangria, but apparently, they have no pitcher to transport the fruity, sweet wine to Thursday's celebration, across campus.

One of Brooke's friends, Angel, explains, "When we first got here, we found a recipe for Sangria. Without a pitcher, we've been making it in a big pot. I'm sure administration would not be happy if we walk through campus with a pot of wine and set that up in the middle of Thanksgiving."

Brooke has three close friends here at Oxford, All from her undergrad years at High Point University. I call the group the Alphabet Girls, A, B, C & D; Angel, Brooke, Chelsea and Deidre.

Angel has a sweet, high voice, and wispy blonde hair that will not hold a curl more than an hour. Her name obviously fits her.

"You don't have a pitcher in a dorm kitchen?" I'm amazed. That would not happen in the 70's when I went to college.

"It's expensive to bring things from the US, so we don't have a lot." Angel goes on, "The kitchen isn't well stocked. We only get whatever the last semester's kids choose not to take back to the US. They left us comforters, blankets and pillows too. When we got here, there was a big pile of stuff here in the main area and we had a free-for-all. Kids that came late got very little."

The group is beginning to show signs of readiness.

"Let's take the bus?" I ask. Silence. "I'm old." Now, I'm pleading.

Graciously, they make a U-turn to head toward the back door, which leads to the bus stop.

The Christmas Market is interesting. I note that in the US this type of seasonal display would be called a 'Holiday Market.' I guess we are a bit more accepting and inclusive of the Jewish population than our English brothers and sisters.

Through the bitter cold, this outside market is bustling with shoppers and yuletide happiness. The Alphabet Girls are filled with joy, reminding me of my youthful optimism.

What happened to my optimism?

I decide to get swept up in the spirit. I change my focus to the love and freedom I have in my life. Thankfulness for what I have, begins to take over. This is the perfect opportunity to begin my Christmas shopping. By the time we all get to the end of the Market, my heart is full, as are my shopping bags of gifts, and it's time for dinner.

We're early enough at the Wig and Pen to get the best seats in the house, a booth seat in the shape of a C, right in front of the dance floor. I hand my credit card to Brooke and announce to the Alphabet Girls, "This night is on me. Order whatever you want." I raise my eyebrows to the Alphabet Girls, telling them I want no arguments. When the drink menu comes, I point out to Brooke the list of drinks.

"Brooke, order a pitcher of one of these, and a gin and tonic for me."

I love these girls. Well-educated and well-traveled. They can converse about anything. Deidra is sitting next to me. I learn her undergrad degree is in French History. She translates from French to English for extra money.

"Deidra, I've been researching Nostradamus…"

Deidra cuts me off, "I know. He was hardly an astronomer that could see into the future that all the history books say. Blah blah blah, ridiculous. At the end of his life, when he wrote those tens of thousands of four-line quatrains, (that were supposedly insight into the future), most of real academia assumes that he had found some really good hallucinogens. Maybe highly addictive hallucinogens." She laughs, pours herself a drink from the pitcher of something pink and continues.

"In his early years, he did groundbreaking research in herbs, plants, and pharmacy, which was totally against the teachings of the Catholic Church. Very dangerous back then. In fact, he was thrown out of medical school. One of the artifacts, the College displays, is the document announcing Nostradamus' expulsion. He left the area for a while to study meditation, but returned to secretly hold classes that turned into a real movement."

I blink, my mouth opens to respond, but I am literally speechless. A movement?

"Oh yeah!" She continues, noting my obvious interest. "He and his sister-in-law developed and sold perfumes, which were widely sought after. He was the first to use musk. But a 'seer' he was not."

I take a deep breath.

"So, he began what kind of movement?" I can't wait to get back to my room to find out where this Medical school is in relation to Beatrix and Beren's Residential Art Center.

"I don't remember. The name of the movement was in French, obviously, but was called White something. Maybe white craft, something like that. Witchcraft, in French, is *la sorcellerie*. Like Sorcerer. Which, in the France, 1500's would get him hung. Apparently, if you could see into the future by divine intervention, that is… invoking the name of God, and or Jesus, that was fine with the Catholic Church, actually that was required. But seeing into the future without first asking God for direction would have been considered witchcraft or sorcery, and certainly a trip to the gallows. Same goes for healing. If you treat a patient in the name of God, even if your patent died, that's OK but healing via any method not approved by the Catholic Church, who ran the Universities, that is witchcraft and a death sentence. Basically, any medical procedure not approved by the Catholic Church was deemed witchcraft." Deidre leans in and raises her voice for punctuation "…even if you healed the patient!"

By now, the music is getting too loud for conversation and frankly, I am too stunned to continue. Just then, Angel screams to us all, "This song is my FA-vorite! Let's go!" So, we break out of our huddle and obediently follow to the dance floor, to dance like we're in a foreign country, where no one will ever see us again.

Even with bellies filled with dinner, we all begin to feel the alcohol swimming in our heads. I decide it's time to go, so we bolt from the Wig and Pen.

At the end of our short cab ride to the dorm, as the girls exit, I drag the empty pitcher out of my purse.

I almost forgot, "Here, Brooke, take this to the dorm."

"MOM!" Brooke looks at me horrified.

"Take it. You need a pitcher for Sangria." I say, while Brooke still will not take the pitcher from me. "Oops?" I say hoping this lame apology will bring her to see that resistance is futile. Brooke grabs the pitcher from me. As she emerges from the cab with the pitcher, the surprised Alphabet Girls burst into cackling, joyous, hysteria. I drive off to my BNB with the girls squealing, 'thank you', 'you rock', 'you're the best Mom ever…'

I love them all. There's such power in being a young woman.

On the cab ride back I ignore the fact that I'm their bad influence and they are my inspiration to live better… I'll think about that at some other time.

I enter the BNB where the Cat waits just inside the front door.

"Michael Nostradamus," I whisper his full name. Wobbling a bit, I salute him just to be silly, then bend at the waist, and whisper even softer, "Yes, I locked you out of your room."

I'm drunk and realize I probably didn't speak as softly as I intended.

"I need to go to bed, Dammie. It's after midnight and I have to meet Brooke at the bus stop early tomorrow. We're going to the Hyde Parke Christmas Market."

I should not be speaking out loud.

Bea and Beren are probably sleeping.

As I begin my slow trek up to my room, I'm reminded again of the still unknown connection between my landlords and Nostradamus. Before long, I'm taking the steps two at a time.

It's only 7:00 PM in New Jersey. After confirming that Dammie is still in the hall, I close and latch the door. I go directly to my computer and to AirBNB.com which lists the town of Beatrix and Beren's arts center.

Bingo. Nostradamus went to Medical School at the University of Montpellier, just fourteen kilometers from Bea and Beren's Arts Center. I sit back to really grasp this coincidence. An adrenaline burst sobers me a bit and keeps me researching.

I find that before medical school, at just fifteen-years-old, Michael was sent to the University of Avignon. In his first year, he studied critical thinking, grammar, logic, and rhetoric. I had to look that up;

Google 'rhetoric' ENTER

Persuasive speaking, i.e., marketing.

When the plague began to take many of his classmates and professors, the college closed. Michael never made it to his second year, where he would have studied astrology. This is the first solid evidence I've found that indicates that Nostradamus was not the astrologer that history has advertised him to be. Or, maybe not the astrologer he marketed himself to be in order to keep himself from the gallows.

I also find that the nobles of France, and all through Europe, would request from Nostradamus a private horoscope "reading" and psychic advice. It is well-documented that Nostradamus required birth charts to be provided TO him. In fact, the few birth charts created BY Nostradamus were found to have many errors. This is more evidence that Nostradamus was not the astrologist historians have recorded.

After Avignon closed, Michael did not return home. Instead, he traveled the countryside, researching herbal remedies and working as an apothecary before entering the University of Montpellier, Medical School.

I had to look that up too.

Google 'Apothecary' ENTER

Pharmacist.

What kind of sixteen-year-old boy, with the country full of plague and the Catholic Church disciplining heresy with imprisonment and worse, would not go back to the safety of his home, back to his beloved teacher and grandfather, but instead strike out on a mission to learn about medicines for himself?

His grandfather must have been, not only a great teacher, but a true inspiration. By this time, I had opened a bottle of red wine. I toast to all grandparents and this one especially.

Michael was twenty-six-years-old when he entered the University of Montpellier to study for a doctorate in medicine. Which means he traveled on his own before entering medical university for TEN years.

As I pour another glass of wine, I cannot imagine how this resolutely independent, free-thinker could last in such a place where no research was approved, in fact no results from research were approved, unless the Catholic Church approved first.

I read that Nostradamus found a friend while there at University of Montpelier. Francois Rabelais, much older but the bond between the two ran deep. Francois was famous for his satirical, off-color, bawdy writings.

I had to look that up,

Google 'Bawdy' ENTER

Rude, Lude, Vulgar.

And just as I begin to wonder how these two could stay out of the Court of inquisition… I find Nostradamus was expelled after just one year at Montpellier. In fact, just as Deidre said, the expulsion document still exists, displayed in the faculty library basement. The document was signed by a student Procurator, Guillaume Rondelet, who discovered that Nostradamus had been an apothecary, (considered a manual trade), expressly forbidden by the university. Apparently having a 'manual trade' at any time in your life was so beneath the Medical College that you could not even apply. Further research finds this student, Guillaume, thought Rabelais to be a good close friend but years later Rabelais writes about a character in a short story, Guillaume, who is an unintelligent, easily duped, snitch.

My guess is, Nostradamus was about to be called to the court of inquisition, but Rabelias duped Guillaume into expelling Nostradamus under other reasons to give Nostradamus an excuse to flee.

Michael did flee. He was invited to live with, and study with, a world-renowned scholar, Jules-César Scaliger. It's here that Michael deepens his understanding of various ideas, including meditation, which the Church would consider witchcraft. After the Catholic Church torched the home of Jules-Cesar along with all of his books, in the name of heresy, Michael returned to the area of Montpelier.

Google, "heresy" ENTER

Belief or opinion contrary to orthodox religious (especially Christian) doctrine.

I find it surprising that the Catholic Church was so relentless. Further surprising that Nostradamus continues to escape their wrath.

I sit back. I grew up in an Italian-Catholic neighborhood. My best friend was Jewish. My family attended Presbyterian Church every Sunday. Our US system of religious freedom seems to be working. In fact, has been working since it was established in the 1700's.

I feel heart-sick that all this pointless fear, frustration, and exasperating destruction was so prominent for centuries.

I continue researching the University of Montpelier and find that two-hundred years after Michael was expelled, during the French Revolution, when all universities in France had to close by order of the King, the Catholic Church brought the Montpellier School of Medicine into the Monastery and continued to operate. (Pun intended.) My guess is that the Catholic Church did not want to lose any more control over this particular medical school.

Google. 'Translate English to French witchcraft' ENTER

La Sorcellerie – a person who claims or is believed to have magic powers.

Yes, this is exactly what Deidre had said.

Synonyms: wizard, witch, magician, warlock, enchanter, enchantress

Google 'White Craft translate English to French' ENTER

Artisanat Blanc.

Artisanat!?!

Sounds like Art Center to me. This is So cool. My adventure cannot get better than this.

I slip into bed. *I can't wait for breakfast!*

Chapter 4

Love is a passion that resembles
a melancholy disease.

Life is good. I wake slowly stretching, feeling lazy. Thankfully, finally, I had a restful night. I have plenty of time before meeting up with Brooke. As a smirk begins to grow on my face, I have to say it out loud.

"Artesian Community Center in the south of France". Laughing, I feel so triumphantly, cunning. In just forty-eight hours, I figured out their secret. Of course, I do not believe in witchcraft, but this is SO amusing.

I'm not ready to get out of bed, but my teeth need brushing, the bathroom calls. I smell coffee. Life is good. So, out of bed I gladly go.

Twirling down the stairs, my spirit is light. I feel as though I can fly. As I land hard at the bottom, I giggle to myself, *'Light as a bird, I am not.'*

I enter the kitchen. Beren and, I assume, his cousin, Dan, are sitting at the kitchen table.

"Good morning, gentlemen."

As I head for the coffee. I notice both men begin to stand. Another cultural difference. I love England. I divert my mission from the coffee pot and extend my hand to Dan.

"Joyce, this is my cousin, Dan."

I make eye contact.

"Good morning, Dan. Very nice to meet you." Then to both, "Please be seated." Gotta Love England's social graces.

Dan is a small guy, both in height and build. He has an accent I can't quite pin down, which, when taking all attributes together, reminds me of a leprechaun. I shake my head and think, '*This trip just keeps getting better.*'

Dan says, "Beren tells me you are here to visit with your daughter for the US Thanksgiving week. How long are you staying?"

"I don't know, exactly," I say as I pour a cup of coffee. "I left my return ticket open. Many of my friends think I'll meet, and be swept away by, the Earl of Sandwich or the Duke of Earl and will never return home," I joke. I am really feeling very silly.

"Well you can tell your friends that you met a man who owns a castle in Ireland," Dan sits back in his chair, bringing his small pot of breakfast with him, crossing his legs under him. Dan certainly can fold up to a very small footprint.

"You own a castle in Ireland?" My eyebrows are up. "Is that where your accent comes from?" I ask.

"Well, more to the truth, I own a third of a castle. My Mum recently titled it to my brother, sister, and me. I live in Portugal."

"You live in Portugal," *(...on someone else's property out of your car.)* "While you have a Castle in Ireland?" I ask, knowing that my landlord and Dan are first cousins, so I assume Dan will be held to the truth.

"Yes, well the history is quite complicated, filled with scandal and even a witch's curse."

"Witch's curse?" I say laughingly, but lean way forward, both elbows on the table on each side of my coffee cup. I cannot be more riveted.

Dan nods yes, as he chews a giant mouthful of lentils. (Yes, he's eating lentils for breakfast.)

He's chewing slowly, creating an awkward pause although I don't feel this guy is pausing for dramatic effect. I'm a bit puzzled by his reluctance.

"I would love to hear that story while I cook my porridge," I coax him, as I rise. "Will you indulge me?" I add with the slightest of English accents, I don't think I've ever said 'indulge me' but add it just for some panache, because I'm feeling silly, and this is England.

"Well," Dan begins, "The Thomastown Castle was flourishing in the eighteen-hundreds with over one-hundred apartments for servants and dozens of horse stables. It was its own big community. One of the titles that was bestowed upon my family was the Earl of Llandaff. By the early eighteen-hundreds the expansion into a gothic-like castle, with new wings and four huge slender towers, was completed. The river was a good distance away but was artificially diverted to provide water for cooking, yes, obviously, but also to feed the lush gardens and fountains. They say that the splendor of the Thomastown gardens, the opulence, was really only second to Versailles."

I'm riveted, even if I'm skeptical of how much of this story is true.

"A little daughter of one of the Mathews' family died. She fell into one of these fountains and drowned."

I gasp, leaning back in my chair, hand over mouth. I didn't expect to hear such a tragedy. My silly mood immediately turns to horror. I have two girls. My youngest, Brooke is twenty-something but I picture them both at two-years-old. My heart breaks for everyone involved.

Dan continues, "Yes, well the Mum of the little girl accused the nanny of killing the little girl through witchcraft and the nanny was put to death. This nanny was just a young girl herself, of English descent and was burned at the stake. It's said that this nanny, was actually a witch and just before she died, cursed my family, that all the Mathew heirs of the castle would 'never realize their wealth'. And, in fact, no one did. The mother of the drown little girl killed herself the day after the nanny was burned. More interesting is that even though the Earl of Llandaff had five sons, only the one son, who was away at war in India had children and ultimately had to sue to inherit the property.

One of the Cousins who grew up in the castle, Theobald Matthews, was a preacher. He was known as the Apostle of Temperance and began the Total Abstinence Society."

I interrupt, "Abstinence? Like sobriety? Abstinence from alcohol?"

"Yes. He went around signing people up to pledge to totally abstain from drinking alcohol. Each time someone took a pledge, he gave them a little metal. The cost of these medals came out of his own pocket, ya know, and he gave out hundreds of thousands of these medals. In fact, in less than nine months, no fewer than 150,000 names were enrolled. This movement spread all over Ireland. He enrolled over 3,000,000 people in Ireland alone, which is over half the adult population. He began signing up people all over England. But the cost of these millions of little metals was too much for Father Mathews.

Because of this, he owed all these debts. In fact, it was the Queen of England who paid Mathews debts to get him out of debtors' prison and gave him a small pension so he could survive and continue his quest. So, even he never realized riches. The castle ended up in the hands of some cousins from France. But that family could not afford to keep it up nor were they good business people to keep the hundreds of workers working and producing. Well, shortening the story a hundred years, the castle went to my uncle…"

I interrupt again. "So, this is your mother's brother?"

"Yes, and he could not afford to pay the taxes. In 1900's the government passed a 'roof tax' so he had the roof taken off the castle so he didn't have to pay the tax…"

"Wait." I interrupt again. "So you don't have to pay real estate taxes if there is no roof, even on a castle?"

"Correct. He was going to lose the property, just lose the whole thing, so he had the roof taken off to save the ownership. Obviously, in just one decade the place was totally destroyed. In fact, many historic buildings in Ireland had their roofs removed which led to the destruction of thousands of historic buildings. When my uncle died, several years ago, my Mum became the executor to my Uncles will, so it's like, she doesn't want to do anything with it because of all this Irish lore and didn't want to upset the locals and it really is just a pile of rubble now anyway. So, when I heard all this story I began to push my Mum to get all this wrapped up and have the Deed switched into our names: my brother and sister and me. But we'll not be realizing any wealth either because even though the blocks of stone are worth a little money, it's cost us everything to just get to this point."

I had nothing to say but, "I'm so sorry. I'm sorry for everyone, the mother and father of the little girl but also the nanny. She was just a young girl?"

"Yea, English. They say she still haunts the ruins."

"From England?"

"No." Dan was somber. "The winters in Ireland can be very long and brutal. Many families in Ireland, the ones that could afford it, have winter homes in warmer climates. The Mathew's family had a home, not as opulent as the Thomastown Castle, in a little English community in the south of France."

I lean way in, eyebrows up, eyes like saucers, "An Estate in the South of France?" I say, way too loudly.

Dan is obviously taken back. "Yes, South of France. That is where they found this English nanny."

I'm riveted. I have so many questions swirling around my head. This entire story is both unbelievable and so captivating all at the same time. Why would this mother accuse her nanny of witchcraft and not just inattention? And were there any 'witch trials' in the 1800's? I thought all that ended by the very early 1700's. I look at the time. My questions have to wait. I've got to get a shower and meet up with Brooke.

"That was an amazing, interesting story, Dan," I say, as I rise with my bowl and mug. "I'd love to stay and discuss it with you, I have dozens of questions. Unfortunately, I have to go now to meet up with my daughter..." looking at the kitchen clock, I add "...by noon." I walk over to the sink. Dammie is there on the counter. I wonder if this Cat can read my thoughts. I look directly into Dammie's eyes and think, 'this can't be true.'

Dammie doesn't even blink. I know it's all so ridiculous. I wash my dishes and place them in the draining board.

As I turn from the sink, Dan continues, "When you get back to the US there are statues erected of Father Matthew. One in Philadelphia and another in Boston. He went to the US when he was in his sixties. He was greeted in New York City like a rock star. Apparently, hundreds of thousands of people met him at the dock. The mayor closed the business day. I believe Father Mathews is the only non-US citizen to ever hold a seat in your, uh, like your parliament."

"Our house of representatives?" I say, now in real disbelief. I check my tone to be more polite but add, "The number of representatives are fixed, each state getting a certain number determined by population and voted on by districts. How is that possible?"

"I don't know. But you can certainly go to Philadelphia when you get back to US and see the statue and the inscription," Dan assured me.

"This gets more and more fascinating," I say, as I think, *this gets more and more unbelievable.*

"What was his name?" I stop to make a note into my phone.

"Father Theobald Matthews, Total Abstinence Society." Dan says.

'Research when I get back; 'Father Theobald Mathews, Total Abstinence Society.'

Brooke and I meet, just as the bus pulls up. I give my wallet to her so she can figure out the money and ticket.

"Adult, same day, round trip," Brooke says to the driver.

"Thank you," I say to Brooke and the driver at once.

"Mom, are you even going to try to figure out the money while you're here? What if I'm not around to help?"

Oh, boy. "I'm sure I can figure it out, Brooke." I say sternly, hoping she takes the warning to be nicer. *All day in London. Here we go.*

We find seats facing each other. These buses have Wi-Fi and electrical strips to plug in your laptop or cellphone. Brooke pops in her earbuds and closes her eyes to rest. I'm amazed how she can nap anywhere, recharging for the next adventure. The motion of the bus is getting to me too. I let myself drift away. Brooke is directly across from me. She is so beautiful. I giggle and think, *especially at rest.*

My thoughts go immediately to the Thomastown Castle. *What of the tragedy of the castle? That poor mother who lost her toddler.*

I can't imagine the pain. I can't even get close to imagining that kind of pain. Why would this young mom accuse this teen of witchcraft and not just of inattention? I look across to Brooke. No. Brooke would not be drawn to a profession of caring for children. Neither would she put up with being accused of witchcraft or anything else.

She would fight.

She would win.

How did this young English girl end up in the south of France? Obviously, she didn't arrive by herself.

Liz. Yes, my Liz. Quiet and filled with love. Children are drawn to her resolve of peacefulness. She would be drawn to a profession of tending to young children. Young children would be drawn to her. She loves without exception, without judgement.

I chuckle to myself because I could never figure her out.

Why would this mother's cousin-in-law dedicate his life to the total abstinence of alcohol? Not just pledge for himself but begin a movement. What could be so profound that he would dedicate himself to this cause after expending all his money and even being jailed?

The bus is slowly rocking me into sleep,

...rocking me into the 1800's.

Out the window, I see the English countryside,

...thatched rooves

...and horse-drawn carriages.

I look to the other window seat. There is Liz. She is staring blankly, straight forward. We have been through some event monumental enough, that we all find it necessary to leave London. The carriage is rocking and there, next to me, is my friend Patrice. Her bright orange hair states emphatically that her many ancestors came from Ireland. This carriage is full. My stepdaughter, Karen and her two children Olivia and Olysah are here as well. These twins usually cannot be contained. In fact, I have nicknamed them Whoa-livia and Whoa-lysah.

However, now, they are silent but not quite sleeping. All of us in unison, rocking, apparently catatonic, to the rhythm of the carriage.

I turn towards Patrice, "Are you OK?" I say in a low tone so as not to wake the sleeping Brooke

Patrice makes no movement, as if I am not there. She scares me.

She has been, for many years, in many ways, my rock. In fact, she is where I get my sense of security. The rocking of the carriage sends her shoulder bumping into mine. I try again.

"Patrice. Will you ever be OK?"

Patrice reaches over and pats my hand. This woman, who usually takes care of everyone, including me, is now debilitated by... something terrible. I try to remember but can't seem to figure out what happened in London, why are we in this carriage? I feel that I alone am now leading this war-torn bunch. I don't want the duty. The carriage stops and one of our attendants opens the door to plead with us all to stop to eat.

These horsemen, who I'm sure, feel awkward, but as the miles wear on, realize that this band of woman need more help than just to get to their destination: An English community in the south of France.

"Miss." He directs his request to me. I am the only one seemingly coherent. "You all need to eat something."

I'm trying to figure out what happened. I'm trying to remember the events that brought us all here. I don't respond.

The horseman says more sternly, this time putting his hand on my arm, "Madame, we are stopping here and not continuing until you all eat something."

"Yes." I say but no one, including me moves to eat.

...and the days, miles and horses ride on in silence.

"Madame Blanc!"

The twins were the first to show life. It is the last full travel day, Olivia and Olysah wake on that late summer morning, hungry.

Finally hungry. Very hungry.

After eating they begin running around a tree, then running after each other. The giggles of two five-year-olds are magical. A blessing, really.

The healing of the Blanc de Noir woman had begun.

We are almost to our destination. I know, because instead of main roads, we're travelling through the center of a small town. Odd. These people seem to know us. Expect us.

One tall gentleman leaning on a rake, especially. I see the light of recognition in his eyes... and maybe more.

"Mom! We're here," Brooke wakes me.

The bus has arrived in London.

Her face, in contrast to the somber mood of everyone in my dream, is exuberant. I'm so relieved, and begin to tear up. I turn away. I don't want to have to explain my tears. *Just a dream.* I tell myself trying to shaking it off. *My children are OK. They are not in pain. Just a dream.*

The quick pace Brooke sets out of the bus station helps to shake the hold this dream has on me.

First stop; Buckingham Palace. We've seen this place dozens of times on TV and now here we are. We giggle as we critique our selfies, one after another, finally agreeing on one that we can post to Facebook. We stroll around Westminster Cathedral, Tower of Westminster, and Big Ben. We walk along the River Thames through what appears to be an impromptu Christmas Market. We take a ride on the London Eye, where we take pictures in ridiculous yoga positions with all of London behind us. Then a ride up the Shard, the three-hundred and six-meter glass and steel tower. From the top, we can see the Tower of London and the Gherkin. The London Bridge, City Hall and the White Cube.

"Let's get dinner in an English Pub near Hyde Park then spend the rest of the night in Hyde Park Christmas market, before the last bus back to Oxford," I say, knowing I can always tempt Brooke with food.

Brooke responds by pulling out her phone and looking for the nearest bus or metro route.

Our transit lets us out near Harrods, which is an upscale department store. We walk through the store where we find a memorial to Lady Di and Harrod's heir who died together that terrible night in 1997.

I learn that a friend of Brookes, who is going to the London School of Economics, will be meeting us for dinner. Brooke has found a Pub so close to Hyde Park we can hear the music of the market while we sit at our table inside. We both take this opportunity to hook up to WiFi, post to Facebook, and giggle at comments made to our previously posted pictures.

"I'm glad my first trip to London is with you," I say with love.

"I love you too, Mommy," Brooke says, reminding me of a simpler time, before the divorce. "Emily! Over here!" My gift of a loving moment was short lived with the arrival of Brooke's friend. I reluctantly let go.

"Emily, what made you choose London School of Economics?" I ask, after the girls settle in.

"I had sailed in regattas all around Europe and fell in love with London. The transit system here is so clean, easy to use and very inexpensive, especially with my student pass. I am getting way more than just an economics education.

There are many famous graduates of LSE. Mick Jagger is probably our most famous but there have been Kennedys and Rockefellers. George Soros is another extremely powerful and wealthy graduate. Juan Manuel Santos, president of Colombia. George Papandreou, prime minister of Greece. Kaushik Basu is the senior vice president and chief economist at the World Bank. The wife of the current Prime Minister of England is a graduate of the Law School. I could go on, there are over fourteen Nobel Prize winners too."

"Wow," I said impressed with both her knowledge of the subject and the swift recitation. "The names I recognize all sound very..." I hesitate, trying to find just the right words. "...very liberal."

"Socialists? Progressives? The idea of open society, one world order? " She says, what I'm not willing to push.

"Yes," I say, surprised. "The business school, from which I graduated, would consider those ideas very much opposed to theirs." I add slowly, choosing each word very carefully. I'm trying not going down that conversational road with this young impressionable girl who probably has never heard the other side of the argument.

To my surprise, Emily laughs a full-throated, head back, honest laugh.

"Yes, Ms. Bartlett, I am aware of Capitalism and all the principles of free markets, small government, personal responsibility, etc. My Dad owns a pretty big company so I have heard and seen the arguments that contradict some of the principles taught here. All is well," She smiles to assure me, I don't have to tippy toe around her. "I see both sides and think the answer to social injustice, poverty, starvation, is a complicated one and therefore the solutions are complicated. Further, I see that proven solutions for one demographic, for one country, and or one ethnic set of people may not be the answer for those that may be standing right next door."

Emily pauses to be sure I'm still with her, then adds, "My personal opinion is that having different cultures, countries with different governments and different monetary systems, makes it less likely that all the whole world will crash into depression, recession and or inflation at the same time. Kind of like protecting your investments by having a diversified portfolio."

"Emily, you obviously are an amazing open-minded woman who knows way more than I. Thank God you are part of the well-educated, new generation who will take over the world, better than anyone I have seen. With all that said, I'm heading to the bar to let you girls catch up. Want anything?"

The bar is quiet with very few patrons. I send the girls drinks to the table and talk to the bartender, Ron Brookhardt. I find out that he has been tending this bar with his Dad since he could walk. Now, he's running the bar with his son-in-law, although his granddaughters will tell you, they're the backbone of the operation. He's tall and strikingly thin but muscular. He rests against the beer taps as his eyes follow several patrons out the door then past the giant front windows. I'm quite sure women have gotten lost in his eyes. Eyes of steel blue. Wildly intelligent eyes. The type that have no questions, just answers. Eyes that have been watching, seeing and understanding more than most. Now, at seventy something, his eyes have seen an abundance of love and pain.

Most patrons are here to socialize. A sign above the bottles of alcohol reads, 'Why do we think Love is a Magician? – Marsilio Ficino'. Another sign at the beer taps, "The doctors of antiquity have affirmed that Love is a passion that resembles a melancholy disease. The Physician Rasis prescribed, in order to recover, among other things, coitus, and drunkenness. - Marsilio Ficino."

I like him, both the bartender and Mr. Ficino.

Brooke, Emily and I head to Hyde Park Christmas Market which is truly the acres wide, winter wonderland it is advertised to be. Thousands of giant metal plates are laid on the ground to elevate what could become a muddy mess. We make our way through the maze of food booths, shopping, rides and music. We all take a ride on a merry go round, find out we do not like mulled wine, and I shop for the daughter and grandchildren I left behind. The sparkling lights make for a real fairytale atmosphere.

Brooke warns that the last bus to Oxford will be leaving soon. I forgot there is a time limit to this. Brooke and I are having one of the best days together since she was very small, but it's time to go, so we head to the exit.

The bus is at the stop, waiting for the published departure time. We take our seats.

Even before the bus takes off to Oxford, Brooke and I both travel off to sleep...

Chapter 5

White of Black

Brooke and I are asleep before the London/Hyde Park bus takes off to Oxford.

My dream begins vividly inside a stable in the South of France.

Ron had been tending this stable with his Dad since he could walk. Now he's running the stable with his son-in-law, although his granddaughters will tell you, they are the backbone of the operation. He's tall and painfully thin but muscular. As he rests against the rake, his eyes follow a caravan of carriages. Women have gotten lost in his eyes... eyes of steel blue. Wildly intelligent eyes that have no questions; just answers. Eyes that have been watching, seeing, and understanding more than most. Now at seventy-something, his eyes have seen an abundance of love and pain. A sign above the entrance to the barn reads, 'Why do we think Love is a Magician?'

The rumors of the aching inside that caravan is like no other. He's heard the gossip of his good community. Some stories of their agony are hard for him to hear. He feels, and his eyes pool up.

"Grampa, what are you looking at? Do you know them?" Comes softly from his curly haired granddaughter.

Ron pulls his empathy back. "I do. I think you know the Blanc de Noir twins," Ron squats down to put his arm around her. Her hug consoles him.

"Olivia and Olisah Blanc? Yes. They come every fall," his granddaughter answers.

"They're in that caravan with their Mum, Grand-mum and Great Grand-mum, my friend, Patrice."

She's not accustomed to seeing her grandfather sad and babbles nervously. *"It's summer. Why are they here so early? No one else is here yet. They're here so early. Can we go visit Olivia and Olisah now? How do you know their grandmum?"*

"I went to school with their Grand-mum, Patrice. They've packed up their belongings from London. They'll be staying year-round now.. I'm glad for them. They're starting a new adventure. We'll visit after they settle in." Ron says slowly. His mono-tone, not matching his hopeful message.

"But you're sad for them?" She asks, trying to understand.

"No," he lies. Then, more honestly, *"My school friend hasn't had an easy time of it these last several years. A new beginning in a familiar place will help her. This is a new, healthy start."* More to himself, than to his granddaughter, after a deep breath, with an even more somber tone, *"I pray for them all."*

"I'll pray too," his granddaughter says.

The carriages are now out of sight. Ron turns to his comforter, "I thought all these years that your Mom was the sweetest girl ever. Apparently, I was wrong." Ron winks with eyes that are no longer welling with tears and a voice no longer filled with pain. He's back to the happy, loving Grampa she knows. He winks again. Relieved, she embraces him very tightly. Instinctively she knows that her hug is comforting him. On her release, she kisses his nose and runs off to play. He stands and again, leans on his rake looking in the direction of the caravan which is now out of sight. Pictures of Patrice and him in their London neighborhood and later in their teens at school, here, near Montpellier, play in his head. In every memory, she always seems to be breaking his heart.

Ron's deep thoughts are interrupted by his son-in-law.

"Who was that, Dad?"

"Those were the women of the Maison Blanc de Noir," he says, mixing English with French.

"The house of White of Black?" His son asks, "What does that mean? White of Black?"

"When you go through a bad situation but still turn out to be filled with love and kindness. Their name is a beacon to all of us to work towards Love, Freedom, and Thankfulness, no matter what we're going through or...have been through," he adds, slowing and lowering his tone. "I believe they shortened it to Blanc. Blanc de Noir fits them, although maybe brought on... or foretold their current position." Ron says, while still looking down the street.

His son-in-law, not sure if Ron is still talking to him or to himself, leaves him to his thoughts, which are obviously consuming.

Ron's attention is pulled toward the purring Cat, now standing on his left foot.

"How do you always know when I need a hug?" Ron says as he picks up the Cat. "Patrice Blanc de Noir," Ron says, out loud, with all the French flair he can muster. He remembers and smiles...

Her hair, deep red, crimson. No light strawberry blonde for this fiery woman. A woman born under the sign of fire. This community has always had secrets, but how did she preside over, and keep these secrets for so long? I can't imagine the Patrice I know keeping her house's black and blue secrets of unspeakable pain. Further, how did that strong, fiery, powerful woman I know, let her *house continue in violence? My friend has never spoken of her bruises. I'm sure not the least of which are bruises of the heart.*

New rumors tell of this household's fiery, dramatic escape.

These women have managed to stay together by wrapping themselves and their secrets in love, like an infant's swaddling blanket. This is their strength.

Then, talking aloud to the Cat, "I'm sure you're anxious to go see her. We'll go for a visit soon I hope, but I think its best we wait for an invite. God help us all, Dammie."

With that, Dammie uncharacteristically wrestles out of Ron's arms and runs down the road, following the path of the caravan.

The bus bumps me awake. I check on Brooke who is, thankfully, sleeping peacefully. I say a prayer, thanking God I don't live in the 1800's.

Rocking with the bus, I settle back to sleep...

I'm standing in front of the hearth in the Blanc de Noir home. Two south-facing windows, on either side of the wood stove, promise little light or heat. They're small and the walls are thick, damp, and cold. The stove is most always lit, even now, on this warm, summer day.

The floor of the great room is stone, weeping condensation. The icy grip of guilt fights the stove.

We've been here one year today, hibernating through the mild therapeutic winter of Southern France. Now, its summer, and we're all healing well. Even Patrice is coming along, though, very slowly.

Rocking too close to the stove, rocking in a chair that is not a rocker, trying to connect to a feeling of warm peace, is the fiery red head, Patrice Blanc de Noir. Patrice rocks a lot now, since we escaped from London last summer. I'm concerned that her near-catatonic state is disturbing to 'my girls'.

"My Girls." I am comfortable now as head of this household. I have initiated conversations with each cohort, individually and in groups, about the events leading to our escape from London. I won't avoid or shrink from the subject as Patrice did all those years. I believe that discussions of our family history will speed the healing of our little coven of females. Patrice voices no resistance. In fact, she speaks very little. I imagine she feels blame that her leadership has brought us all this pain of permanent separation. Self-blame always leads, eventually, to shame.

All her life Patrice had been known as, "Lucky Pattie." She doesn't feel lucky now.

Patty was, at one time, a strong, competent, and 'always in the right place at the right time' kind of woman. But over the last twenty years, she has lost her lucky luster. Her husband, once covert about his violent, abusive ways, fueled by alcohol, found that even daily brutality was not questioned in our London neighborhood.

Back in her young life, Patrice was always surrounded by a rainbow, of sorts. Her mother told her that was because her father was born under the sign of water and her mother was born under the sign of the sun.

Patrice was a good, generous woman who never kept her pots of gold to herself but instead, showered others with Love, Joy, Kindness, and small gifts. Most famous, were her random, silly rhyming words of encouragement.

In contrast, and breaking my heart, I see her now rocking in this chair, which is not a rocker... rocking to cradle her innocent damaged soul.

She will have to learn to live with visions of scenes she did not see but imagine vividly. Guilt that is not hers. The nightmares, that began before we left London, are driving her slowly insane. While trying to sleep, she hears screams of "help me," but she's blind and can't help the young victims. The pain of her choices is so great she can only look back, One. Frame. At a time.

Patrice looks out of the tiny windows. This French town's summer is unseasonably hot, but only the weather is turning warm. This day's light is waning to a deep, dark, indigo blue. She has seen that color before. When a bruise is especially brutal, it turns that same violent violet, then, deep blue. Rainbows as well begin with heartfelt, crimson, blood red, orange fading into a sickly yellow. She weeps. These last months she has hardly spoken a word. I reach out with one questioning, gentle hand.

Patrice turns to look at me in a rare cohesive moment.

"I am hanging onto my feelings of Love with both hands. My guilt, and visions of the worst of humanity are trying to strip me of this. Give me time. Love will win."

I can say nothing in response except, "I love you, Mom."

"I know, sweetie. I'll be OK."

I tend to the hearth. There, on the left, hangs an old billows, once full of color, now faded. Handmade, fifteen years ago by Patrice's son, my husband. One of the first presents he brought home to me with a poem. I was born under a Gemini sky, an air sign. My husband, Stephen, born under the sign of fire.

My heart began to beat hot red on that cold frosty day.
I watched you, so young and already searching for who you are,
You found focus on your breath, and at once you're the air.
You're free. You move and you're the wind.

Strong caution to my heart of fire.
A flirt and tease will feed into a blaze of smoky suffocation.
Where love ends and lust begins will vacillate,
Undulate with your howling winds...

Stoking our heart fires' dance
...throughout the rest

...of earth's history.

Yes, my heart of fire beware...
She breathes and she's the air
She moves and she's the wind.
She's free to feed my fire within.

I was too young to see the violence of his words until it was too late. Still, I can't part with the now useless billows. It's a reminder of how brilliant he was. How attentive and generous he could be with his time... and with his apologies. It was a reminder of a time before he fell out of love with me, and in love with alcohol... falling in step with his father.

Back then, just as the poem says, both our lust and the billows were powerful...and would ignite even the tiniest ember. Over time, both my love for him and the billows, were irreparably damaged by too many nights, of too many tears that tore at my trust. My sense of security and then, ultimately, my virtue was reduced to ash.

How much suffering will a woman, who claims to be righteous, tolerate?

I have aged quite a bit since our marriage. I have matured, but still in search of my center. In response to the worst of the violence, I found the ability to quietly plan, wait, and hope. Last summer, in London, my mettle was tested. My husband and his father had morphed into united dark forces.

The good residence of this town in the south of France will never know the circumstances surrounding last spring's escape from London. My plan for our new beginning is well under way. I vow to give my children and grandchildren a life without fear.

As I pick up the billows, instantly...

I can feel something is coming.

In the door, rushes the high energy twins, home from school, who are, always running. Mostly running in circles, after each other.

I refuse to rehash that horrific time in London. I'll focus only on what happens next. A story of women who took drastic steps, to take charge of their health, retreat to a place of peace, and healing, and yet I fear...

I can still feel bad things are coming... soon

As a rule, we all travel in circles. We land in exactly the same place. Yes, different locations, different actors, different time, but find ourselves in exactly the same drama unless you change who you think you are.

I stare into the fire which mesmerizes me, ignoring the twin's loud disruption. I have always been able to see the future in little bits. Patrice has taught me to quiet my mind so that I can see more of the messages in the ether.

The flame is dancing. I feel the power of the Blanc de Noir women around me, stronger and more focused than ever. We're fighting some evil horror. I calm my breathing. I'm sure I'm just getting the messages from the past. I pray these are messages of the past. "Oh help me." I mutter out loud, not really clear who I'm talking to. Please, no, we're not going to have to go through something more... The feeling gets clearer now. Yes, it's a horror we'll struggle with in the future, and we're fighting with a new band of cohorts who are more mature, more powerful. A growing population of actors will add to our campaign with every step. We'll have to fight something horrifying. But what? I can't see.

I step closer to the fire. Still not close enough, I kneel on the hearth to get even closer. I'm sure the answer is there.

What is the fight against? I want to see. I feel as though my eyes are closed, I can't open them to see. All at once I know. And now I can't bear to see... but it's too late.

I can't stop getting even closer.

The heat is burning my skin, my eyelashes. I see fountains and music. In a flash, and very clearly, I see Elizabeth, MY Elizabeth. My Elizabeth as a sweet young girl. Innocent. She's in excruciating pain and screams, "Mummy! Help!!"

"NO! NO! NOooo!" I scream myself awake, and disrupt all the passengers on the bus.

I am both breathless and crying.

'It's not real,' I tell myself. NO. It's not. Thank God. I want to call to check on Liz in New Jersey. **Right. Now.** I wonder if the bus's internet is up. I'm looking for the password but something is preventing me. Brooke is leaning forward right in my face. "Mom!?"

Breathless and in a whisper, "I guess I had a bad dream," I say to Brooke, as I try to see around her and through the dark for the internet password.

"Y'a think?" She says in serious sarcasm, then very loud to the startled passengers, "Just a nightmare. Everything is OK." She turns to the bus driver, "Sorry."

Brooke switches her seat to the one next to mine, grabs my hand, and puts her other hand on my leg.

"Just a dream, Mom," she pats my hand, "Are you alright?"

"It was just a dream." I say to Brooke but also to myself.

I'm thankful for my children. I try to focus on that. The ride continues in silence until we arrive at the Oxford College Center.

It's past 1:00 AM. After a long hug, Brooke heads south toward her dorm. I head north and choose not to take the dimly lit shortcut through the park to my BNB.

Dramatically, I think to myself, 'Thank God for this Canadian Goose Down Hat, saving me from freezing to death.'

I'm having a fearful, fast walk through another frigid Oxford November night.

Note to self, advise everyone I meet not to visit England in November.

I'll need the key soon to open the door.

My gloves are not going to let me find the key in this backpack easily. I curse.

I'm going to have to stop cursing.

I'll begin a list of New Year's Resolutions...I chuckle... Yes, resolve again this year.

My thoughts are so disjunctive.

Unwillingly, I take off my glove, juggle my backpack to find the key, panic sets in as I wonder if I even brought the key. I stop... trying to find my calm... before I try to find the key.

"I know it's there." I say, trying to find both the key and my composure.

I stick my hand in blindly and sure enough, viola! The key. I sing out loud, "Thank you," to the key finding powers that be.

I close my eyes and breathe again to find my calm. I'm obviously still shaken.

I open the door. There, waiting just inside... is the Cat.

"I've been dreaming about you." I say with a comedic but scolding, accusatory tone. *Ha. As if the Cat could get in my head.*

I travel up the stairs, hoping no one opened my bedroom door. I don't want the Cat to beat me into my room.

Once inside, successfully without the Cat, I close and lock the door.

I take stock of my vivid dreams from the bus ride and shudder. It's almost 2AM here, but just 8PM in NJ. I quickly Facetime Liz.

Liz answers.

"Oh, I love you," I say before she finishes her hello, "I had a ghastly dream about you."

In her best, you poor-little-thing voice. "You did? Poor BA-by," Liz says.

I raise my voice, "It was a seriously horrifying dream, Liz." Trying to impress upon her that my dream needs to have the proper respect of a horrifying nightmare where she is the one in trouble, "In fact, you won't believe the crazy things going on here."

"Great, Mom, yes," Liz says, distracted.

"Liz?"

"Yea. Yes. I'm sorry, Mom. The boys are not in bed yet and they're tired and cranky. Let me call you back."

"It's almost two in the morning here, Liz. Please, DO NOT call me back."

"Two in the morning?" That got her attention. "What are you doing up? Really, Mom?"

Is she patronizing me?

"You have a bad dream in England and decide to call ME? Are you all right?" Liz lowers her tone, "Is there wine involved?"

Holy crap. She IS patronizing me.

"Liz, I had a dream while on the bus with your sister, from London to Oxford. I just got in now. I screamed so loud I woke everyone on the bus."

"Oh my God, Mom." She doesn't try, to suppress a laugh. "Oh, I'm positive Brooke loved that, and as much as I want to hear this story, I have to put two super heroes to bed." She turns the phone for me to see my two grandsons who are in Superman and Flash, pajamas. Instantly, I change from highly indignant, to filled with love.

"Wave." Liz says to the boys.

I wave back, my heart bursting with love, even knowing Liz is brushing me off.

"Blow kisses, Mom mom," Liz says quickly, afraid I may continue my rant.

I blow kisses, and wonder if my heart is big enough to handle the love I have for this trio.

"Say good night to Mum mum. Bye." Liz hangs up.

Did she just say MUM-MUM? Oh my Lord, I have to go to sleep. I may be losing my mind.

I lay in bed and try to change the narrative in my head. Unfortunately, no matter how I begin, all roads of thought lead to that vision of Liz screaming. Burning.

I chant to myself, "It's not real, it was just a dream. My girls are fine. The boys are safe." But the fact is, even though my children and grandchildren are safe, in the 1800's an innocent little girl drowned, and all the people in her world, for generations, were shattered. Devastated is maybe a better word.

I roll over and grab my phone.

Google. Devastated define. ENTER

- Destroy or ruin, wreck, lay waste, raze (to the ground), level, flatten. Cause (someone) severe and overwhelming shock or grief.

Yea. Devastated is a good word.

Two hundred years? It's gotta be time for forgiveness and healing. I begin to pray for this family I've known for just three days, which thankfully brings my own peaceful sleep.

Chapter 6

Why do we think Love is a magician?

"Ma…. Mom? Joyce!" Brooke startles me awake.

"Brooke! What's wrong? Is everyone OK?" I'm sitting up in bed, a bit dizzy.

"Nothing's wrong. It's AFTER NOON? When did you get to bed?"

"Two." I say, still trying to get my bearings.

"Liz said you called her last night all freaked out. You've been sleeping for almost TEN HOURS!"

"Oh, thank God. I obviously needed that. Let me brush my teeth, then I need coffee." I realize Dammie is now inside my room. I roll my eyes at him and reprimand Brooke. "You left the door open."

"Mom, if you don't get on London time, you're going to miss everything." Brooke says, completely ignoring my agitation.

While looking into the mirror, with toothbrush in my mouth, rolling my eyes again, "Yes, Brooke," I say, wondering if my parenting skills are really all I think they are. "OK. Let's go. I need coffee." I'm hungry. "…and porridge", I add with a smirk.

I stick my face into Brooke's, "I'm going to have Porridge." I say over-zealously, with the message - I am in a great mood and you should be too. "Maybe I'll get to use the great big red antique coffee beeeean grinder." I add just as enthusiastically. She gets the message. We canter down the stairs loudly. By the time we hit the foyer, we're in sync. Life is good. Ten hours of sleep will do that.

"Good morning, Ladies." Beren awkwardly holds up a screw driver. He's fixing a kitchen drawer with contents all over the counter above.

As I walk directly to the grinder. "Brooke, are you hungry?"

"No. Thank you, Mom. The girls are waiting for me. We're having lunch together before afternoon classes. We thought you may want to join us."

"Oh no. I'm going to give this wonderful, freshly ground coffee the attention it deserves, make a giant bowl of Porridge, then take a long bath. Yesterday's all day London trip obviously wiped me out. I'm old. Please tell the Alphabet girls, thank you for the invite, but I'll make it up to you. Tell them to have a light lunch, I'll take you all out for dinner. Anywhere you want. Let's go back to the William Penn."

"The Wig and Penn?" Brooke rolls her eyes.

"Yes, let's go there."

"Let's go somewhere else. We don't really eat at the Wig and Penn, just drink. There's a cool place that's tucked into an ally called the Turf Tavern. We'll go there. I'll talk to the girls." Brooke talks as she walks down the hall towards the front door and all her winter gear.

"So, how was London?" Beren breaks in to change the mood.

"Lovely. We covered so much of London and ended the night at the Hyde Park Christmas Market. Excuse me." I say as I set the coffee to brew and walk down the hall to see Brooke off.

All bundled up, she hugs me tight, whispering, "I'm glad you're OK" and heads out, turns and says much louder, "Please don't call them alphabet girls," instead of good bye.

"I love ya too, honey." I say, after she closes the door.

Beren is gone. I'm left alone in the kitchen with the best coffee ever, my porridge, and a mounting curiosity about this family. I have to get upstairs to google Father Mathews, the Apostle of Temperance. I'd also love to know the time period the Irish were burning witches. I thought that all stopped by the early 1700's. My Dad was born in 1914 and his Mom was born in 1869. It's hard for me to believe there was a young woman accused of witchcraft and burned in Ireland around that time. Is this all related to Nostradamus or do I have way too much time on my hands and want this all to fit?

I was so absorbed by my thoughts, I didn't notice Dammie sitting on the kitchen table, licking my mostly empty porridge bowl.

"Eww!" I say, as I grab the bowl and my coffee cup. "That is not appetizing." I whisper harshly as I rise to put the porridge bowl in the sink and turn to fill my coffee cup again.

Dammie jumps off the table and onto the counter following the porridge bowl into the sink. Dishes go crashing to the floor. "I'm not going to be blamed for this, Michael." Bea and Beren obviously allow their Cat to walk around on the kitchen counters. Gross. I bend down to pick up the fallen dishes, with that, books come crashing down.

I reluctantly put my coffee down to pick up after this Cat, I now hate more than ever.

Why did they leave me alone with this Cat?

I begin to put the books back into the bookcase located just above the sink. "Eat to Live", by Joel Fuhrman.

I have that one.

"Chopra Center Cookbook", Deepak Choprah.

I have that one too.

"Techniques in Home Winemaking", by Pambianchi. "The Green Pharmacy", by Dr. James A Duke. Another book of the same title, Duke also. Looks like a newer version of the first. I pick out that book to read the cover. 'New discoveries in Herbal Remedies for

Common Diseases and Conditions from the world's foremost authority on healing herbs.' I'm pretty sure Michael Nostradamus would not agree with that rhetoric. These are not cookbooks. 'The Complete Book of Incense, Oils, and Brews', Cunningham. 'The Elixirs of Nostradamus'. My eyebrows go up. I read the front cover aloud, "Nostradamus' original recipes for elixirs, scented water, beauty potions and sweetmeats. The first English translation 1996."

Oh I'm sure my landlords will not mind if I take this to my room. I press the book to my chest, grab my coffee, and head upstairs.

Before exiting the kitchen I turn to Dammie, with a bow, "Thank you." Just behind him is an old wooden sign. "NO!" I gasp out loud.

'Why do we think love is a magician?'

All these coincidences are beginning to pile up, which is making this vacation one of my best ever. Of course, I don't believe in witchcraft, but this family is very interesting.

It's 1 o'clock. I'm meeting the Alphabet Girls at 5. As anxious as I am to google 'the Apostle of Temperance', this book comes first. I run upstairs and make the decision to keep the door open.

The chapters on Elixirs has a forward by Wulfing von Rohr, which reads, in part:

"… Most of Nostradamus' biographers cannot agree whether there was direct contact between him and Rabelais: however, Manafred Dimde, the most important German Nostradamus expert, considers that **he can prove close co-operation in the realms of medicine and magic and in the constitution of a secret society.**" I'm riveted.

I page through the Elixirs. The first recipe I turn to is for 'cleansing the face', which starts with putting a 'good sized piece of mercury' on segments of lime. Since I'm very sure mercury will make Swiss cheese of your brain, I will not be following any of his other recipes. In fact, I know the term 'mad hatter' came about, in the 1800's, when hat makers lined hats with mercury. Finding out much later, the mercury made the hat wearers go mad.

Then, I come to Chapter 18 which simply says,

"DEAR FRIENDLY READER, at this point, not without very good reasons, I have omitted from my translation into German the eighteenth chapter, because it teaches such things as are not fitting for a Christian or God fearing man to know and I therefore felt it better not to make any mention of them."

Oh yea. If Nostradamus did not go mad by handling mercury, I'm guessing he found some other hallucinogens, and probably addictive hallucinogens, which is exactly what Deidre had said.

I look up to the clock. I've been on my bed reading for over an hour and Dammie is sitting at my feet.

"Cool book, Dammie. Now let's find out why we think love is a magician." Then add, "I bet you already know." And that quickly, Dammie is not so bad.

I move to the desk and my laptop.

Google, 'Why do we think love is a magician?' ENTER

Quotes by Marsilio Ficino.

"Why do we think love is a magician? Because the whole power of magic consists in love. The work of magic is the attraction of one thing by another because of a certain affinity of nature."

Whoa. I've read "The Secret" and "Ask and it is Given", both books on the laws of attraction, but I thought these were relatively new ideas. This guy, Ficino was saying this back in the late 1400s before Nostradamus was even born. The most advanced scientists in Nostradamus' time knew nothing about light waves, radio waves, sound waves... and yet Ficino uses the words instrument and vibrations... and messages in the ether. Sooo cool.

Back to Google. "Marsilio Ficino" ENTER

http://www.iep.utm.edu/ficino/

'Father of Natural Magic.' Ficino published *Three Books on Life*. The third presents Ficino's theory of natural magic, which has since become the definitive Renaissance consideration of the subject.'

Ficino writes… 'To avoid the perils of melancholy and preserve your health you must purify your spirit with three things: Wine and aromatic foods, pure-sunny air, and music…' These are the same quotes as on the sign in that Pub near Hyde Park.

I really like this guy, Ficino.

As I read further, I realize, Ficino's three books on life deal not with the health of the body, but the health of the soul. Defining true love, teaching ethics, and the importance of thankfulness.

Ficino goes on to say that music and the human spirit are very similar, in that, they both 'live in the air, moving in an organized way, which can carry intellectual content.' He writes that he is, 'disappointed that priests do not care more for the instrument, (the spirit), which, he is certain, can measure and grasp the whole world'.

Ficino's use of the term 'instrument' is striking. I'm reminded of my Dad, an early pioneer in sophisticated electronics, working on top secret radar projects for the US Navy during WWII. In the 40's, 50s, 60' and 70s he led the revolution in telecommunications technology, holding patents for numerous two-way communication inventions while gracing the cover of magazines like RADIO and FM/TV several times. My Dad was a true genius.

At a very young age I was immersed in the amateur radio communication of HAM radio and Morse Code. His 'call letters' W2CDG were known throughout the world. On a clear night, he could 'talk', through Morse Code, all the way to other HAM Radio geeks in Europe. He taught me, the big antenna (instrument) atop our home, picks up dots and dashes' riding on radio waves at different frequencies.

It works exactly like our eyes. Our eyes are specialized instruments that can differentiate between different light waves. Our brain interprets those signals so we can understand them.

Our ears too are just instruments. Specialized to differentiate between different sound waves.

Radios can tune into, different radio frequencies or 'channels'. Each frequency can contain a different message.

My Dad said that since our brains send out brain waves, we may be able to develop equipment that, not just can detect these waves, but decipher the message on those waves. MAYBE, he theorized, we all already have equipment that just needs tuning in and the volume turned up.

I sit back. Ficino wrote of information, (like music), that is in the ether. Further, Ficino believed, it is our SOUL that can decipher these messages. In his writings he begged his fellow priests to care for their soul, because it's through the soul we can receive and interpret.

He wrote all this in the 1400's. Brilliant. I like Ficino. He reminds me of my Dad.

Now it's 4 o'clock. If I want to meet the Alphabet Girls for dinner, I have to start getting ready now.

"OK Dammie," I say to the Cat who has been sitting at my right elbow on the desk watching me and my computer. "I appreciate the company but I have to get ready for dinner." To my surprise, Dammie gets up and runs out. My door, still ajar.

I'm consumed with questions, but I have to go. What is Ficino's connection to Nostradamus if any? Was Beatrix's Artisan Center really the magic society begun by Nostradamus and Rabelais? When did Europe's laws put an end to burning witches? What really happened with that poor young English nanny? Was this Irish Apostle of Temperance really admitted to Congress? I'm going to need to start a time line... But I can't keep the Alphabet Girls waiting.

The sound of giggles coming up the hill to the bus stop, where I stand freezing, pushes the fifteen and sixteen-hundreds out of my mind. After a very short bus ride, but a very long walk through a maze of alleys, (I'm sure we walked passed a couple places twice), just outside the city center wall of Oxford, we find the hidden Turfs Tavern. Very cool. The place is packed but we find a table to fit five and immediately begin to realize that the entire pub is filled with soccer players. Yes, dozens of athletic, handsome, 20-somethings. The Alphabet Girls are glowing, and very quickly, the soccer players notice them too. I was ignored but spent my time in appreciation of youth. They all had so much energy, heart on their sleeve, willing to take a chance on love or rejection. I admire them all. I really want to ask Deidre if she knows of any Nostradamus/Rabelais connection, but she's so happily distracted, I can't bring myself to pull her away.

I think to myself, *'like bees to a hive'*. I notice that the team colors are yellow and black stripes, which magnifies the illusion of bees. I giggle to myself.

"You find something funny?" Comes a deep masculine voice from behind me.

"Hello." I say startled.

"You were just laughing. What is it you find funny?"

"Bees to a hive? Yellow and black team colors..." I trail off, hoping I won't have to explain myself any further than that.

"Ah, yes. Well, it's gold and dark blue to be exact, but yes, I get it. You and all your 'hive' are American?" He asks.

"Yes." I stick out my hand. "Joyce. Joyce Burgess."

"Chas. Chas Michaels. I'm the Bees' coach. Well, one of the coaches."

"Have you played already? Or are you about to play?" I say, uncomfortably. I'm not very good at small talk.

"We're just coming from practice. We'll be playing tomorrow. I believe your girls are getting invited." He nods, pointing at the 'hive'.

"No doubt." I say, because I can't think of anything else to say. Unlike the Alphabet Girls, I'm uncomfortable with first meetings, especially this one-on-one. Chas is standing too close and my bar stool is already up against the wall.

"Where in the US are you from?" Chas asks.

"New Jersey." I say, knowing most people think NJ is a factory polluting, parkway-slash-turnpike, industrial accident. I always want to add, 'It's the Garden state.' But I don't.

"Oh, yes I worked at ITT, a very long time ago, in Clifton. Northern New Jersey."

"I know it well. I grew up in Rutherford, the next town over. The last thirty years I've been living at the beach." I used to say 'the Jersey shore' but since the crude show of that name got popular, I now use this phrase. Still uncomfortable, I try to get the conversational ball in his court. "What did you do there at ITT? My Dad used to work there, a very long time ago."

"I ran the place. I'm retired now. Just Coach Chas now. What was your Dad's name? Maybe I knew him."

"No. You were probably fifteen when he retired." I laughed.

"Oh?" he said smirking. "And how old were you when he retired?"

"Fifteen." I say, instantly regretting this whole thing, while hoping I wasn't insulting this guy, who looks my age, but I could be wrong. Needing to change the subject, "Maybe you can help me with something. There's a picture of our US President Clinton behind the bar. Why would there be a picture of one of our Presidents behind an English bar?"

"Ah. Well your Bill Clinton was a Rhodes Scholar and therefore, went to Oxford." Chas pauses with a big smirk.

"Ah, yes." I feel like an idiot. I should have known that.

Chas continues, "Well the amusing part of the story is, this is the bar where he... Quoting Bill now, he 'did not inhale and did not break any laws of the United States.'"

I laugh a full throated, mouth open, laugh. "Oh." I say simply. "What other amusing stuff do you know about the Turf Tavern?" I say, much more relaxed and realizing that this guy has nice eyes and a very large chest. I blush and look down.

"Well," he continues, noticing my blush and probably noticed my quick, but too long glance, at his chest. "They say, there's a ghost roaming 'round, if you're into that kind of thing." Seeing my eyebrows go up, he continues, "Oh, yes. Reportedly 'Old Rosie' haunts the place. She drowned herself after learning her lover was killed in the Civil War."

"What was her 'lover' doing in our civil war?" I ask.

"The English Civil War." He corrects me.

"She drown herself in alcohol?" I question.

"No. In one of the many moats in the area." He says, trying (not too hard) to be polite.

"Aw. Poor Rosie." I say, realizing I seem to be embarrassing myself. This conversation is not going well.

"So what did your Dad do at ITT?" Chas, tries again.

"He was an electronics engineer. He worked on the big radio units way back, WWII era stuff until he retired around 1974." Explaining the gap in time, I add, "My Dad was 45 when I was born."

"Well, you're right. Before my time." Chas says as I look around, trying to find one of my Alphabet Girls to get me out of this conversation. Chas continues, "Well, I'm sure the girls have, certainly by now, been invited to the game tomorrow. It was nice meeting you, I hope you'll come with them, Joyce." He extends his hand.

"Uhm, maybe." I smile as he takes my hand with both of his.

"I do hope to see you there." He leans in, and looks down, directly into my eyes.

"Maybe." I say, my voice, only a bit, but still noticeably, higher. I blush again. Chas is tall and handsome-ish. I wonder why all this meeting and dating in my 50s can't be easier.

This was awkward and I'm instantly relieved he's gone.

Just as I begin to feel self-consciously alone, Angel appears with another glass of wine for me, the other girls are right behind her with our food.

"Having fun?" I say to them all.

"Yes." Brooke says, "Hey Mom, wanna go to a football game tomorrow?"

"Sitting on bleachers for hours in an Oxford November is not going to happen. You guys go." I say hoping they drop this.

"You were talking to their Coach, what'd he have to say?" Asked Brooke.

"He's cute". Angel said, not waiting for me to answer Brooke.

"The game is tomorrow at one." Said Deidre.

"Did you think he's cute?" Angel asks while looking in Chas' direction.

"Angel! Eyes on me. Oh Lord. We were just talking about the ghost that haunts this place. Yes, I think he is handsome-ish but he lives in Oxford and I live in New Jersey." I add, "The Garden State."

"Ghost?" Chelsea is intrigued.

For the next two hours we eat fish and chips and talk about Ghosts, then share a dessert of Sticky Toffee and Date pudding with Cornish clotted-cream ice cream.

Life is good.

"Deidre, I've been researching Nostradamus and his University of Montpellier classmate, Rabelais. I have read from multiple sources they began a school, a secret society that studied medicine, meditation and magic. Do you know anything about that?"

"Yeah, I've read they started a secret research school under the cover of Freemasonry. Back then the term 'invisible college' was big. Invisible because there's no actual classrooms. A bunch of guys show up at a restaurant or bar and share research and knowledge in different subjects. As you can imagine, the Catholic Church was not a fan.

That whole area around Montpellier is filled with weird characters thinkin' they're witches and warlocks. I've never been there, but I've heard it's very strange." Deidra says.

The girls want to get back early. They have papers due etcetera and all are going to yoga early tomorrow. So, we reluctantly leave in search of the bus stop.

"Why don't you join us for yoga tomorrow, It's not until 8AM?" Angel says. She misses her Mom and has been fawning over me a bit.

"Where?" I say, with a pained look. Then directed at Brooke, "Are you going?"

Angel answers, "This will be Brooke's first time."

"Are you all going?" I turn towards Deidra.

"Yes, Angel has convinced us all to go. I think you'll like it. It's different. We're doing movements in the first part of the meditation. I get the theory behind it. Makes sense."

"It's held at my church just a couple blocks down the hill from your BNB!" Angel is really hoping I go.

I give in. "Come by ten-minutes-to-eight. I'll be ready." I say, as I get off the bus and give each girl a big hug before parting ways.

They all hug me back with a thankfulness that reminds me, they're all here without their own Moms. "Love you guys."

As always, the walk home from the bus stop is a bit scary and insanely cold. As I come down the walkway to the B&B, I see lights dancing in the front living room window. There's a fire in the fireplace. Lovely. I hope Dan is up. I have so many questions.

Chapter 7

What God wills, will be.

After removing my tedious winter garb and hang it all on the coat rack, I notice the Cat is sitting. Watching me.

"Hello Michael." I say. We're on a first name basis.

I round the corner to the living room, and there is Dan.

"Please, stay seated." I insist, as he begins to unfold from his perch, legs crossed, somehow comfortably sitting on a very small foot stool just in front of the fireplace. He can fold up to a very small footprint. I add, "Someone started a fire. Lovely," as I'm really thinking of the nursery rhyme, 'little Miss. Muffet sat on a tuffet.' THAT must be a tuffet.

"Yes, how was your evening?" Dan says, as he smokes a cigarette, flicking ashes in the fire, and exhaling up the chimney. I wonder if smoking is allowed in this house.

"Wonderful. I've been thinking about you and your family history." I say. The understatement makes me smile.

"Yes. I've had a chance to talk to my Mum today."

"Oh yes, how is your Dad?" Realizing this poor guy has had a lot to deal with this week.

"He's doing very well, came out of surgery like a champ. Apparently, he needed a triple by-pass."

"I'm glad he's recovering well. Is your whole family here now?"

"Yes, my brother is still at hospital with my Mum. He said he'll be here before midnight."

"Glad to hear it. I didn't get to look up your Apostle of Temperance." I say, as I take a seat on the couch.

"You'll find a lot of crazy stuff researching the Mathew's Family. My Mum reminded me of some of the details today, of the time period that all that crazy stuff happened." He pauses to take a drag of his cigarette and to be sure I am still interested.

"I'm riveted." I say honestly.

"OK, so the really crazy story is of Francis Mathew." Dan said as he waives his hand in the air, as if announcing a grand entrance to a ball. "1st Earl of Llandaff."

"Before he was given the title, when he was very young, he got his thirteen-year-old girlfriend pregnant, and they…"

"She was thirteen?" I interrupt.

"Yes, back then, that happened very often. Girls, especially, were married off very young. But of course, a scandal. They named the baby Theobald Mathew. That son disappeared, no doubt sent to a relative. Some say died young. No one really knows."

"How do you know that?"

"Well, there were courts, still are courts, 'the office of arms' and such where you registered your offspring. Registration is very important to protect your lineage, your titles, and to be sure your name continues on. There is a saying, 'every lord needs an heir and a spare'. So, this Francis Mathew, the 1st Earl of Llandaff, listed Arnold in registrations which are dated, signed and notarized." Dan pauses to make sure I have no more questions and to take another drag.

"Anyway, six years later, he got this same girl pregnant again. By now she's nineteen, and this time, Francis marries her. Ellisha Smyth Mathews. They got married in September then, snuck down to Paris to have this baby, February of the next year. This was his first legal heir, Arnold Nesbit Mathew. Now, even though Arnold was a legitimate heir under English law, Francis and Elli sent him to a relative's house to be raised."

"Were they living in the Thomastown Castle?" I interrupt.

"Well, they were living in Thomastown on the land but the building was not a grand structure at that time.

Anyway, they had their third son, Francis James, finally naming a boy after himself. Then a fourth son, Montague. Then, after his wife died and he remarried he had a fifth son, George Tobias Skeffington Mathew…" Pause for another drag and hand wave, "… and finally a daughter, Ellisha, named after his first wife."

Dan lists, as he holds up his fingers. "Now with five sons,

One, Theobald, who was born out of wedlock and disappeared, then

Two, Arnold, born in Paris, sent to live with relatives, but the legal heir. Went off to fight in the Indian war.

Three, Francis, later known as the 'black sheep',

Four, Montague,

Five, George, the youngest.

You'd think there would be lots of Mathews' grandchildren running 'round, but no. Only Arnold, that second son, the one born in Paris and sent away, had children.

Now, when the father of all these boys, Francis, the 1st Earl of Llandaff, died around 1810, Francis the third son, the black sheep, told the court that no Last Will and Testament was found. With the help of a sleazy legal advisor, Francis convinced a court that Arnold, (The actual heir) was dead with no heirs, and he, Francis, the Black Sheep, was the rightful heir and began using the title '2nd Earl of Llandaff'.

With the approval of the court (remember, the rightful heir was serving in the army in India) and no objection from any of his family, the black sheep sold all his father's property, except the Thomastown property. Apparently, the assets in Wales were quite extensive, enough to pay off a bunch of gambling debts and expand this Thomastown property into a giant gothic-style extravagance.

This new expanded castle was enormous. There were over 100 rooms just for the servants, huge horse stables, and much of the river was rerouted to feed the spectacular gardens."

"How do you know all this to be true, and with so much detail?" I say, trying not to question the validity of this story, but still so curious.

"Well, in short, the rightful heir, Arnold, was not dead at all, and whose son had a son, my great-grandfather Arnold Harris Mathew, filed a petition to restore his title and lands. All these details with all the supporting documents are in the court papers. In fact, the story was summarized and published in Country Life Illustrated around 1900." Dan paused to take another puff, flick and exhale up the chimney.

Dan waits a bit to be sure I want him to continue. "While all these shenanigans were going on, there were other Mathews' families living in the Castle and on nearby estates. That's why Thomastown is called the seat of the Mathews. James Mathews and Anne Whyte Mathews had two sons, both born at the castle in the late 1800s. One of those sons, became the Apostle of Temperance, Theobald Mathews. In an estate near the castle, called Rathcloheen, lived John Mathew and Cherry Pennefather Mathew, who were having children around 1830 as well.

We all think one of these children was the toddler that drown. The witch-nanny was accused of putting a sleeping spell on the Mum.

It wasn't too soon after that, the Apostle of Temperance began his Total Abstinence Society." Dan pauses again to smoke.

I take this opportunity to question, "So your theory is, a little child drown, but the nanny was NOT on duty that day. The mother, who was probably supposed to be watching her own child was so stricken with guilt that she blamed the nanny. I am further guessing that the Mother was intoxicated when the child drown and intoxication was the reason for the inattention. Theobald knew this secret and so he pledged to bring as many people to sobriety as possible to atone for this poor, innocent, nanny's death. Yes?"

"Yes." Dan said.

"Wow. Now, that is some family history." I realize Dan's head is down. His mood is quiet. He's obviously taking personal responsibility for this injustice just for being a member of this family.

"You can't take this as your guilt." I say, trying to mitigate the verbal damage I just aimed directly at him."

"I know most people don't believe in witchcraft, but witchcraft or no, the curse certainly did come true and continues today."

I don't have anything to say to help this poor guy. I try to slightly change the subject. "So Cherry Pennefeather is a real name?"

"Yes, Short for Charity, and it's PenneFATHER." Dan corrected.

"What exactly was the witch's curse?"

"The curse was, 'No Mathews would realize their wealth'." Dan said as if he has said that phrase hundreds of times.

"But obviously, the real heir, your great grandfather reclaimed the titles the fortune and the castle?"

"Oh, so that's another crazy thing. All through the time when all these shenanigans was goin' on, Arnold was serving in the military in India.

After Francis, the 'black sheep' passed away, the court appointed the young daughter, Ellisha as the administrator. So Elisha, writes to Arnold Nesbitt in India and addresses the letter, to 'Arnold the 2nd Earl of Llandaff', acknowledging his rights, and assuring him she will take great care of the property. As you can imagine, Arnold is not happy with the whole Mathew family because he was not allowed to live with his own parents, sister and brothers, while other relatives were allowed to live in the castle. So 15 years after the letter, Arnold finally travels to Thomastown. He finds Elisha had died and willed the entire estate (which was not hers to give) to her French cousins the Viscount Chabot. Instead of fighting, he just left for London and swore he would never return and never talk to any of the Mathews clan ever again. So Arnold, never realized his wealth either.

The Chabots owned the property just a short time and then the Daly's ran it but that is when the place started to deteriorate.

Anyway, bringing this story up to my grandfather, just before 1900 Arnold's son's son, my great-grandfather, petitioned the court to fix his inheritance. Unfortunately, by then the castle was in ruin. The Daly's were known to be 'slum landlords'. They just collected rents but did nothing in maintenance for decades. To make matters worse, in 1950 the roof was removed to avoid the 'roof tax'." Dan says as he flicks his cigarette ashes into the fireplace and drinks tea from an oversized cup.

"Wow. That's some story." I say.

"Yea. Many people have said it would make a good book."

"I was thinking the same thing. This would make a great movie." I say, as I notice the time. "I have an early meet-up with my daughter, I have to go to bed. I'm sorry I'll miss your brother. I do want to talk more about this, but for now, I have to go. I'm one of those people that needs more sleep than most. Good night, Dan."

"Pleasant dreams, Joyce." Dan says, rising to be polite.

As I climb the stairs I think *'it's a very interesting history but the real story is the witch's execution in the 1830s AND the fact that this guy believes the curse.'* I begin to take the stairs two at a time.

I go directly to my computer.

Google "Irish witch craft" ENTER.

I find a list of witch trials by country, which lists Ireland as having just four and estimated as many as ten, while Germany lists over EIGHT THOUSAND known trials, and estimated as many as twenty-six-thousand! Whoa.

Ireland folklore is full of good fairies, and other good hearted mystical beings. So accusing someone of witchcraft is not, at first, a bad thing. Which explains the almost non-existent witch trials. I find that while the famous Salem Witch Trials were conducted in Boston, late sixteen hundreds, fifty miles from the Thomastown castle, in one trial, they executed 20 people. I find another trial held in the early seventeen-hundreds, again one trial but eight woman executed.

I find the British 'Witchcraft Act of 1735', which states that witchcraft has ceased to be an act punishable by law.

Dan's story, although fantastic, is looking to me as just that, a story. Since the British ended witch trials with the 'Witchcraft Act of 1735' and the Apostle of Temperance began his campaign in 1835... Not really plausible that Theobald, the Apostle of Temperance, somewhere around 1830, saw a witch, accused and put to death.

Back to Google. "Ireland witch trial 1830" ENTER

Bingo! 1865, Bridget Ellen Early, County of Clare.

Google "Directions County of Clare to Thomas Town, County of Tipperary, Ireland. ENTER

50 miles from Thomastown.

Bridget was an herbalist, at the ripe old age of 72, after four husbands, reported to talk to fairies. She was accused of witchcraft, found guilty before the court of Ennis and put to death in 1870. I find that in Ireland, witches found guilty were strangled first then burned.

"Oh, dear Lord." I say out loud. "That's not going to help me sleep well."

I need a timeline. I begin to scribble.

1735 Witchcraft law, banning accusations of witchcraft

1790 Born - Apostle of Temperance, Theobald Matthew

1835 Theobald Mathew begins his campaign (45 years old)

1870 Bridget Ellen Early put to death at 72 years old.

Yes, a nanny put to death in the 1830's is entirely possible for Ireland.

I'm still trying to find the history of the Thomastown witch trial…

Google 'Witch trial. Tipperary County, Ireland' ENTER

I find Bridget Clearly again. Accused of talking to fairies. But the dates don't match and the circumstances don't match…

I look back through my search history. –

1870 - Bridget Early, put to death at 72. Yup. That's what I listed.

1895 - Bridget Clearly 24 years old, is put to death, accused of talking to fairies.

This website reports that Bridget was just 24 year's old, living in a home with her husband and father-in-law. This home, was supposedly built on the site of a fairy ring fort.

"Of course it was." I mumble. The two men accused poor Bridget of being abducted by fairies and was possessed by a witch. Without a trial, the two men immolated her.

I have to look that up.

Google 'Immolated' ENTER

Apparently, the two men poured boiling oil down her throat until she exploded. "Oh Lord." I say out loud. I notice the Cat is at my elbow. "Now, there's a woman who picked the wrong family to married into." I turn to Dammie, more seriously, "The sick part is, Michael, this really happened. Those are some seriously messed up men." I pause, sit back and try to understand how two grown men could do such a hideous thing. SUCH a violent thing. Was alcohol involved? Maybe mercury, or some other 'home remedy' was involved?

Google, 'harmful home remedies of the 1800's' ENTER

"19 wildly dangerous home remedies of the 1800's"

A quick review includes ingesting kerosene, boric acid, turpentine, ammonia…

"Dear Lord, Michael. Says here, if ingesting this stuff gives you a sore throat, take a Cocaine lozenge. Yeah, that'll fix it… and create an addiction ending in, who knows? Well, ending in emulsifying your lovely wife." I pause. "Two hundred years ago, these were real suggestions, this was a real family. This poor woman really was held down and…" I turn to Dammie, "…ex-plod-ed."

"Let's try to find out if Bridget was 72 or 24. One of these reports is wrong." I start another timeline;

1870 Bridget Early 72 years old.

1895 Bridget Clearly 24 years old.

"Wait!" I say out loud. "Bridget Clearly is not Bridget Early. Two different women. So, Bridget Early died the same year Bridget Clearly was born! Holy, crap, Michael." Gasping, "Bridget Early accused of talking to fairies, while Bridget Clearly was said to have been captured by these fairies and exchanged for a changeling. Further, she lived in a house said to have been built on a fairy cemetery."

I sit back. This is really creepy. Too creepy. Especially, before bed.

I shut the laptop with a snap. Dammie backs up.

"Yeah, that'll give us nightmares." This is not a very good bedtime story. "I'm going to bed. You have to go." But Dammie is already gone.

I slip into bed praying for sweet dreams, then, praying for poor Bridget. Both of them. Selfishly thankful, I don't live in the 1800's Ireland. I don't care what kind of 'medicine' those two men were on, holding that young girl down and… boiling oil… I moan audibly and roll over then abruptly sit up, as if I could get away from the horrid thought by leaving it on my pillow.

I need some space. Maybe if I brush my teeth, drink some cold water, spend some time in the very, well-lit bathroom… and I'm up on my feet.

At the bathroom mirror I stare deep into my own eyes. So dark brown. All the vile images that can abduct me in my sleep are hiding behind a very sheer curtain. I can feel them. A house of horrors awaits. Once asleep, I can be strapped and trapped into the ride, and shown the worst of human nature. Grotesque figures of two strong men holding down that poor woman. She was just 24, about the same age as the Alphabet Girls. Did she fight and curse at them, which would only strengthen their resolve that this was not their beloved wife/daughter-in-law? Did she beg for mercy? Did she just give up and weep? I can imagine Angel weeping. Deidre would fight, Chelsea would beg for mercy. No matter which, the end would be the same.

"Emulsification." I say it out loud, maybe to rid the images of some if it's horror.

Brooke. Brooke would keep her cool and be cunning. I imagine Brooke would somehow break free. Maybe tell the duo she was pregnant or maybe fake being exorcised of the fairy beasts. Brooke would see the entrapment coming and never arrive. Brooke would never be with a man who could do such a thing in the first place. Brooke would never be with anyone more than a minute, male or female, who would be violent. Yes. Brooke has never been attracted to drama. Somehow, playing this scene with Brooke as the lead has chased away the fear and frustration. I feel better. If the boogie man comes to get me, I will send him Brooke. She will vanquish the evil.

"Vanquish the evil." I say out loud, waiving my toothbrush, with a chuckle. I've got to get some sleep.

I go back to my bed. I throw the pillow across the room, just in case those horrid thoughts are resting there. I know it's ridiculous, but I do it anyway. I won't be researching witchcraft before bed again.

After a deep breath, I try to focus on good things. My kind-hearted Liz. I bring up images of Liz through the years, her big, happy, innocent face. She is happiest when surrounded by children, especially her children. Slowly, I allow myself to descend into sleep.

My dream begins happily with the face of Liz the Kind-Hearted. She's in a street market much more like the small Oxford market than the Hyde Park market in London. She's dressed in a beautiful, light-blue, full-skirted dress of the 1800's. Her eyes are a tranquil, matching blue. She reaches out to a caged chicken. Her touch is calming...healing. She moves as if in a dream. Her empathy is visible, a halo, extending around her. While children are drawn to her, most adults will steer clear. They find her simple innocence so perfectly crystal clear it acts as a mirror, filled with truth that can shake the sinful to their core.

Liz moves along the line of merchants, exchanging smiles and pleasantries. As she comes up to a candy cart, her face lights up. Liz chooses sweets she knows the children will like. As she counts out the coins, the canopies above this cart suddenly blow up, almost taking the tent poles with it. The peddlers busy themselves re-securing their tents. Finally an old woman rises to take the money, but she is looking past Liz with widening eyes.

"Beware, Elizabeth." The old woman says in French in a deep raspy warning.

"Excuse me? Do I know you?"

"I know you, Elizabeth Blanc de Noir, and your family. You'll need them now. I'll call for them to come."

Liz holds out the payment for the candy bewildered, but the old woman grabs her wrist and pulls her in. The old woman's hands shake while her fingertips squeeze on Liz's wrist. *"Hold onto your Love, with both hands. Be kind to yourself, our treasured Elizabeth."*

There is screaming in the background, sounds of a stampede of horses. Liz turns to see the Mathews Calvary of destruction is coming closer. Two dozen Mathew's guards are on horseback, destroying the market and heading directly for her. Liz stands still.

"Liz! You must hide." Behind her, a familiar face. Tall, handsome, military.

"Good morning. What's going on?" Liz says calmly but bewildered, ignoring his urgency.

"A tragedy. Lilyanna is dead."

"No!" Liz whispers in horror, pulling away from his grasp, her peaches and cream skin turning red, and around her lips now pale white.

"Yes, she drown in the main courtyard fountain."

"No! Where was Cherry? That can't be." Liz is pleading for this news to be false.

"She was the last to leave the party last night. She was too hard asleep with drink."

"Impossible. It's afternoon." Liz is still trying to find a way for this horror to be a mistake.

"*Elizabeth, she was still drunk from last night's dance. Elizabeth, they're blaming you.*"

"*Me? But, when I left the children, they were still in their beds...*"

"*Elizabeth, run with me. They're blaming you. They say it was you that put a sleeping spell on Cherry. They're calling you a...*"

"*Witch!*" One of the Mathew's guards spots her, raises his arm and points directly at Liz, shouts again, "*Witch!*"

"*Elizabeth, run with me now. Please, come with me. Elizabeth.*"

But Liz stands silently, resolute. She whispers under her breath, "What God wills, will be." Repeating the Welsh motto on every Mathews' coat of arms. 'Y fyn Duw a fydd'.

Without a word to defend herself, or to weep, she is taken suddenly, abruptly, abusively. She is swept away with the guards that leave just as swiftly as they assaulted this market.

The crowd is left in collective quiet. The secret in the air becomes so thick, it's visible. The crowd is still, silent, and unmoving, in contrast to the ether which begins to swirl in an organized, visible vapor... until this tempest reveals its vortex... Which has a life of its own.

Just as the squall seems to be building to a full blown tornado, it vanishes.

The handsome friend looks down. There, on the ground, are scattered candies and coins jolted from the hands of this sweet Elizabeth, The Kind Hearted. His fury builds to screaming...

"*NO!*"

Chapter 8
www.LiFT.foundation

"No!" I wake breathless. This sucks. It's just 2 AM. Maybe this vacation is not as cool as I had first thought.

I'm up and out of bed, back in the bathroom, with all the lights on. I may not be brave enough to go back to bed.

"This sucks." I say out loud to my exhausted reflection. At once, I see the toll that multiple nights of restless sleep have taken from me, creating an old lady in the mirror.

I sit down on the side of the tub, not braving the image in the mirror.

Back in the 1830's, a woman who lived in a castle was blessed with a child. Horrifically, she realized too late, she neglected this sweet innocent blessing... to death.

'It's not my fault' is a strong lie, which succeeds in pushing away the pain of blame... the beginning of the road to shame and unbearable agony. Looking further down that road... to admitting to friends and family, your Mother, your sister...

Your husband... that you just neglected his daughter to death. Unimaginable humiliation, disgrace... which would never end until death. Suicide.

Even an epic, obvious lie, like accusing a young innocent of witchcraft can be the difference between - walking the earth as a humiliated, irresponsible mother verses living as a witch's victim, forever exclaiming, "A witch killed my child. Poor me."

That was Lady Mathew's choice on that summer day in the 1831.

This is not a fake story, but a real family with a real nanny and real little child. Drowned. This was a real woman, a Mother, a member of a huge prominent family, with a choice.

I refocus - My daughters' are healthy, happy, and most importantly, safe. My grandsons, are certainly by now, tucked into their shared bunkbed, having superhero dreams, safe and sound. But in the 1830s, in Ireland, throughout the Thomastown Castle community, there was a very sweet nanny, living in a toxic environment of a jealous, powerful man, the 'black sheep' of the Mathews family, who was not the heir to the castle. Somehow he convinced his brothers, sister and cousins to con a court... to give him absolute power, not just over the title, but over the vast wealth.

I can imagine that Cherry Pennefather stayed out very late, drank too much on the eve of a day where the sweet nanny had a morning off. Just because Cherry gave into the addiction of drink, doesn't mean she didn't love her toddler. In fact, the horror of finding her daughter drown must have been worse one-hundred fold when she realized it was the result of her drunken over-sleep.

Yes. I can see her immediate reaction could certainly have been, 'It's not my fault'. In a time where witches were blamed for sickness... Yes. I can see this all reasonably happened. I empathize with this Mother who would rather breathe her last, right then, instead of facing her family, friends and her husband along with the unfriendly Thomastown community.

Certainly, if this cousin, Cherry Pennefather was part of the scheme, asked to back up HIS lie to give the 'black sheep' all that power and money, she could now blackmail the powerful 'black sheep' to go along with HER lie. Yes. I could see, and unfortunately, in this 3AM, on vacation in England I FEEL this, All. Too. Much. He who has information that can pull down the black-sheep in power, has power himself, in this case, herself... Black mail the Black-sheep.

Further, how could Cherry Pennefather NOT be jealous of the sweet, young Elizabeth? A young girl, whose heart is attracted to the service of nanny-hood and probably by now showing signs of young adulthood. She's just as beautiful inside as out. Yes. A perfect storm, fueled further by jealousy.

I feel the excruciating grief, fraught with guilt, of this mother finding her toddler drowned, then seeing a path out. Blame someone else. Blame the nanny.

This household will go along with the lie. Thomastown Castle was steeping with abuses. Alcohol abuse probably being the least of them. Secrets which have the power to take down this mighty empire. The seat of the Mathews.

Yes, these motives and actions are all assumptions and speculation, but what is true: This poor nanny, in the 1830s, after the devastating death of a precious toddler, she cared for, she loved... was accused of murder by witchcraft. Then inhumanly strangled and burned on the Thomastown Castle property. An innocent young girl put to Death, but first excruciating pain of her heart.

I sit on the side of this tub, my eyes closed now. Swaying at the edge of sleep, knowing that though these events happened hundreds of years ago, I still see so clearly... feel so deeply... with a frustration that only complete helplessness brings.

Did this nanny really curse this family to 'never realize their wealth'? Is Bea here to take the spell off or keep it going?

I rise, turn off the lights, so exhausted, I'm sure my demons can't conjure anymore horror. I grab the pillow on the chair. In this state of exhaustion, it can cause me no harm, and I drop into bed.

Focusing on my grandsons is the easiest way to begin filling my heart with love. Yes. They are most certainly now, in bed, in super-hero PJs and dreaming sweetly from a day filled with their loving Mommy, my Elizabeth the Kind-Hearted. When they're older they'll be strong handsome champions of any evil in their path.

Exhaustion takes me... unconscious, I have no defenses.

My dream begins:

I am again, in front of the fireplace in the house of Blanc de Noir. My mother-in-law, the red-headed Patrice, is cleaning. The doors bang open, I twitch and expect the worse. It's only the *girls running in with baskets of flowers.*

"Whoa-livia, Whoa-lysah! Please slow down." They seem to be always running. "Brooke, Karen, you two should know better." I say, pretending to scold. They know I'm so happy they're all out of the spell of the London trauma.

Patrice hugs them all, one at a time, while she takes their gifts of sweet smelling, fresh cut flowers. Then, she begins the process of beautifying this home, gathering multiple vases. I close my eyes and breathe in deeply, trying to identify the scent of each individual flower in the assortment, now laying on the dining table. Eyes still closed, while I take a second breathe... and smell... FEAR. I abruptly open my eyes but see nothing. I still smell fear and hear...

Elizabeth's voice from very far away... "Mommy."

"Ron!" Patrice says in elation, which snaps me out of my trance. Ron, Patrice's childhood friend who owns the near-by stables in town. In this last year, Ron has been the guiding star in Patrice's healthy recovery. Patrice drops her flowers to run to him for a hug and kiss, but stops short. "What is it, Ron?" Patrice says with intense apprehension.

"I smell fear." I say simply with an aching for Ron to give us the bad news quickly.

"A message has come from the people of the seat of the Mathews, The Thomastown Castle." Ron speaks clearly, trying to keep calm and strong.

"My Elizabeth?" I say choking.

"I'm afraid so." Ron says.

"She's dead?" I ask directly.

"No. But soon." Ron is anxious. "We have to leave now."

"Tell me." I am demanding for more detail.

"No one is sure but those that can see, have seen a singular tempest in the ether." Ron says, now sweating.

"...and?" I am close to screaming, though my voice is very deep.

The message is, as best as anyone can see, *"Come now. Bring the power of the house of Blanc de Noir."* He looks to Patrice, *"We believe Elizabeth needs you. I know you're just recently getting back your strength but... it would take a very large portion of the community, to send a message that clear, that loud... All. At. Once."* He stresses.

"The power of the Blanc de Noir?" I question.

"Yes. Patrice has a reputation for her wide reaching power."

"Power?" I'm confused..

"Yes. She was widely considered the most powerful in the craft until..." Ron hesitates and looks to Patrice.

"Was? Until what?" I press again.

"Well, yes. Was, well..." Ron hesitates again and looks to Patrice for permission to explain.

"Yes, Dear." Patrice walks to me slowly, taking both my hands with both of hers. Looks me straight in the eyes. *"Until Elizabeth was born."*

"Elizabeth? My Elizabeth?"

"Yes. I'll explain on the journey. We have to go NOW. There'll be many who have gotten this message. They'll arrive before us to help." Patrice turns to the twins. *"Tell the stables we'll need all the horses, ready as soon as possible. Brooke, Karen, we'll need to pack up food from the kitchen."*

"My carriages are on the way over. There'll be a small caravan at first, but more will be joining us." Ron is encouraging.

"Ron. I want a horse. A carriage is too slow. I'll go now. Right now." I insist.

"No, sweetie." Patrice is apologetic. "We need you. Elizabeth will be communicating through you. You're her Mother. It's complicated, but we have to stay together. We're most powerful together. Together." Patrice says almost in a chant.

Olivia and Olysia repeat, "Together."

Thankfully, the next thing I hear is my alarm. The girls'll be here in thirty minutes, and I need coffee. These dreams are not restful.

I try to shake off my nightmares. The bathroom, thankfully, has very bright lights. I'm going to refocus on my mission for this morning; dress for yoga and get out to meet the Alphabet Girls.

I leave the attic in a better frame of mind. The house is quiet. I softly descend the stairs. As I round the last turn, I catch Bea, exiting with a big duffle bag. I wonder where she's going so early. Thankfully, she's left a big pot of freshly brewed coffee.

The girls are right on time. I bundle up and join the gaggle of happy, healthy girls, on their way to morning yoga in Oxford. I feel so blessed. The church is just a couple of blocks away and very soon, we're pulling on the enormous front doors and entering the main cathedral. Beautiful. Statues rest inside alcoves where parishioners are praying and lighting candles.

Angel whispers, "Yoga is in the basement."

Reverently, we pass through the back of the church. I make a mental note: This is a great place to bring a drawing tablet and pencils.

We hurry down the stairs through double doors into a single basketball court. The room is only big enough for the court and one bench for the players of each team. Looking up ten feet, I see bleachers for spectators.

The girls lay out their yoga mats. Brooke has one for me. The front of the gym has three huge twenty-foot-long bright white banners hanging down from the second-floor bleachers. The first reads LOVE in red, graduating to orange from left to right. The next, FREEDOM in Yellow to Green and the third says, THANKFULNESS in blue to deep violet. I say out loud, "A rainbow."

Angel looks up. "Rainbow?"

"Yes," I say pointing to the banners. "ROY G BIV. **R**ed, **O**range, **Y**ellow, **G**reen, **B**lue, **I**ndigo and **V**iolet. Colors of the rainbow. Beautiful. Vibrant. Must be satin. Only satin shines like that." I add.

"Yes. It's a theme with LiFT yoga." Angel says. "You'll see. It's all about doing yoga while you meditate. Getting your feelings in sync."

'In sync' with what? I wonder.

The yoga mat in front, obviously that of the teacher, is bright white, with a logo that says www.LiFT.foundation.

"LiFT?" I ask Angel.

"**L**ove, **F**reedom and **T**hankfulness. You'll see. It'll all make sense." She hands me a note pad and pen. "After the meditation part you'll want to write down your thoughts. We've all had some really interesting coincidences. That's why I don't skip this class. It's only once a week."

Deidra adds, whispering, "The lady is really creepy, but that just adds to the intrigue."

Brooke cuts in, also whispering, "Mom. Look. It's Bea!"

"Bea?" ...and in walks Beatrix. My landlord, who ran an Artesian Center in the South of France, near the University of Montpellier. Bea with the crazy Cat. Bea with those Eyes... I hope she can't read my thoughts. I wave and blush.

"Oh, hello Joyce. Are these your Alphabet Girls?" Bea says.

"Yup, these are them. They've been telling me wonderful things about this class." I say, because I don't know what else to say.

"Aw, well, that's very nice." She nods to Angel. "OK class." She claps twice. "Let's get going." She lights up incense at each corner of the group.

For the next hour Bea takes us through yoga poses as we are instructed to feel love towards others. Then, alternately feel others loving us.

Feel freedom, and feel thankful. Each pose lends itself to these feelings. We go smoothly from one posture to another, instructed how to refine these poses to fit the ability of the poser.

Her voice was keeping me alert but in a trance.

Finally we sit, imagining we're safe and secure, on a garden bench. Again, we feel love towards nature and all that exists. Then alternately, we feel the love of all existence filling our heart, freedom, and then thankfulness. We bend our head down in reverence and both hands on our heart. "Anything is possible in love." she chants.

Truthfully, this is a powerful hour. Bea instructs us to breathe and listen. No more thinking. Listen with all our heart and when we are ready, open our eyes and write down whatever we have heard or a picture we've seen. If there is no message, begin writing whatever comes to mind.

One by one, we begin to 'wake'.

I write.

'Take care of yourself.'

I doodle, which comes out looking like a bird.

Brooke is the first to speak. "We gotta get out of here. Classes start soon and I have to go back to the dorm for my backpack."

"Ok." I'm ready. Bea and her banners are already gone.

The Alphabet Girls are energized but focused on getting out of here and back to their dorm. On the way out I grab a flyer. 'www.LiFT.foundation'.

Just two blocks later, "Thanks girls." I yell, as I take my left through the gate of my BNB.

"Don't forget, the game. I'll facetime you, Mom." Brooke yells over her shoulder, never slowing.

No one is in the kitchen so I take my coffee and porridge to my room, then begin running a hot bath, with bubbles.

As I soak in this hot tub, I close my eyes and try to take in all that's happened. 'Everything happens for a reason,' I say, as a reminder to myself. I'm trying to relax but really want to look at that LiFT brochure. I curse and get out of the tub, grab a towel, sling it around me and run out, grab the card, and head back into the bathroom… there is the Cat.

"Turn around." I say, feeling like an idiot.

He jumps onto the windowsill casement, and settles himself, looking out the window.

Apparently, www.LiFT.foundation has no physical address or phone number. I wonder if the foundation is based around Montpellier University. I wonder what's on this website. I'm trying to relax in this bubble bath but my curiosity is screaming. I'm sure a long hot bubble bath will do me good, but not right now. So, out of the tub I hop.

I pull up the website and read for almost an hour, but can't find where this foundation is located. No address. No phone number.

The website www.LiFT.foundation begins by claiming…

LiFT - The next several pages will show you a method to transform your life. We'll give you all you'll need to: tune in and turn up the messages around you, define your unique skills, talents and gifts, show you the path to your 'best life', and how to evoke the power of attraction. It's all here. We won't leave out key features then ask you for money to divulge those secrets. There are no magic potions, crystals or videos to buy. It's all here. In fact, this one page 'Quick Start' will allow you to begin now.

BEWARE - We urge you to refrain from asking. Asking for anything except to be guided to your unique loving path. Just feel and listen. Requests, if not structured just right, in a loving environment, can hurt you and all the people around you. This one page QUICK START and the pages following, must be practiced… and when you're ready… you'll stumble upon the second level.

Try it for yourself, just for fun. Let us know…

QUICK START:
1. Get comfortable, holding onto the freedom statements from below.
2. Every breath OUT (either out loud or to yourself) say "I love you", while you think of all the people you love. FEEL love for them. Then, when you're ready,

It is the feeling of love that will ride your brain waves. Your brain waves travel on a frequency between 1Hz (Deep Sleep) and 30Hz (highly awake and focused). It is the message you send out ON that frequency that will be 'heard'. Just like tuning into any radio frequency, one hour opera may be 'riding on that frequency', while the next hour may be Elvis.

3. Every breath IN, feel "I love you", while you FEEL these same people feeling love towards you. Then, when you're ready

4. Every breath out, say to yourself, and feel "I'm free".

Although you are free to choose your actions, thoughts and feelings right now, you are not free to change the past. Also you are not free to avoid the consequences of your actions. With self-discipline, free-will can be a blessing. If we give into vices, free-will can be hell on Earth. Consistency wins this game. Habits are built in consistency, both good and bad.

I am free physically to better serve with Love, Truth and Thankfulness.

I submit to the unlimited abundance of good health.

I go easily toward healthy activities with Love and Truth

---

5. With every breath out, say "Thank you". Think of all the things for which you are thankful.
6. Repeat the process using this new paragraph.

I am free emotionally to better serve with Love, Truth and Thankfulness.

I rejoice in the circular parade of characters that bless my day.

I respond with Love, Truth and Thankfulness.

---

7. Repeat the process using this new paragraph.

I am *free financially to better serve with Love, Truth and Thankfulness

I submit to the unlimited financial abundance.

I prosper wherever I turn. I deserve financial health.

---

*"free financially", means to: Save & grow your investments, until the income stream, (interest, dividends and capital gains) will sustain your humble living, freeing up your time to serve

humanity with Love. This is the reason to strive for financial freedom: To Serve.

Identify and enumerate your unique talents and gifts that set you apart from others. Seek out careers that utilize your uniqueness, to bring you closer to your highest purpose. THIS is 'your best life'. Read, out loud your list of unique talents and gifts, then read the sentences below.

"With these great gifts comes great responsibilities. I am ready now.

I see the loving path clearly. My smile lights the way brightly.

The entire universe is conspiring to bring me what I need to serve in Love.

I am Love. I am Truth. I am Freedom. Thank you."

Ultimately, the entire Universe sends you 'who you are'. Not what you pray for, what you need or what you deserve. 'Who you are' is what you feel right now and consistently. You are free to direct your focus on whatever you want.

Understand that this "Quick Start" is all you need. EVERYTHING else that follows here is just superfluous. That is: superficial tricks to help you to get into the habit of, and intensify, the FEELINGS of Love, Freedom and Thankfulness.

'Tune in and tune up the message,' is exactly what my Dad would say. That's all we need, to see into the future... see the right path more clearly and even find lost items.

There's a warning to be careful not to ask for anything. I am reminded of all the Genie in a bottle stories which always seem to end in a big fail.

I read the QUICK START: It's all in printable word documents. English, German, French, Spanish, Italian.... Unfortunately, I have no printer. There's no physical address or phone number. At the very end, I can buy bracelets that say "LiFT", "My body heals quickly", "In Love, anything is possible", "I see the loving path clearly, my smile lights the way brightly", along with Tea cups and yoga mats with the LiFT logo.

I'll ask Beatrix tomorrow morning. Curiouser and curiouser...

Right now, I need to focus on getting ready to sit on cold bleachers for hours in this Oxford November. This is not going to be comfortable.

After blow dryer, curling iron, and makeup, I head downstairs. Maybe my landlords have an old blanket. Noone's around. I hope all is still going well with Dan's Dad. I slip out the door without a blanket.

I'm at the bus stop, and again, I can hear the Alphabet Girls giggling before they appear. I smile and I'm reminded of the LiFT phrase... "I see the loving path clearly, my smile will light the way brightly." Yes, this is certainly a loving path.

Quickly, there's a crowd at the bus stop. Everyone is heading for this game.

The bus is already crowded when it rolls to a stop. I find a seat with Angel. We're not all sitting together. The two girls across the aisle are on the brink of hysteria. One girl, directly across the aisle screams, "Have you seen Chas Michaels?" She stands and shows an image on her phone.

"Chas Michaels, the Coach?" I mutter to myself.

Angel leans in to whisper, "Isn't that the 'handsome-ish' coach with the big chest?"

"I'm hoping not." I say to Angel. Then, to the girls in the seat in front of us, "What's going on?"

"Oh, my Goodness, the new Rugby calendar just came out. Chas is DEF-inately the hot-EST!" She screams.

"The Coach?" I say repulsed and a little too loudly.

"No! Chas is a player and is like... twenty-something." She fires back, just as loud and just as repulsed for suggesting such a thing.

The bus goes crazy with young girls, all holding up their phone, all screaming different names, all insisting their pick of 'the best looking player' is, in fact, The Best.

I get glimpses. The boys pictured in this calendar are not naked, but close to it.

I turn to Angel, "The College allows this?" I have to raise my voice to be heard over the frenzy of the girls on the bus.

"Oh, it's to benefit charity." Angel defends, screaming back just as loudly.

"Still, awkward." I say with distaste.

The girl from the seat ahead adds, "Oh it's to benefit breast cancer research."

"Save the boobies!" Screams a male student from behind me.

I smirk, "OK. That's funny." I admit.

Everyone on the bus is erupting in cheers. I look towards Brooke. She gives me the 'what are you gonna do?' shoulder shrug and adds loudly, "Welcome to Oxford Rugby, Mom."

I give her a head tilt, sarcastic smile and thumbs up. 'Great', I motion back to Brooke as I notice, I am the only adult on the bus.

Just as the insanity gets to a fever pitch, the bus comes to a stop and we all unload. Angel and I, find the rest of the Alphabet Girls and head into the stadium to find our seats on the fifty-yard line just three rows up.

"How did we get these great seats?" I ask Angel, as we settle in.

"The higher ups really like Brooke." Angel reveals, looking at Brooke.

"Really?" I say to Brooke as a question.

"The Dean of International Studies got a couple of my papers and asked to meet me. He said 'if I ever needed anything' to ask. So, I called him this morning before yoga, left a message that I could use five tickets to this game. When I got back from yoga, these tickets were in an envelope pinned on my door."

"Well, wow. Great. Nice to know people." I say while shaking my head, rolling my eyes, and wondering why anything 'Brooke' still surprises me.

I don't know the rules of Rugby, I don't know the players, and honestly, most of the time, have no idea which team has the ball. So, for the next couple hours I'm looking around at the big picture. This beautiful, new stadium is full of happy, screaming, twenty-somethings. Heart-warming.

My own college experience never included the luxury of going to sporting events. I was too busy working. As I glance over at Brooke, having fun with her college mates, I'm blessed to have been able to give my daughter a work-free college experience.

Life is good. The crowd is excited and cheering. I'm reminded of the yoga meditation, swinging between love of all that is in the universe and the universe loving me back. Is this the way to find messages in the ether? Was Ficino correct? If I practice this meditation, will I be able to hear the messages that surround us? Now, THAT would be cool. I'll be sure to be at the next week's session. I get out my phone, find next Wednesday and add the appointment. 8AM LiFT with an alarm to wake me at 7:15.

"Mrs. Bartlett." Angel brings me out of my thoughts. "I think that handsome-ish coach wants your attention."

I look down to the side lines. "Where?" I say, to Angel.

"Right here." Angel leans back into her chair. Chas is standing in the aisle. I blush.

"You're enjoying yourself." Chas has caught me playing with my phone. I blush more.

"Yes." I say because I'm not going to say no in this way-too-public conversation. I can feel, not just all four of the Alphabet Girls intent on this exchange, but much of this section of the stands. Ugh!

"What are you doing after this?" Chas says, as I blush until my ears run hot.

"I don't know yet. I'm with my daughter and her friends."

All the girls answer at once, but Brooke breaks in loudest. "Oh no, Mom. We all have to go do papers and study…"

Angel adds. "I have lots to do, gotta go back to the dorm. We all do."

I turn to them, giving them the evilest of eyes I can muster.

"Say yes." Says a random girl in the crowd behind me.

I turn back to Chas, "Well, I guess I'm free."

"Great. I'll meet you at the Cartoon Bar, across from the Ashmolean, right after the game." Chas says, and he heads back to his team, not waiting for an answer.

I'm only now realizing the game is just about over and I have a date.

1735 – 'Witchcraft act" removing 'witchcraft' as a crime.

b. 1738 – (Father) Francis Mathews, 1st Earl of Llandaff

b. 1746 – (Mother) Ellisha (Smyth) Mathews

b. 1758 – (1st Son) Theobald Mathews (born out of wedlock)

   1763 – Great Flood

m. 1764 – (Marriage) Francis and Ellisha

b. 1765 – (2nd Son) Arnold Nesbitt Mathew

      (1st true heir - born in Paris)

b. 1768 – (3rd Son) Francis James (Black Sheep)

b. 1773 – (4th Son) Montague Mathews

b. 1779 – (5th Son) George Tobias Skeffington Mathews

b. 1781 – (Daughter) Ellisha Mathews

b. 1790 – (Nephew) Father Mathews

      (Total Abstinence Society)

d. 1806 - Francis Mathews, 1st Earl of Llandaff dies

1810 - Francis Mathews, (3rd son, The Black Sheep)

     gets control of his father's wealth

1812 - Thomastown Castle enlarged, gardens are constructed

1824 – Amendment to "Witchcraft Law" passes

     Making it a crime to ACCUSE anyone of witchcraft.

1831 – Nanny accused and found guilty of 'witchcraft'.

1838 – Father Mathews creates Total Abstinence Society.

Chapter 9

A toast to our coven of cohorts.

The Cartoon Bar in the MacDonald Randolph Hotel is easy to find. Inside I discover beautiful, raised-panel woodworking, fireplace, giant leather chairs, and big red-crescent booths. I wonder if I'm dressed for this.

"Hello." Chas welcomes me looking directly into my eyes, I blush. "I secured us a booth in the back."

"Great." I say, thankful I don't have to sit on an uncomfortable bar stool while having an uncomfortable conversation.

"What can I get you?" Chas says. His hand moves to my elbow, as he guides me to the booth.

"A white wine will be great. Pinot Grigio."

"The Cartoon is known for their cocktails. How about a signature martini?"

"Ok." Fine.

"Vodka or Gin?" he asks as he looks at the bar.

"Gin," I say simply. I'm nervous.

Chas raises his hand, two fingers up and immediately gets the bartender's attention, "Two Corpes Revivors, Sweetie."

Sweetie? I bartended my way through college. Not attractive to call the wait-staff, 'Sweetie'. But I smile as he leads us to the booth.

"So, you're from Rutherford, New Jersey. I'm sure we can find some things to talk about. I'm assuming you've been to Rut's Hut." Chas says, as he motions to take my coat.

"Yes. But I still have indigestion, to this day, from their signature fried hotdogs." I say, laughing.

"Ok, well, we probably won't agree on food choice, then. How about concerts?"

"Well, I worked my way through college so I didn't have time for concerts."

"None?"

"Not-a-one. I was 27 when I went to my first concert. Springsteen. I'm not really a music buff, although I do like classic blues, and a little rock. You?" I say trying to keep the ball in his court.

"I'm a jazz guy, myself." He said.

I'm not a jazz fan, so I try, "You have a business degree?"

"Engineering."

"You ran ITT with an engineering degree?" I'm interested.

"Clearly, you see the problem, where the board of directors did not." Chas admits his time there was not a success.

"Oh, I'm sorry." I say, very sorry this conversation is so painful, apparently now for us both.

"That's OK. It all brought me here to Oxford and coaching. I'm near my son and this is where I have been happiest." He says, finally an honest endearing moment.

"You have other children?"

"Nope, just Chucky." Chas says, as he takes the drinks from the waitress. "Thanks, sweetie." Directed to the waitress.

My eyebrows go up. Really? Sweetie? If he calls me sweetie, this ends now. Does he even remember my name? I look up. He's looking directly into my eyes. I sit up a bit straighter and lean back just a bit. Ugh!

"You did say gin, right?" Chas smirks, knowing he's made me nervous.

"Yes." I say, trying to find body language that says, 'I'm not nervous nor am I terribly uncomfortable.'

"Taste it. It's great."

"OK." I say, as I take a sip. "So, how long have you lived here in Oxford?"

"Just two years. I followed my son here. We had been living in London and before that, New Jersey." He says, with a ridiculous 'Jersey Accent'.

"You know we don't talk like that." If he lived there he would know that.

"I know. But it gets a chuckle from my friends here in UK." He says, unapologetically.

This guy's an ass.

"So what do you do when you're not visiting your daughter?" Chas says as he takes another sip.

"I'm an accountant." No. We are not going to talk about me. "So. I've been to the Botanical Garden and the Ashmoleon, any suggestions? Where is your favorite tourist spot?"

"I like this place." He holds up his drink and grins. He's getting drunk and lazy. The one empty glass in front of him says he's had at least one drink before I got here. "No, really." He laughs. "This place has a long history. No ghosts here, but it's where the freemasons of Oxford meet."

"The freemasons are a secret society. So how do you know this, Chas?" I say, accusing him of disclosing a confidence.

"Well, first, free masons don't have a secret society, Joyce," He says poking at my accusation. "Unless they have the worst kept secret in all of human history. It is a society WITH secrets. Why? Are you interested?"

"Yes." I say, and echo, with all my body language. I turn towards him and lean forward.

"Well, way back, in the days when building giant castles was a great profession, needing big-time, math, architecture, and engineering techniques, these Masons, who were paid handsomely for their work, needed to protect their techniques for obvious reasons. See. I do know some basic business, 'the laws of supply and demand'. Too much competition would drive down their prices. So, they created a Society of Masons that protected the secrets of design, architecture, and engineering. THOSE were their secrets. There are levels of membership, apprentice, journeyman, and finally, master mason. Each higher level would be taught higher level secrets of the craft and be responsible to safeguard those secrets."

"The Craft?" I break in.

"Yes. Still to this day, it's called 'the craft'. Back then, the Catholic Church tolerated no secret society for fear the Jews or Protestants, or whoever would hide from them and grow strong. But they had to tolerate these Mason societies because the Masons were needed and protected by the super-rich and powerful, including the Royals, to build their castles and the Catholic Church, to build Cathedrals. The Court of Heresy could not touch the freemason's secret meetings."

"Very cool." I say, thinking that there always seems to be a real power struggle, chess game going on between religious leaders and heads of state. Power and land.

Chas continues, lowering his voice to a whisper and leaning forward, "Some of the 'secret' documents leaked out were a collection of fantastic stories where God, the Great Architect, founded Freemasonry, and that Christ is included in the list as Grand Masters. Other leaked documents claim that Masonic science existed before creation. Still others say they came from aliens." Chas leans back and chuckles loudly.

"Totally believable." I say, sarcastically. The absurdity is really not funny.

What of my Nostradamus and Rabalias secret society? I can now see why the medical and scientific community wanted to have a society where the meetings were secret to keep their medical research free of the Catholics and the Court of Heresy. Understandably, Europe quickly was littered with 'Free Masons' and the craft. Sorcerers only?

"Men only?" I ask simply.

"There have been woman inducted, but rarely. Every lodge is different. There's always been a 'women's auxiliary' called Lodges of Adoption, and a similar, related organization 'Order of the Eastern Star'. They have the same levels, Apprentice, Journey Woman, Mistress and..." Chas leans in, raises his eyebrows and whispers loudly. "Perfect Mistress." He leans back and raises his martini, staring straight into my eyes. "I think there's a book with that title."

"I'm sure there is and I'm pretty sure you have a well-worn copy." I'm also pretty sure I know why this guy is divorced. I realize I may have gone too far, so I purposely change direction, "I thought the Free Masons had to be Christian?"

"No, no, no." Chas said, now on a roll, leaning forward, elbows on the table, obviously knowing this subject. "You are talking about the now famous 'Illuminati, Knights of the Templar.' Only THEY had to pledge to Christianity. In fact, the alter of the Mason meetings here and in the US, have a King James bible, the Jewish Kanach and the Koran all open on the altar where their most sacred ceremonies take place. These symbols, sitting together symbolize the coexistence, even brotherhood, of Judaism, Christians, Islam and the Druse within the Masons."

I am shaking my head. "Wow. Interesting. Makes sense. Many of the founding fathers of the US were Masons and therefore saw that coexistence, tolerance among different religions was not just possible but made for a more healthy society."

"Yes." Chas continues somberly. "Europe's history is filled with wars, overlapping other wars. Whoever's in charge always wants more power and control." Looking right in my eyes, leaning forward, Chas continues, just a little too intense. "The more you own, the more money it takes to keep it all going. Keeping the armies happy, keeping the castles maintained, appointing judges that will do your bidding, keeping the schools in line with the politics of the religion du jour. All very expensive. So you need more land, to earn more rent, and you need more people to charge and collect taxes. It's all a vicious cycle."

I have a feeling he is talking about himself. I wonder if he had a run-in with financial problems brought on by too much… too many toys, too much real estate… add a divorce… that's a mix that'll bring, even the President of ITT, to financial ruin.

Chas continues, "In theory, your constitution is supposed to prevent that, 'protected by an educated voting population'." He chuckles and with drink in the air, "God help us all."

I question his laughing, "So, you're saying the education of the US isn't good enough to keep the US constitution going?"

"Oh no. I'm skeptical of all worldwide education, economics, and politicians. I'm an equal opportunity skeptic." He's getting drunk.

"So, do you have any solutions? You seem to be suggesting it's all so hopeless." I say, wondering where he went to college and how he got his position at ITT as 'running the place' further wondering if that's even true.

"No. No solutions. I do have a quote from your Thomas Jefferson, 'Self-government is not possible unless the citizens are educated sufficiently to enable them to exercise oversight' "

"So, you don't think the US citizens are educated sufficiently?" I ask directly.

"No. No, I'm not saying that they are not educated. I'm not saying that at all."

"OK. So, if you agree education of citizens is the answer, and you agree that our citizens' education is sufficient, then why do you seem so cynically hopeless?" I know I'm close to being rude, but I want to know what this guy is truthfully thinking.

"Well, that's a good question. I guess I don't know what I'm trying to say." Chas says as he leans back and takes a long gulp from the martini glass, now almost empty.

I don't like this guy. He's getting drunk and obnoxious. "Well, on that note, I have to meet up with the 'hive'. Thank you for the drink, Chas." Abruptly, I grab my coat and rise. I'm so uncomfortable.

"OK. I guess you're welcome, then." Chas says, a bit bewildered and raising his glass to me as I make my getaway.

I wait to put on my winter garb at the front door instead of at the table. I know I was rude and abrupt but I had to get away from him. As I open the giant door to escape, I catch a glimpse of Chas walking towards me.

Outside I spot a bagel store, quickly duck in, move as quickly as I can to the back where, thankfully, I find a ladies room and hide.

Looking in the mirror I feel like an idiot. My eyes are dark. 'Two burn holes in a blanket', my Grandmother used to say. I'm almost 60, hiding in a bathroom, running from an innocent drink with an intelligent man.

"Ugh!" I groan as I pick apart every syllable of our conversation and realize I may have been the one who was rude. "I gotta get outta here." I say, out loud to no one in-particular.

I don't know how to get back to my BNB, except to take a very long and cold walk. If I bump into Chas I'll be so embarrassed. Hoping this store has WiFi I finally come out of the ladies room to find the password. I'll be able to facetime Brooke and set a dinner meet-up somewhere right here in this neighborhood. I can always bribe Brooke with food.

"Hello."

"Hey, Mom. How is everything?" Brooke says, as the rest of the girls try to squeeze into the frame of this facetime....

"I'm fine dear," knowing they all want to know details of the 'date', "The Coach and I had one drink. We're done now." I quickly change the subject. "I want to know if you guys want to come into town here to have dinner. It's dinner time. On me."

"We're cooking. Come up!" Says Angel. She is so sweet.

"Did you start cooking already? Come out." I coax.

"Mom, we've already started cooking. In fact, we're already in our pajamas. Come up. Can you find the bus that comes to our bus stop?"

Angel adds, "Sleep over. We'll have a pajama party."

Brooke smiles at the suggestion, "We'll find some really fun PJs for you."

Angel adds, "So, how was your date?"

I look up to be sure Chas did not walk in while I'm here distracted... "It was just one drink. I'm obviously not ready to date yet." I say too honestly.

Angel says, understanding this did not go well for me, "I'll make dessert. Come up. I'll make something chocolate."

I can't say no. In fact, I start to tear up at her empathy. Or maybe it's pity. "OK." I say extra loud to fight back tears. Everyone but Brooke disappears from view. I'm sure they realize I'm getting emotional. "Can you find the Cartoon Bar and direct me to the right bus?"

"Sure. I'll message you the map." Deidre yells from the background. They are out of sight but obviously still listening.

"I love you, Mom. Be safe. You should be here in thirty."

Deidre, as promised, sends me the map and I venture out into Oxford, alone. It's dark now. As I walk to the bus stop I wonder, why did I act like that? I wasn't drunk. I'm not mean. Usually. This guy brings out the worst in me. Before finding the bus stop I find a liquor store. I can't carry enough wine to share with five people so I buy a big bottle of vodka and two frozen orange concentrates.

Waiting at the bus stop, I look down to find another dime. More correctly, a euro-dime. I ride the bus thinking of all the dimes I've found in the last thirty months. The probability is too small to calculate. I think of Angel. Yes, the universe is a very powerful thing. Curiouser and curiouser.

My focus switches again to this last encounter with the Coach and the things I should have said. 'The worst of me' is not attractive. I wonder where that loving focus from yoga, and from the game, has gone.

It's a short walk from the campus bus stop to the dorm but I have time to refocus on all the good things. I decide that some people bring out the worst in me and I need to stay away from them. I chuckle. I don't think it'll be hard to stay away from Chas. He's probably had quite enough of me. But others, like these Alphabet Girls seem to bring out the love and thankfulness; the best in me. With that realization, I come around the corner of the dorm and they all run out to meet me with a big group hug. Their empathy is sweet. Life is good.

The dorm living room is buzzing with activity. A group of two-dozen students is gathering with suitcases to leave for Italy. Their bus arrives, they pile outside and I'm thankful for the quiet and privacy.

"What are the plans for tomorrow? It's Thanksgiving." I ask Brooke.

"I want to take the tour of the 'Bod'. It's the library, the building is beautiful. The tour takes over an hour and includes underground tunnels" Brooke says, "I have the whole day planned."

"Are we all going?" I ask all four.

"My Mom will be here." Chelsea is obviously excited. "Tomorrow is Thanksgiving. She's in charge." She says, with a big smile.

"I'll go." Angel and Deidra say in harmony, and begin to laugh.

"Mom, you'll love the tour of Christ Church too. Some of the scenes in Harry Potter were filmed there. Angel is a big Harry Potter fan too." She turns to Angel, who is at the stove. "My Mom has read all the Harry Potter books, usually the day they came out. She and my sister would fight over them."

Angel drops the spoon. As she runs out of the room, screaming, "I have Harry Potter PJs! I'm sure they'll fit you."

After changing into Angel's PJs, I come out to the girls at the giant kitchen table. The head of the table is set, waiting for me. I show them the big bottle of vodka and they all scream. Angel jumps up to grab new glasses. I hand Brooke the OJ concentrate. She jumps up to make a batch of OJ in their new pitcher and we settle back down to a salad appetizer and the most delicious chicken parmesan, with thick spaghetti, I have ever had.

The pajama party has just begun and the conversation turns to Yoga, to Bea, to LiFT, and soon, I am telling the story of the Thomastown Castle, the curse, the young nanny-witch, then, the possible parallel story of Bea and Beren, their time in the South of France, and their - Ficino, - Nostradamus, - Artisan Center, - freemasons connection...

Yes, there's alcohol involved, but we are solemn in our mission to solve this puzzle and rid this family of their curse.

After the dishes are done we move to the empty giant community living room. Everyone else has left for the long weekend. Chelsea builds a great fire and we begin to build our plan.

"We are our own coven." Angel exclaims, almost spilling her vodka.

"I think a coven has to be six." Deidra says, then realizing she may be putting a damper on the mood adds, "Sorry, I'm just sayin'."

As if on cue, someone opens the big heavy living room doors.

"Mom!" Chelsea exclaims, now slurring just a bit, "My Mom can be our number six!"

We all stand and break out in cheers.

Brooke, raising her glass, "Let's toast to our coven of cohorts!"

"Well, good God, wait till I get a drink so I can toast too. Then you can all tell me exactly what is going on here. Don't skip any details 'cause I'm still on Chicago time and not ready for bed."

Chelsea's Mom is obviously perfect.

"Can you all wait till I get in PJs too?"

"No!" They all scream in unison.

"Joyce." I say as I offer my hand.

"Kim." She says, with a big smile. Then, calling to Chelsea, who is making her drink, "Honey. Vodka, rocks, no OJ, Please. Make it a double."

We are going to be good friends.

As Chelsea hands her Mom the glass, Brooke repeats loudly, "Toast to our coven of cohorts,"

We all stand again to toast.

"Alright. I wanna know every detail."

This is the best vacation EVER.

Chapter 10

If it harms none, do what you will.

Chelsea begins telling her Mom the story of my BNB friend Dan and his Mathew's family history in detail.

When she's done, Kim takes a deep breath, stiffens her back and says, "Ok. So, what we know for a fact is, a little girl, around 1830, did drown. We also know that the Matthew family did not accuse their nanny of in-attention but instead, accused her of killing the little girl with witchcraft, specifically, a sleeping spell cast onto the Mother. Which leads us to believe that the Mom was 'in charge' and over slept, when the drowning happened. The Mom probably felt such shame, therefore, wanted to blame someone else. But the nanny was not supposed to be watching the little girl when she drowned. That's why only witchcraft would explain how it could possibly be this Nanny's fault.

We know also, for a fact, that immediately after the drowning, the uncle priest, Father Theobald Mathews, went on to dedicate his life to abolish alcohol consumption. Which leads us to believe that the Mom was probably over slept because she was drunk when the little girl drowned. Further, Theobald and probably the entire Matthew's extended family knew the Mom was drunk and overslept."

Kim's shoulders drop and her tone changes dramatically.

"That poor Mom, when she found her little girl drowned… she must have been so…" she pauses to find the right words. "…distraught with grief and guilt. I understand how her immediate reaction would be to blame someone else. Anyone else.

If the Mom was drunk, then it is even more plausible, she would make such an appalling decision to blame the nanny. And since the nanny was not around, accuse her of casting a sleeping spell.

Unfortunately, once a decision like that is made, it can't be unmade. I'm sure she needed her family to get behind the accusation, then no one can roll it back."

Kim looks at me, "Is that what we're all thinkin'?"

"Yes." I say a little too loudly. "This really happened in 1830-ish. I looked it up. There were a couple of witch trials in Ireland at that time and even a few decades later. Burning witches was still going on then."

Kim, still somber, "Oh that poor child. So what are we 'investigating' as a 'coven of cohorts'? I think we pretty much got this."

Chelsea answers her Mom, "Well, the heirs think they have been cursed, still to this day, and there's all kinds of weird other stuff going on at Brooke's Mom's BNB. We think the owner is a witch, from the same coven."

"The same 'coven' as the Nanny?"

"Yes!" Chelsea says simply but with wide eyes.

I interrupt, "There's waaay more to this. It's a really long, intricate bunch of puzzle pieces." I tilt my head, raise eyebrows, and point to my watch… "Wanna hear it?"

"Oh, good God, yes. But now I must insist on PJs and more Vodka. Do I smell chocolate?"

The Alphabet Girls erupt in gaggling, all at the same time. Chelsea leads her Mom to put away suitcases and get into PJs. Angel goes to the kitchen to cut up the chocolate lava cake. Deidra heads outside to bring in more firewood. I gather empty glasses to refill with ice, OJ and vodka, while Brooke fills big glasses with water and lemon.

"Gotta hydrate." She says with a smile.

We all assemble back in the great room.

"Well?" Kim looks at me.

"Well," I answer, "it all started with a little old priest in the 1400's named Marcilio Ficino. It seems, from some of his quotes, this guy somehow knew about sound waves, light waves, radio waves."

Deidra interrupts, reciting Ficino's quotes, "Why is love a magician? Because the whole power of magic consists of Love. The work of magic is the attraction of one thing by another."

I'm impressed. I know Deidre has studied French history but this guy is Italian and she has memorized his quotes.

Deidre continues. "'Love is like a melancholy disease.' In order to recover, he prescribes among other things, coitus and drunkenness. I'm paraphrasing." Deidre admits with a smirk.

Kim raises her glass in a toast, loudly exclaiming, "Here, here, to coitus and drunkenness."

"Mom!" Chelsea exclaims a bit disturbed, but raises her glass.

We all follow. "To coitus and drunkenness!"

I really like this woman.

Deidra goes through Ficino's famous trilogy about listening with your 'instrument' to the information in the ether. Like music, there are messages all around us. We just have to take care of our 'instruments', which Ficino later defines as the human soul. Deidra finishes with, "He is regarded by most as the 'father of natural magic'."

"Heavy. This Italian priest started a witches' coven in the south of France?" Kim questions with a look of doubt.

"Oh, no. Nostradamus. About 50 years later." Deidra continues. "Ficino was greatly admired by Nostradamus. His works quote Ficino many times. Nostradamus went to medical school at Montpellier in the south of France. Actually, he was kicked out after a very short time because he questioned the accepted medical practices being taught and approved by the Catholic Church at the time."

"Like leaching?" Kim interjects.

Deidra says sarcastically, "Nostradamus believed in ridiculous things like bathing with soap, often and the healthy benefits of fresh air." adding, "Nostradamus was mostly known for researching and developing medicines and perfumes."

"Elixirs." I say, slurring a bit.

"And seeing into the future." Kim adds.

"No!" Both Deidra and I answer at the same time.

Deidra explains, "Most authorities on Nostradamus agree that he just got into some hallucinogens. When you write tens of thousands, four line senseless, nonsense, some of them are bound to mirror future events."

"I have heard that one of his quatrains, particularly dark, mentions Hitler. He called him Hizler." I add, not wanting to disprove Deidra but, curious.

"Hizler is a river in Germany." Deidra says simply, and a bit dismissively. I give her a pass because I brought the vodka.

Kim tries to get back on course, "OK. Not a seer. You've convinced me. So, why is Nostradamus important?"

Deidra continues, "Most historians believe he, that is, Nostradamus, after he was kicked out of Medical school started a secret society that researched medicine and meditation in a town just north of the University of Montpellier."

Angel could not help herself but to break in. "And Brooke's Mom's BNB owner has been running an Artesian Center in that same town in the south of France for twenty years! AND if you google 'translate white craft to French', you get Artesian Center!"

"Mom, this BNB owner is the same woman that runs that strange Yoga thing I've been telling you about." Chelsea goes on to describe the free masons history, hierarchy, and the books I found in the kitchen bookcase. "We think this woman…"

"Bea, my Mom's landlord." Brooke adds quickly.

"Yes, Bea. We think Bea is like, the Grand Mistress of this white craft, natural magic, witches coven under the guise of freemasonry."

Kim takes the fork out of her mouth, which has been there for some time while she listened intently, eyes round, while trying to grasp all the strings she's been presented and says, "Freemasons, overwhelmingly, are all men. What you seem to be describing is the order of the rainbow girls. It's the freemasonry for really young girls like teenagers before they're old enough to join the auxiliary or the 'Order of the Eastern Star'. Rainbow would certainly explain the rainbow in the LiFT logo and 'white craft' which all rainbows are just a refraction of white light. I'll buy into everything you've said so far. So. Well, what's the mission? You needed a sixth to make a coven to what purpose? To wait until the owners of your BNB are out and search the house for her book of spells?"

Silence hits the group.

I'm speechless. My eyebrows go up as I begin to blink. The girls also are stunned into this continued silence. I didn't expect that. "Uh, wait till the owners are out?" I repeat. "… and search the house?" I stop. I look around. The girls are motionless.

Kim breaks into a Cheshire grin. "If she is... this Bea, your landlord, is in fact, the Grand Poobah of witches, then she's got to have a spell book. Right? Probably one each for ointments, scents, yoga, meditation... and probably still has the Apprentice first degree books from when she was just learning, then another set of journeymen books, and finally the big, badass, 'I'm the Grand Poobah, keeper of all the secrets' book." She pauses. "Right?" she asks honestly.

"I guess." I say, as I blink and repeat slowly, "If this is all true, she has the 'big badass, I'm the Grand Poobah, keeper of all the secrets' book." The girls are still totally silent, looking between Kim and me. I begin again a bit louder, "Yes. I guess she does have that book right there in that BNB, where I have a room." I say getting even louder, "Let's our coven of cohorts go get that book of spells!" I say, yelling.

The room erupts in high-pitched, euphoric screams, as every one of us six rise up on our feet.

No one feels the breeze but we are startled by the fire roaring up. The squealing stops at once. We all look to the fireplace. Just then, on the opposite side of the room, the big, great-room doors slam closed. In unison we turn our heads to the opposite direction, to the doors.

Silence.

A draft like that could only happen if someone opened an outside door. I run out of the room to catch the 'spy' as the room erupts in screaming. I run down the hall to the only exit I know. Brooke is right behind me. NO one is there.

"There's no one there?" I question the validity of my unspoken assumption that the fire rising up and the doors closing must have been from this door opening, letting in a breeze.

"There's a front door!" Brooke yells as she turns to run to the other side of the building. We are running together, and together we push through the big double, front-doors while still running. We are well down the front stairs and out onto the sidewalk when the doors slam closed behind us. I continue down the path to the left, Brooke continues right.

"No one here." I yell as I come to a halt and realize I am out in the frigid November sidewalk in Oxford with no shoes or socks.

"No one this way, either. These doors locked when they closed. We'll have to go around to the great room doors. We'll probably scare the heck out of the rest." Brooke says with a mischievous grin.

"Cool!" I say with a smirk, and we begin to run.

Brooke bangs on the windows of the great-room. As we thought, the room erupts in screams. Chelsea opens the door for us.

"No one is out there." Brooke says.

Everyone is laughing and talking at the same time, except for Angel, who is crying. I go over to her and give her a motherly hug. I notice she's shaking. "It's OK." I start to chuckle. "Com'mon Angel. We'll get more cake. Chocolate solves everything."

"I can't have any more sugar. We have really good vegan chili in cans." She turns to the coven. Wiping her eyes, says "Anyone want chili?"

The cohorts erupt in the affirmative. It's been five hours since dinner. Everyone is in the kitchen at once. Opening cans, grating cheese, getting out pots, refilling vodka, more logs on the fire, more water with lemon. Very quickly we're all sitting back in the great-room with bowls of vegan chili topped with cheese shreds, water glasses filled, as well as the fire stoked, and of course, refill our vodka glasses. Brooke changes her seat to sit with me near the fire.

Kim starts, "So what is the connection between the Mathew's family and the witches? They're not related, right?"

"Good question." I say. "Dan's Mom is a Mathews' descendant. But Dan is related to Beren through his Dad. So neither of my landlords, Bea nor Beren are Mathews.

But, what if Bea, is with Beren, to keep an eye on the Mathews family? If so, then either that coven wants to be sure the spell stays on or is trying to take the spell off. I don't know."

"The first rule of witchcraft is 'Do no harm'." Kim says

"And how do you know that? In fact, how do you know about the rainbow girls?" I accuse.

"Yeah, Mom." Chelsea is not smiling, her tone matching mine.

"Well I was a Rainbow Girl when I was in Grammar School, Junior High, and High School. Of course, the focus in the US in the 60's and 70's was leadership skills and community service, which is exactly the mission of witchcraft. 'If it harms none, do what you will' is the creed of witches."

"Mom!?" Chelsea is obviously shocked.

"So, you're a witch?" I say with a smirk.

"No. I was a rainbow girl. I also know that karma is a very real thing. So, if those witches put a spell on this family, they will have bad karma ten-fold."

"Mom!" Chelsea is more and more jolted.

"So, what else do you know?" I'm so curious where this is all going.

"I know that we were taught to do good works, to work for the community, to see the big picture around you, and lead others to do good works."

"Like steal the spell book?" I interrupt.

"Well... I was thinking more like FIND the book, get the book to a copier, then put it back." Kim defends. "Borrow would be the word I will use."

I'm reminded that 'Elixers of Nostrodamus' is still in my room.

"We can take pictures of the pages with our cell phones." Brooke adds from under my arm. We are all getting sleepy. Angel is already asleep. A night of vodka and full bellies of vegan chili will do that.

"Let's sleep on all this." I suggest.

Kim asks, "I don't want to wait until next Wednesday to take this yoga class. Anyone remember the process enough to guide us all through a meditation?"

Brooke suggests simply, "Angel."

We all look over to sleeping Angel.

Chelsea gets up to shake Angel awake, "Angel!"

"I'm asleep." Angel says, complaining.

"Wake up. We want you to guide us through a LiFT meditation. Com'on. It'll be fun."

"Tomorrow morning before we go to the Bod." Angel says, as she rises, like a zombie and heads to bed.

"Actually, the LiFT website description, includes a cup of tea. Let's do the meditation in the morning with tea." I suggest.

"I'm assuming coffee will work too?" Kim adds.

"I'm sure." I agree.

Angel has already left the room. The fire is out as is the bottle of vodka and the coven of exhausted cohorts head to bed.

Brooke shows me to her bed where we both plop, without even brushing our teeth.

"Good night, Brooke. Thank you for dinner. Tonight was fun." I say with my eyes already closed.

Brooke responds with an incoherent mumble. She's already sleeping.

Dreaming begins instantly.

And in that instant, I am back in the 1800's.

I am in the belly of a ship, which is not going fast enough toward Ireland and the Thomastown Castle and Elizabeth. My heart is bursting. My Elizabeth has been accused of witchcraft. These witch trials are swift. I pray for a fast, direct wind. I'm restless, and having visions of the Thomastown Castle militia building a pyre to burn...

I need some air.

On the top deck, looking out from the starboard rail at the open sea, I'm mesmerized by the moon reflecting on every white cap. I re-direct focus, just as Patrice has shown me. Soon, I see clearly: Elizabeth sits in a cell. She will not defend herself. She stands resolute, not because she's stubborn, but because she's filled with love...

She sees truth clearly, truth is the other side of love.

She is aware of the probable outcome and accepting of it. Her grief is for her little Lilyanna.

Elizabeth, my Kind-Hearted empath, feels for Charity Pennefather, as well. Yes, Liz will feel sorry for her accuser. In fact, Liz will understand and forgive this mother who is so obviously, deeply flawed and now, so obviously, deeply, guilt-ridden. This mother is guilty of sleeping while she should have been watching her own child. She is guilty of putting one late night of more dancing and more drink ahead of her own daughter. Now guilt on top of guilt, for blaming and setting into motion, that which cannot be taken back... accusations of witchcraft leading to a sentence of death by fire.

Elizabeth sits in a cell, feeling sorry for everyone involved. Everyone but herself.

I am back on the ship and watching the reflection of the moon dance in the ever-changing waves. Elizabeth has been in the Thomastown Community for a while now. She must have friends who know she could never be capable of this act of bad intention. She must, by now have friends who will help her escape. Our English community must be a united, irrepressible bunch to have sent that message. The strength of that message keeps me encouraged that Liz has a community of powerful supporters around her.

I pray, 'Dear God, keep my Elizabeth safe and sound. Deliver her from evil.'

I put my hands on the rail and wish my comforting hands finds hers, to bring her solace, and my prayers of love, find her heart. I begin to weep in empathy.

"Elizabeth." I am now crying out her name.

"Mom!" Brooke wakes me with a kick.

These dreams are weighing on me. No more vodka.

The sun, such as it is, in November in Oxford, is coming up. I get out of bed to brush my teeth and put on a big sweatshirt. Brooke's bed is too small for us both to sleep comfortably. I find the great room where the couch is calling my name. The fireplace, which earlier was roaring, now sits dark. I walk up to the hearth and find that even though there is no light, there is heat. I am reminded of the poem in my dream. I wonder if I am, in fact, a child-of-the-air sign. I do spend my summers racing my small nineteen foot sailboat. I know Brooke, was born under the sign of water and is aptly named, attracted to all activities on the water. I bend down to blow on the dark grey dust and watch embers glow.

I wonder if Chas was born under the sign of fire. I painfully remember the meeting we had in the Cartoon Bar. I'm sure, if he sees me again, he'll head the other way. Exhaustion takes me to the couch, where I close my eyes and pray for sleep. I fear those familiar, horrid feelings of loneliness and isolation will begin to build.

Blessed sleep takes over.

I'm still on the deck of the great ship. My hands are still on the rail, but now completely covered by the masculine, strong hands of Chas. I turn to face him, looking up, into his eyes.

"My Elizabeth." I whimper and burry my face, wet with tears, into his chest.

He leans in to wrap his arms and coat around me, "We'll be there soon." His deep voice resonates through his barrel chest. I nuzzle into his white shirt, padded with musty smelling chest hair. His words give me little comfort.

"Will we be in time?" I speak directly to his white shirt. I'm begging for more assurance. My right hand feels its way slowly up his chest to wipe my own tears. I hate crying.

He gets ahold of my chin, trying to get me to face him. I pull away. No one can comfort me. I need to be with my Elizabeth.

He won't give up. He pulls my chin up again. I feel his breath. I open my eyes to find him looking deep into mine.

"You need sleep to face whatever awaits us."

My right hand moves instinctively up to his face, while my left hand moves around to his broad back. "I know you're right."

Chas holds me so tightly in his warm cape, then sweeps me up into his arms. I'm dizzy.

Dear, God.

Chapter 11

Wherever you go, there you are. - Confucius

"Mom? Mom!" Brooke wakes me.

"Dear God, Brooke. I'm awake." I lie, and blush, wondering just what have I been moaning.

"Mom, you were crying." Brooke says softly.

"Yes. My dreams have been just horrid lately." I try to stay more to the truth.

"Come on, Mom. I hear alarm clocks going off. Let's make breakfast for everyone. We have eggs, cheese, and toast." Brooke says, as she turns to begin working in the kitchen while I enjoy the moment to wonder where this dream was going and if I'll be able to finish it tonight.

"Happy Thanksgiving." Kim walks in followed by Chelsea "Please tell me there are coffee beans from which we can concoct a caffeine elixir." Kim says with a smirk.

I really like her.

Over the next half hour all the Alphabet Girls make their appearance and take their place at the table. Each with an open laptop. It's a quiet room.

Kim breaks the silence. "The girls, all reading at breakfast, remind me of my Dad. We always had reading material at breakfast. Very quiet mornings at my house."

Deidre looks up first. "I was just looking up the Apostle of Temperance. Seems he was going around taking pledges of total abstinence from alcohol, which became a real plus for any town he campaigned in. And he was, in fact, appointed to the United States Congress and has statues erected to him in Philadelphia and Boston."

Brooke adds. "I found that petition from Dan's great-great-grandfather which was reported in Country Life Illustrated, just like he said."

Deidre breaks in excitedly, "So, the poor guy that got cheated out of his inheritance, Arnold, guess where his grandson was born? Montpellier!"

"NO!" I say excitedly, getting up to look at her screen.

Chelsea looks up, finger on her screen, "Hey, I found a John Mathews who married a Charity Pennefather in 1823. They didn't live at the Castle but a smaller residence nearby named Rathcloheen. I guess they named their homes back then."

"When the 'house' was big enough." Kim breaks in.

Chelsea continues, "So, if they married in 1823, certainly, they would have had toddlers in the early 1830's. And get this, reportedly, a Miss H. Pennefather of Marlow, died from falling out of the Thomastown Castle ballroom window in 1881. The article suggests alcohol was involved."

"I guess Miss Pennefather never took the pledge." Kim tries to be ironic.

"Wait. I have a different account of that event." Brooke interrupts, reading from her screen, "Hortense Mary Pennefather, who later married Hugh Hamon Massy (was probably the Miss H. Pennefather of Marlow) who, at a party at the Thomastown Castle in 1881, which is 50 years AFTER the nanny was killed, stepped through a window onto an imaginary balcony, toppled 30 feet and was caught, completely unharmed, by some gentleman who had stepped outside for a smoke."

"Well," Kim interrupts, "THAT doesn't sound like she was cursed."

Deidre cuts in. "Yeah, names, dates and circumstances will be reported completely differently when you really get down to researching anything, even in the 1800's. The papers would print anything that would sell the publication."

"In 1881, the castle was already decaying." I say.

"Still to this day. Look at all the fake news." Kim says, with a smirk.

I add, "OK check this out. Wikipedia says Arnold Harris Mathew, 4th Earl of Landaff of Thomas Town, born in Montpellier, Herault, France, August 1852. Died December 1919. They still had a winter home there in 1852, apparently."

I add. "OK. Unless we have more research to report... What do we have on our schedule for today?" I say, mostly to Brooke. I'm tired but ready to get on with the day.

"I just reviewed that www.LiFT.Foundation web site. I'm ready when you guys are." Angel says, rising to lead our LiFT meditation.

"After LiFT, we'll shower and meet at the BOD." Brooke says. "Are you guys all coming?"

"I'm in." Kim says as she looks to Chelsea for approval.

We all move into the living room. Angel sets up in front of the fire place while we all move the furniture to the walls. Angel goes through the steps of the yoga/meditation just as Bea had done yesterday morning.

We repeat, "I Love you," and all I can think of is Coach Chas and his chest. Now, I have the added benefit of smelling him as well. I'm sure this is not what the meditation is designed for me to 'see' or 'feel'. I change focus to feeling the love I feel for, and from, my grandsons.

I sit quietly, waiting for a 'message' from the universe. Nothing. The notepad and pen in front of me remain blank. I give it another try.

I write, 'Dear God, thank you for this day.' Nothing.

I begin again. 'I love you. The truth is… " Hmm. Nothing.

One more time. I close my eyes and imagine my grandsons, I love you, I say with more love than is possible. "I Love you." I repeat with them in mind. Again, "I love you." Now with the image of my grandsons looking directly at me and saying to me, "I Love you Mom-Mom." My heart fills. Tears appear, my nose gets stuffy. Yes. I'm ready now and begin to scribble randomly…

I love you my sweetie pants boys. I draw a heart and a bird. The bird is chirping, I draw music notes. I write down, 'Chirp Chirp' I smile and keep writing Chirp, Chirp, Chas." Whoa. CHAS? That was a surprise.

I tear the paper out of the notebook and crumble it up. I could not imagine the embarrassment if one of the Alphabet Girls saw this page. I rise with the crumbled paper and throw it into the fire of the great room. The blaze envelopes it quickly and I am instantly reminded of that young Nanny burning….

Oh, Dear God, I have to get out of here. "I'm heading to my BNB for a shower." I say with way more desperation than I had intended to reveal, and rush out holding back tears.

While taking the sobering, Thanksgiving morning walk back to my BNB, I begin to reevaluate last evening. The further away I get from the turn of the century Oxford dormitory, and the Great-Room with its giant fireplace, the idea that I will search this BNB and even further let these graduate students search this BNB, is wildly distasteful. In fact, it's down-right embarrassing. Did I agree to that? As I remember, I encouraged the idea?

What bizarre plot have I gotten myself into? My landlord, Bea, is not a witch, certainly not some 'Grand-Poohbah' of all witches from a sect started by Michael Nostradamus. I have been focusing on this passing family's painful past to the detriment of attention that should be spent on Brooke.

Brooke should be my priority while I'm here. I can really be an asshole.

With the rising sun, I see so much more clearly. I take a deep breath and exhale all the superfluous distractions I seem to... need, want, attract? I'm not sure which. Probably a complicated mix of all, plus some. All this ridiculousness occupying my thoughts instead of finding out more about Brooke. I have limited time here. How does she feel today? What is she thinking about? What is she studying? Who are, and does she like, her professors? I have asked her none of these questions.

I mutter, out loud this time, "I can be an asshole."

I wonder what Brooke thinks of me. I have no idea.

I resolve to make this day all about Brooke.

Another deep breath and exhale out. My breath is visible in this frosty cold, and therefore reinforces the idea of purging. I breathe out again, imagining all the distractions exiting my body and dissipating.

"Joyce!" I hear my name yelled from the main front doors of the building where Brooke takes most of her classes. Oh no! Not Chas. I pull my scarf up and wool hat down. My eyes are bloodshot and have a horrid case of makeup meltdown. I look up to the sky and beg any powers that might be up there, to let me get to my BNB without being seen.

"Joyce. Wait." Chas says, obviously closer now. This is inevitable, but I don't slow.

From directly behind me, "Walk of shame?" That stops me with a turn and foot stomp.

In a harsh whisper, I say, "I had a sleep over with my daughter and her friends at the dorm. Is it possible for you to get your mind out of the gutter and just be civil?" Turning again, I continue my escape to the BNB. '*That should get rid of him.*'

"Oh God, I'm sorry. I was joking." Chas says as he runs ahead of me and turns.

"Not funny! Please leave me alone." I say, as I step up my pace and walk past him.

"I'm sorry. I can be an asshole." Chas says, as I recall, just seconds ago, I said exactly those same words to myself. I recall also the bathroom of the bagel shop where I struggled to understand how our meeting at the Cartoon Bar went so wrong, so fast.

Softened, I stop, put my head down and mumble, "Me too."

Chas catches up and stands in front of me. "Excuse me?"

I'm not sure he heard me, I take a deep breathe to say very clearly, "Yes. I can be an asshole too. Maybe it was just your turn."

Chas straightens up and looks out passed my shoulder. Obviously my statement took him by surprise. "I. I wasn't expecting such self-deprecating... well honesty..."

I cut him off, "Fuck you! So, I tell you I can be an asshole too and your first response is to agree with me? Fuck you, Chas."

"No. No. I didn't mean that. Wow. You Are a Jersey-Girl. No, I meant you took me by surprise."

I've moved passed him and walking now at an almost run. He is running to get ahead of me and turns, grabs my coat's shoulders with both hands. "Dear God, Joyce. What I was about to say is, you make me nervous and I drank too much and I say really asshole things and it's all my fault. All of it."

He pauses. I'm looking down because at this point my eyes are welling up with tears. I'm afraid if I look up the tears will stream down my face. I want to scream out to the world, 'I am not unbreakable!' But that would begin an emotional collapse.

When I don't respond, he continues, "My fault. All of it. I was drunk by the time you arrived at the Cartoon. I'm surprised you stayed so long. The crack about walk of shame... I have no excuse for that. I am... deeply sorry."

I can't speak. I am at the edge of an inescapable rip tide of tears, in danger of getting swept out, to drown in my own salt elixir.

"I want an opportunity to show you, I'm not always an ass." Then quietly, "I want to spend more time with you."

I still can't speak without breaking down. The awkward silence gets way too long.

Still looking down, I say, "Let. Go." because that is the only thing I can say without tears.

Chas lets go of my shoulders. "OK. I really am very sorry. If I see you again, I promise to think before I speak."

"Yes." I have no idea what that 'yes' means but it was a short word I could speak without cracking and I needed a remark with which to exit. A short remark not filled with drama. 'Yes.'

I walk quickly back to the BNB. My head is filled with images of Chas at the bar where we first met, Chas at the game in the aisle, Chas at the Cartoon Bar, Chas in my dreams. Chas in my subconscious after a meditation... I clearly need to attract and be attracted to, a different kind of a man. A kind man who... will bring out the best in me. Certainly not one who brings me to the brink of emotionally drowning.

Now inside the BNB, while running up the stairs to begin this new path, I remember the book on Nostradamus's Elixirs needs to be returned. I cannot, fast enough, grab the book and head immediately back down stairs to replace it into the kitchen bookcase.

Out of breath, I return to my room and plop onto the bed. What have I gotten myself into?

While unpacking my phone, Brooke has left me a message. "We're all going back to bed. Trip to the BOD rescheduled for later afternoon. Meet us at the bus stop at 4PM. Thanksgiving dinner is scheduled for 7PM. Love you."

Thank God! I set an alarm for 2:30, put the phone on the dresser, and close my eyes. I am beyond exhausted.

I re-play the scene I just left. *'Walk of shame?'* "Fuck. You." I say hushed, but out loud. And why would I want to spend time with an asshole? I sigh a long, cleansing exhale. And him? Why would anyone want to date me? I can be an asshole too. "Admittedly," I say, out loud to myself.

I roll over to the other side of the bed trying to escape my lack of self-worth. Ridiculous to think I can, by rolling over, leave the painful thoughts on that side of the bed. I'm reminded of the Confucius saying, my Dad repeated often. 'Where ever you go, there you are.'

Maybe a hot bubble bath? I'll focus on Brooke and all the questions I'll ask her today. It's Thanksgiving. I'll make a list of the things I'm thankful for. Yes. That gets me out of bed.

As I turn on the hot water and load the tub with bubbles, I begin thinking of this idea of LiFT. Meditating, while feeling Love, Freedom and Thankfulness. I wonder, 'what is the frequency of brainwaves, versus light waves, versus radio waves, and microwaves? Are brain waves, while feeling love very different than while feeling fear, frustration or hate?

Turning off the water and slipping into the tub I begin the meditation... 'I love you... I am free... thank you.' Over and over, I go through the routine. I modify the yoga positions while sitting in this warm, bubble-filled tub. "I love you." I say aloud while hands on knees with palms up. "I love you." Shoulders pulled back.

"I'm free." I say out loud, as I lean forward, arms out, resting on the tub sides. I imagine a breeze lifting me. I lean forward a bit more and feel myself flying out the picture window of my new Oxford penthouse. I glide down the steep hill weaving through the chimney stacks. I get to the bottom of this hill and the commercial district, where I bank hard to the right, with my head up, gaining speed, then soar up as the wind lifts me. I dive into the botanical gardens, swaying east then west, then bank hard again. The centrifugal force gives me enough momentum, enough 'lift', to climb back up to the college, circle around the dorm, and then back across the campus to finish, stepping in through my window. My hands and arms are now back into the water at the bottom of the tub. "Thank you" I say out loud and I find thankfulness in the warmth of the tub water, then thankful for the journey. "Thank you".

I make a mental note that the definition of LIFT includes planes, sailboats and birds that soar. Not all birds can fly without constantly flapping their wings. Those that can 'soar' use the rising air currents to glide, sometimes higher. The air currents don't push a plane higher, instead, the lack of air pressure above the curved wing, LIFTS it higher.

I sit back, immersing myself up to my chin, naked, into the warm, soapy water, 'I love you.' Focusing on my breath only, out loud I say, "Thank you for this day, the truth is...' and wait.

Nothing.

I say again, 'I love you.' Shoulders back. I hold out my hand, as if someone will rest upon it, a note for me to read.

Nothing.

"I love you." Both hands on my knees, palms up.

Nothing.

I rest in the bubbles. If the universe wants to tell me something, now would be a good time.

I hear Bea talking loudly to Beren. "It's getting late. Did you put out the trash?" Obviously they are in different rooms or even on a different floors.

"I'll do it right now." Beren answers back just as loudly.

Jokingly, I ask the universe, "Are there chores to do in this realm of the ether?"

"Apparently." Comes the answer. I chuckle.

"What else do I need to know?" I ask out loud.

'You have everything you need.' Comes the answer.

I guess, if I want to lose this extra fifteen pounds, I seem to be carrying around... yes, I do know 'how'.

I want my business to grow, yup there too. I do know how. I don't want to get much bigger. I work enough and earn enough for now.

I search for a wish. But I guess I do have everything I need. My children and grandchildren are safe, learning life's lessons on their own, as it should be. I realize I have everything I've ever wanted. Life is good. All is well.

"Thank you." I say out loud. A smile, comes from deep inside.

Even though my children are healthy, good, and kind. My parade of friends fill me with compassion and fun. My business fills me with exciting challenges, as well as financial security. I fill my summer with sports and fall with travel... a loving, caring partner would complete the list.

As the water drains from the tub I begin to feel empty and cold. I wrap my head in a thick, white cotton towel and put on a matching huge bath-robe, walk into the bedroom, and climb under the covers. As I warm up, I fall hard into a deep, much needed, restful sleep.

Chapter 12

Following Alice in and then out
of the rabbit hole.

During the ninety minute tour, we learn the BOD houses over 11 million works and is one of the UK's 'copyright' libraries, housing one of every book printed in Great Britain. Brooke leans in to whisper, "I wonder if the LiFT foundation publishes in UK. If so, there will be a copy of it here."

"Good thinkin'. Let's try to remind each other to look that up when we get back to the dorm." I whisper back.

"I'll create a reminder." Brooke says as she takes out her phone.

We tour, not just the BOD, but the 15th Century Divinity School, Gladstone Link, Duke Humfrey's medieval library, the spectacular Radcliffe Camera, (Camera meaning 'room'), and finally the underground reading room. We all thought the reading room would be more of a collection of raw, cave-like tunnels, but was actually very modern and well lit, reminding me of the new Dickinson Library in my home-town in North Jersey.

Brooke says, obviously disappointed, but trying to be positive, "Well, Thanksgiving dinner is in one hour and we have to make the Sangria."

Kim askes Chelsea, "Do you have all the ingredients? Fruit, brandy, orange liquor and red wine?"

Chelsea replies, "We sure do, and a big pitcher too, Mama."

The Alphabet Girls, after a short pause, all look at me, and, like on que, burst into laughter. "Brooke's Mom pinched a pitcher for us from the Wig and Penn." Chelsea explains.

Kim looks at me with an approving grin, "We'll need those skills to pinch the white craft, natural magic school book... Or do you think it's a collection of books?"

Brooke answers first, "It's probably a collection of books. The same researchers who study the biology of movement would not be the same who study fragrance."

Angel adds, "Or meditation."

Deidra adds, "...or music and song." She quips. "Yes, there's got to be separate books."

Kim adds with a smirk, "I wonder how to get into the group that studies sunshine, wine, and coitus."

While the group laughs at Kim's joke, I get even more nervous with the thought of this group rummaging through my BNB.

I try to discourage them, "Alright, I think the chances of us finding a time, when no one is in the BNB, so we can all just rummage the shelves, is slim."

"'Just rummage the shelves...' Mom?" Brooke says, questioning my devotion to the mission.

I feel exposed and try to clown my way out by snapping to attention with a salute. "I'm devoted to the mission at hand, Captain Brooke." But I'm afraid my point was made and our little band of cohorts' mood has dampened to the prospects of us searching the always-guarded BNB.

Angel warns, "Be careful of the spoken word. If you say it, it's more likely to come true. We have a divine mission."

I question sarcastically, "Divine?"

"Yes." Angel defends. "The entire universe will conspire to bring us to the remedy, for the sake of this Mathew's Family and their oppression from the spell."

We're just outside the dorm. Kim stops, raises her head, looks to the sky, and in loud proclamation, "Show us the way, for the sake of all generations of Mathews to come!"

"All-righty, then." I say, trying not to be patronizing. "I'll look for the opportunity to present itself. Angel, I admit, the entire universe is a very powerful thing."

With that, Brooke's reminder alarm goes off. While we all begin the work of getting dressed for Thanksgiving dinner, Brooke sits at the kitchen table "I'm going to search for those school books. Where do I start? Nostradamus? LiFT?"

Deidre answers first. "The books are probably in French. If you are a student at this school, you have to know French, so the books may not be translated into English."

Angel disagrees, "Well, let's keep positive. Remember the power of the spoken word. If you say it's probably not going to be there, then there is less of a chance we find it, even if it's there."

"Well, Love, Freedom, and Thankfulness, translated into French will not bring you the initials of LiFT. That's a good sign that the books are in English." Deidra says. "If the nanny really did come from an English community in France, then, I'm betting on an English school."

Kim sits with Brooke, to help search for a set of white craft books.

"Brooke, where is Thanksgiving dinner tonight?" I am trying to get everyone focused on the next experience.

"It's in the student Village. We can walk." Brook says, distracted.

"Are we planning anything for afterwards?" I ask, finding myself tired again. The vodka and very little sleep from last night has my energy failing.

"Chelsea," Kim, speaking to her daughter, "Let's try to remember, except for four hours rest, I've been up for 72 hours."

I continue that line of thought, "I'd like to get a good night's sleep tonight so we can have a fun-packed weekend. No more classes until Monday, right, Brooke?"

"No more until Monday, Mom."

"And no papers due? No studying for a Monday test?"

"Nope, we're all free until Monday."

After everyone freshens up, and the Sangria has been made, (and well tested), we venture out, once again into the unrelenting Oxford November where a celebration of the US Thanksgiving is already underway.

From my seat, at the head of the long cafeteria table, I can see the Alphabet Girls bubbling over. I feel such love and appreciation for these young girls, full of kind, happy energy.

"They are impressive, are they not?" Chelsea's Mom leans in to whisper in my ear.

"Amazing girls. I'm very glad they found each other. It's hard to find loving, like-minded spirits." I say, still watching the girls.

"I have a group of seven woman from college. We try to get together one weekend a year. You? Do you still have contact with College-mates?" Kim asks sincerely.

"No. I was busy working while at College. My connections to my past are mostly to High School Mates." I say, exposing more sadness in my voice than I intended.

"Do you connect with them much?" Kim says as she puts her hand on mine.

I smile, with a chuckle, "Connected? That's an ironic choice of words. I'm afraid I was a wild child well into my late 20's. My 'connections' may have been..." I pause, "Well, connected." I pause again, and add with an Italian accent, "Ya know?"

Kim sits, waiting for more.

"I grew up in an Italian neighborhood at a time when Saturday Night Live's, Steve Martin would proclaim, 'I'm a wild and crazy guy'. I thought that was something to aspire to. 'A wild and crazy girl.' I'm lucky I got out without a police record." I pause, looking down at my wine while still frames of my past flash in my mind. "I'm lucky to have escaped with my life." I look directly into Kim's eyes and put my hand on hers. "Literally." I look back down at my wine, as I lift my glass... "But that is not a conversation for Sangria in a cafeteria. We'll need a bottle of gin, plenty of limes and an Uber on call." I laugh, while I take my hand away, meaning, 'this conversation is over'.

"Oh, it couldn't be that bad. Really?" said Kim.

"Worse. I look back now and... I think I was a good girl thinking that being a bad girl was a good thing. If you can follow that." I say

"Got it. So you ARE going to look for those books, then." Kim says smirking then a big laugh.

"Yup." I say simply. Yes, first chance I get. Alone.

"Come on." Kim interrupts my thoughts of 'the neighborhood'. "Let's get ourselves another red wine before it's gone. You know these college parties..." Kim and I get up to refill our drinks. We mingle with the professors, the parents, and then, mingle with our girls until the party is done. We're the last ones there and help clean up.

On the way back to the dorm I put my arm around Brooke, "Hey. Brooke. I'm going to sleep in my own bed tonight. Yours is too small for both of us to get a good night's sleep." I'm fading quickly.

"I agree with you there, Mom. In that case, this is your turnoff. Straight up to the bus stop. You know your way home from there, right?"

"Thank you, my love." We stop to hug. "Text me tomorrow morning. Let me know what you want to do." And with that, I take off striding toward my BNB.

My thoughts are still with my past. The wine is taking over and memories I usually choose not to remember, take center stage. I change focus.

I count two glasses of Sangria before we left the dorm and four maybe five red wines at the cafeteria. I have to stop drinking so much.

Apparently, I have auto-piloted to my BNB. The glow from the living room windows is flickering again. I open the door and hear crackling of the small logs and feel the heat coming from the living room. Someone has built a fire.

The Cat is sitting. Waiting. "How long have you been there, Dammie?"

As I get rid of my hat, scarf, coat, gloves, I can hear two male voices coming from just around the corner. That must be Dan and his brother. I smirk. I wonder if Dan's brother believes in this curse as much as Dan. Dammie escorts me into the living room and jumps to the middle of the one empty couch.

As I enter the room both men begin to rise.

Dan is unfolding from his 'tuffet', "Joyce, this is my brother, Geoffrey. He's here from Dallas, Texas."

"Hello, very nice to meet you. I've heard about your Dad's surgery, is he still doing well?" I ask Geoff.

"He's well. Yes, very well, indeed. Thank you." Geoff replies as he and Dan settle back into their seats.

Pleasantries over. While still standing, I blurt out excitedly, "Dan, I have been thinking about your family's curse, I have the solution to your problem..." Before I can finish my sentence both brothers lean forward. I don't have to wonder any longer... Yes, both brothers do believe in this curse. In fact, Geoffrey, who had settled back into his chair and re-crossed his legs is uncrossing to have both feet squarely on the ground in front of him so he can lean even more forward. Both men's body language signaling much greater interest than I expected.

"The solution to your problem is... you need another witch to remove the spell!" I say because I am drunk and all that interest peaked my mischievous nature.

"We know that, Joyce." Dan says, stopping just short of condescension.

Unbelievably, BOTH men lean back to settle into their seats and Geoff even re-crossed his legs. My eyes went wide. Two grown-ass men could not be this convinced that their family is under some witches spell.

My face flushes hot with blood that is, well... at this point around five percent alcohol. "No. You don't understand... I'M A WITCH." I say, mostly just for effect and partly because I feel indignant that anyone would condescend to me. (I'm sure that phrase is not proper but I'm drunk.) To my shock, BOTH brothers, again lean way forward. The barricade that was the crossed leg comes down, this time with a stomp.

OK. You want the truth? No one in that room is more shocked than me. Shocked both that I pronounced my witch craftiness (if that is a word) and shocked at the reaction of these brothers to my proclamation of witchdom, (I'm sure this is not a word either, but if I'm making fake drunken proclamations I can make fake descriptors.)

I continue, "Dan, you said it yourself. Everything happens for a reason and I'm sure I'm here to Solve. This. Problem." I look from one brother to the other. At this point, enough moments have gone by where I am a bit more wary that these brothers are just placating me, conning me. Just playing along with a fun game... I evaluate their body language and interaction. All tells show no sign of deception. Oh my Goodness, could this be possible?

Yes. I see the ridiculousness that I am wondering if they are conning me while I am conning them. The Cat moves over, inviting me to sit.

I move to the couch, sitting just on the edge of the seat, "Obviously the poor nanny was innocent. But the curse you say is on your family is against the witches' creed:

'If you do no harm than do what you will.'

I can take this spell off your family, but we need to find out two things... one, EXACTLY what was the curse and two, who put the curse on your family? Was it a good witch or a bad witch?" I'm just makin' this shit up as I go.

Geoff is first to speak. He has a Texas accent. Fleetingly, I wonder how he and Dan can have completely different accents. Both inherited the castle, so they must have the same mother... my thought is cut short. "The curse, as we know it, as handed down from generations is, 'The Mathews will never be able to realize their wealth'."

"That is a black witch's curse. Dark magic, which means you have been harmed for generations but they have been experiencing bad Karma as well. Ten-fold! Any curse of a dark witch can easily be removed by a white witch," I sit up straighter and squeak, "like me." I flush red from my awkward movements, possibly telling my con. Hoping neither sees me as the fraud I am. I make a mental note, 'You're drunk. Stay in control'. With that, the Cat runs out of the room.

I wonder again about Bea. Is she protecting the curse or trying to take it off? I lean back looking out the living room door for eavesdroppers. I don't want, either Bea or Beren to hear this conversation... My internal dialogue asks loudly, 'Because?'

In a moment of clarity, I am back in the real world of alarm clocks, accounting, and chores that are mindless but must be done none the less. Reality that is lightyears away from vacations abroad with twenty-four hours a day to wander and wonder. My internal voice answers honestly, "You don't believe in witches or curses, black, white or otherwise. Therefore, I don't want anyone to witness this pretense because...

I would be embarrassed.

I pop out into the light of reality even further, like Alice coming back out of the rabbit hole. I view this exchange from my landlords' perspective. They may feel I am taking advantage of their guests, who are also their relatives...

...For. My. Own. Amusement.

With that realization I flush with embarrassment. I'm playing with these poor grown men. I excuse myself. "I really must go, gentlemen. It's been a very long day for me, trying to keep up with the twenty-somethings."

Geoff is on his feet. "Oh, Joyce. Please stay. We're just about to open a bottle of Cabernet. It's still early. Just 9PM, 2PM in Dallas. Please stay, really, for just one drink."

"I'm going up to brush my teeth and change into my sweats. I may be back." I say as I'm already moving out of the room.

I bolt up the first flight of stairs, then pass Bea and the Cat coming down the second flight. Finally in my room, I shut the door and lean against it. 'Who am I? What do I believe?' After a long pause with no answers, 'I need to brush my teeth'. At the bathroom mirror, I look directly into my own eyes... 'Who are you?' I ask out loud. "I don't know. It's all so complicated." I mumble out loud with my toothbrush still in my mouth.

As I brush, I search for one phrase, in which, I truly believe. Pause brushing.

I got nothing.

The water runs very cold now, I splash my face then add soap and towel. As I rock back to sit on the side of the tub, face in the towel, elbows on legs. What the fuck am I doing here? I had a drink with an intelligent guy and ended up running out of the bar, then hiding in a bathroom. Which part of that was my blame? I let the cohorts believe I will let them rummage through this B&B and now I feel pressured to let them do something I know isn't right. Am I an asshole? I've been here a week and have barely spoken to Brooke of anything substantive. I push people away, at minimum keep them at arm's length then feel an aching for connection. Brooke is here. I'll see her tomorrow. I love her. I do. I'm certain I would lay down my life for her. Liz and the boys, too.

There.

I find a phrase I can say is truth.

I love. I love deeply.

LiFT says I'm 'free'. Am I free to change the narrative in my head? Am I free to remove the negative things I say when I talk to myself... about myself... and replace them with self-love? If this is true, then why are so many people walking around with self-doubt? And without the level of self-discipline we all want to obtain?

The truth is, we are free to try, and unfortunately we are also free to give up. We are all free to do whatever we want, right now, but we are not free of the consequences. The repercussions can be quick and painful. But the bottom line is, We Are All Free. Another simply truthful statement.

I am Free.

I move to the foot of the bed, wobbling to sit while taking off my left boot. One boot off and I flop back, eyes closed, boot still in hand. I had no idea I was so tired.

I should change into my PJs and set my alarm... but I don't.

Soon there will be Morning. I look forward to the morrow. Lady Macbeth went mad thinking of tomorrow. Yes. I 'strut and fret my hour upon this stage and then I will be heard no more. A tale told by an idiot, full of sound and fury signifying nothing.' Lady Macbeth and I have been good friends since Junior High while reading Shakespeare's book of the same name.

In my tomorrow there will be coffee... and porridge.

I smile, eyes still closed and throw my boot off the bed while bringing the right leg up, remove the remaining boot and throw it just off the bed. Still lying on top of the comforter I remove my sweater and throw it across the room. Instantly, I regret this. I'm cold, and begin scooting, eyes still closed, up to the pillows while removing my pants. I maneuver under the heavy comforter, the sheets are cold. I don't like sleeping without clothes, but my PJs are so far away.

Fading into deep sleep, I think of that rabbit hole I came out of tonight to see truth and stop the insanity. How much effort that must have been for Alice to get out. But Alice was young and had youthful energy... and there were all those drugs... I believe Alice's author, Lewis Carroll, was a graduate of Oxford as well. Curiouser and Curiouser. I wonder, while here at Oxford, if Mr. Carroll was on the rugby team...

Chapter 13

Be sure you know who you are

and what you want.

My dreams are disturbing, waking me often and abruptly. Through this pounding headache, I wonder about the location of my aspirin. After calculating the probability of throwing up the remedy, I decide to lie still until falling hard back into dreams that are disquieting. Disjunctive.

Only my last dream is memorable… Unfortunately.

I'm sitting in a dark, cave-like bar. The bartender is talking with the two men on my right. He has very dark, curly hair, and a crooked overbite. I sit up straighter, trying to get his attention to order a drink. As he continues his conversation I notice his eyes. Inside. There's a flicker. Not a flicker of light, but more like a whirling pinwheel of black, shiny graphite just behind his wide pupil. Focusing even closer, but leaning back, I shudder. This isn't a random flicker. It whirls clockwise, then counter clockwise, with a steady rhythm. I draw away further but my focus narrows, like the closing of an aperture on a camera. I flush as I realize my heart is beginning to beat to the rhythm of these whirling tops.

Slowly, he turns his attention to me. I push farther away from the bar. My chair begins to tilt back then tip. Instinctively, I reach out to the bar to stop my fall, but instead His hand catches me, all the way up my arm, to my elbow. He pulls me in violently, way over the bar, up to his face. We're nose to nose.

"Can I get you something?"

I can smell stale cigar on his scotch-soaked breath. I can't speak.

He speaks again. "You're playing with fire. I suggest you be very sure who you are and what you want before you come in here again." He grows bigger. Taller. His nose pokes mine. Still looking straight into my eyes, he roars with a scotch-cigar musk that makes me gag. I will not breathe. Him. In. He screams, "JOYCE."

I wake reeling with nausea. I maintain my stomach but not my composure. I'm shaking.

"Wow." I say, out loud. Slowly, I rise out of bed and head for the cold water and aspirin. "Toothbrush." I say, again, out loud.

Looking in the mirror, brushing my teeth and carefully brushing my tongue, I vow to take a couple days alcohol free to 'rehab'. In a moment of inspiration I go back into the bedroom to grab the open bottle of red from the desk and dump the rest down the sink. The smell makes me turn my head away.

"Coffee." I say, out loud, over my shoulder, feeling good about my new pledge.

Grabbing my phone, I notice Brooke has left me a text message. - 'All day Winery tour with Alpha Girls and Kim too! Includes lunch. Meet at bus stop 11AM.'

All-righty, then. Shortest sobriety ever. Right now, I have to maneuver down these stairs if I want coffee.

The 11:10 bus was, for the most part, empty. Brooke and I take a seat in a row with two bench seats, facing each other.

"Brooke, what do you believe?" I say, point blank.

"Random." Brooke is not following. "Are you OK? What are you talking about?"

"Witchcraft." I say, trying to be general. "It's obvious that, back in the 1500s during the time Nostradamus was alive and throughout the 1800s while the Mathew's Castle was bustling, Witchcraft was a convenient label for anyone who believed in ideas against the organized religion of that region. Meaning, a person who society should be afraid. A person society should be afraid of because of special powers they possess which make them dangerous. Powers that must be banned from that society. Powers that can only be vanquished by killing the possessor of those powers."

Brooke says, shaking her head no, "You're missing the point that back then, most people felt those 'witch powers' were born to some or bestowed to some but no one else had any power at all. Aside from the fact that the word 'witch' assumes evil intent. On the contrary, white craft, natural magic, and LiFT has an attitude that everyone can possess these powers through instruction and practice. Further, the instruction is all good. You heard Chelsea's Mom. "If you do no harm, do as you will." Her Rainbow-Girl-thing was all about helping society. Hey, even 'The Wizard of Oz' had Glenda the good witch. Secondly, all people are neither ALL good nor ALL bad, we're all… complicated. It comes with the blessing of having freedom of will."

"Wow." I am impressed. "Very well thought out."

Brooke continues. "Everyone defines 'witch' differently. Some immediately think of the 'Wicked Witch of the West', some think of Glenda. Some think of the witches in Macbeth stirring a brew in the dead of night, some see the characters in 'Witches of Eastwick'."

"Witches of where?"

"It doesn't matter, you get the idea." Brooke says, "The understanding of two people having a conversation has to do with the life experiences of each of the participants. For instance, most people find the scent of lavender calming. Most bath salts have the scent of lavender for that reason. It's used on sheets to help you sleep. But, what if you had a bad experience in a field of lavender? What if you saw your Dad or brother fall off a lavender-harvesting tractor which cut off his arm, or worse? Lavender would not help you feel peaceful. Quite the contrary."

Brooke continues. "So, like Nostradamus, if I name my school, which promotes Love etc., and include the word 'witch' more people will be turned off. But, if I say 'this is a place to learn a craft, like masonry, then add the word 'white' then more people, who want to do good in the world, will be inclined to join, or more correctly, practice. Everyone wants power. To tap into and control the powers of attraction is the ultimate power." Brooke says.

"So, what about Angel. She goes to church every week, where ever in the world she is. But yet, she goes to this LiFT meditation. In fact, the Catholic Church allows LiFT to conduct their meditations in the basement of their church. Maybe my question is, 'Where does the Judea/Christian values end and LiFT and or witchcraft begin?" I ask.

"Mom, you'll have to ask the church that." Brooke says. "But frankly, I think any church, synagogue or mosque would have a hard time saying the LiFT message of feeling Love, Freedom, and Thankfulness is somehow against their belief system."

"Good point." I say, still uncomfortable and wondering about the activity in the BNB. "What about this whole, curse on the Mathews family, witches in my BNB, Nostradamus's research center for Meditation… or not? What do you believe?"

"Well," Brooke pauses thoughtfully and looks forward. "We know there was a nanny accused of witchcraft. That is a fact. The Mathews believe they are cursed. Their belief in the curse is a fact. Nostradamus did, in fact, begin a research club of some kind, based in meditation, hidden from the Catholic powers that be, and in Montpellier. We know Bea ran an 'Arts Center near Montpellier. Certainly we DO NOT know if that is one in the same."

I cut her off, "Even when her Cat is named Nostradamus, her WiFi password is Nostradamus?"

"Yes. Circumstantial evidence only. Evidence that, 'more probably' she is a member of THE 'residential art center' that is the remnants of the Nostradamus club. That we do not know for a fact.

We do know Bea is into this LiFT meditation to a point where she instructs. There is a LiFT meditation foundation somewhere. I'm not sure what you're asking. I think the question, 'do you believe in witchcraft' can only be answered if you define what you mean by 'witchcraft'." Brooke says.

"Do you believe there are messages in the ether? That, with meditation we can 'see' and or 'hear' those messages? Can we meditate to tune into and turn up these communications? Can we tune in and or tune up our feels that will bring you things using the laws of attraction?" I pause, then add, "How much of the 'laws of attraction' do you believe? Can we control people and things in our surroundings with meditation techniques?"

"That's like, two dozen questions, Mom. I'm not sure this bus ride is long enough for my answer." Brooke quips.

"Give it a shot. Com'on. Kick in that Psychology degree. Pick one question."

"Well." Brooke takes a deep breath and again, looks forward. "I believe that God is Love… And yes, I believe that the feelings we have are powerful, the most powerful feeling is Love." Brooke shifts, turns, looking at me now. "I believe that God is the power in the universe that most call Love. Every sermon I have heard, whatever the religion, if I swap out the word God or Jesus with Love, the message is the same. In fact, it makes more sense and therefore, even more powerful. I believe, because I see love in action and know for a fact, that Love is all powerful. I don't need blind faith."

"IS?" I say, testing her. "So, if God IS Love. That is, God equals Love, and you believe, I'll quote you, 'God is the power in the universe that most call Love'. You must, then also believe that Love is the power in the universe that most call God. Yes?"

"Yes." Brooke says thoughtfully, "Or Buddha, or Jesus Christ or Mohammad. Yes. Further, my Psychology studies have shown me that Love, when paired with truth is healing. We all lie. The most damaging lies are when we lie to ourselves. Only when Truth is exposed, understood, accepted... only then, do we begin to heal. In Psychology step one is to find truth, expose and admit. The Catholic practice of confession seems to push people to look inward and admit their sins and the priest forgives us, frees us from the guilt."

"Well." I say eyebrows up, "Then, you have been thinking about this."

"But, your questions revolve around the messages in the ether. We all remember the party, where your friend was talking, and while still distracted by her own story, turned and put her hand over the phone. We asked her if she was about to make a call, she looked at us like we were crazy until she realized she had her hand on the phone and suddenly the phone rang. It was her daughter, who had a flat tire and needed help. Everyone has a story like that. So, I don't think it is opinion whether there are messages in the ether. There definitely are. The question to be answered is... is this LiFT meditation the way to 'tune in and turn up' those messages. We'll only know that by research. We have to practice. We'll have to write down what we hear and see if we are right."

"Me too!" Angel comes to sit next to me. "Next time we meditate, let's ask for something."

"Well," I say directly to Angel, "The website warns not to ask for anything, especially when we're still learning."

"Maybe we can ask for... I don't know, something small. Just to see if it works." Angel says.

"Like?" I say. Wondering if this is a good idea.... Because I realize, I believe there is power in meditation.

"Brooke, do you believe the power of attraction can be harnessed?"

"Mom, you've found hundreds of dimes in the last couple years since the divorce. I'm guessing, yes. Somehow you are 'attracting' them."

"Check this out." I say to Brooke as I pull out a dime from my coat. "I found this at the bus stop, before coming up to the dorm for the sleepover."

"So, what is it, you're saying to yourself that's attracting dimes?" Brooke says. Then after a pause. "Got ANY idea?"

"No." looking out into the passing landscape. "I do know that the probability of find an average of 20 dimes a month for this last couple of years is astronomical to a point of impossibility."

"Let's meditate and ask the universe, why." Brooke says, then looks back and calls, "Angel. Come guide a LiFT meditation."

"My Mom and I are in." Chelsea says, as she walks down the aisle. Obviously they have all been listening. "Deidra!" Chelsea screams as she squeezes in with Angel and Brooke. Kim sits next to me.

"I've been listening." Deidre reassures us all as she sits in the bench seat across the aisle.

"I'm ready." Kim says. "Let's do it! We have just under an hour more on this bus ride"

The rest of the bus ride is quiet except for Angel, guiding us through stages of feeling Love, Freedom, and Thankfulness. Over and over, we all try to connect with the feelings that will tune into the messages in the ether. At the end, we all hold out our right hand to symbolize the good we give to the people and environment around us, then hold out our left hand to ask for... an answer."

As the bus comes to a stop, "I got nothing." I say, breaking the silence.

We parade off the bus to wander the turn of the century winery and taste-test their best.

This tour is filled with wine tastings, epic stories of intuition, cheese parings, and even some Yorkshire pudding, but sadly, no more dimes and no answers. Tired and tipsy we climb back onto the bus.

By the time we arrive at the Oxford student bus stop, I'm happy to be going back to the BNB and my attic bed. Life is good, but tonight, I am the kind of tired that only three drunken nights in a row can bring to a fifty-something, in a strange time zone, run ragged by a bunch of twenty-somethings on a winery binge.

As I put the key in the door, I realize I barely remember the walk home. I do remember taking another run at pledging allegiance to rehab... at least, just for tomorrow.

As usual, the Cat is waiting for me. I slowly unload my hat, scarf, gloves, and coat onto the hall rack.

"Hello, Dammie." I say, hoping the door to my attic room is closed. I'm about to head up the stairs to bed when I notice the smell of baking.

My landlords, call me into the kitchen. "Joyce?" Bea yells. "Come join us for tea and scones."

"Yes. I'm home. Smells amazing. You've been baking." I don't want to join them. I'm tired, look tired, drunk. But I must be polite and if I can pour some tea and grab a scone for my room... that does sound wonderful. I need some carbs to soak up some of this alcohol.

As I begin the walk to the back of the house, I notice the room between the living room and kitchen, which has been tarped off while being painted, is now unveiled. I am drawn into the new 'reading room'. Bookcases line every wall, a small round table in the center is topped off with a plaster bust.

"Hey, cool!" I say, surprised by the echo. As I spin clockwise to take in the full effect, I see three drop-down desks have been built into the bookcases and on the last sits a copier. "A copier!" I say loudly to congratulate my landlords for thinking of just about everything... "A copier." I repeat and chuckle to myself. This is definitely better than finding a coin.

"Yes, we finally put it altogether." Bea says. "That is one of Beren's pieces." Bea is referring to the bust on a table in the middle of the room.

"Yes, Bea has done a smashing job with the room, yes?" Beren asks, always surprising me with his thick, English accent.

"Yes, beautiful. Both the bust and the wood work." I say, while I move into the kitchen, trying to scope out the scones and tea.

"Feel free to fill a plate with scones, I made way too many, and there are small pots for tea in the far cupboard. We're just heading up to ready for an early dinner with family then onto the hospital. It'll be a late night for us." Beren says, as he and Bea finish at the sink and head upstairs. Beren has an easy way about him.

A copier. I shake my head. The universe is making this very easy. I think I may copy a couple pages of that Nostradamus book. Certainly the part that says Nostradamus, along with his classmate Rabelais, started a center to study meditation. Also the page that states the translator will not translate because the content was Godless.

I set down my cup of tea and plate of scones to grab, "The Elixirs of NOSTRADAMUS" where I find and read again, Quote:

> "In 1530 the great French poet (and mystic) Rabelais received his doctorate in Montpellier... Manfred Dimde, the most important German, Nostradamus expert, considers that he can prove close co-operation in the realms of medicine and magic and in the constitution of a secret society."

I mark that page and page 43 for copying.

> Dear Friendly Reader, at this point I have omitted from translation into German the eighteenth chapter, because it teaches such things as are not fitting for a Christian or God-fearing man to know and I therefore felt it better not to make any mention of them."

So cool.

I rise from the table, head to the copier, raise the lid to copy, and there's a paper already on the glass.

White Craft School
Entered Apprentice
Syllabus I - English – Entered Apprentice – Spring Semester

MTR morning classes on Meditation - weeks 1-8
    Quick Start   www.LiFT.foundation
    Let's begin - Natural Science
    Building your own Personalized LiFT Binder
    The science of frequency
    Meditation advanced practice and process – Listen

MTR late morning classes on self-exploration - weeks 1-8
    North South East West – determining who you are
    Choosing your Occupation – to serve
    Choosing your Recreation – to serve
    Choosing your ceremonial instrument. An aid to ceremony
    Beads, Baubles and Gemstones making jewelry.
    Choosing and meeting your magical creature. An aid to extending your power

MTR (kitchen) classes on elixirs and perfumes – weeks 1-8
    Teas and other herbs– basic study
    Aromatherapy – basic study
    Cooking as meditation, storytelling and gifts for the souls.
    Music - enhancing meditation and directing mood

MTR Afternoon classes on Ethics and Community Service – weeks 1-8
    12 principles of Basic Ethics
    Knowledge is power – never stop learning
    Charity, Service, and your purpose.
    (Building Blocks of initiation to Fellow Degree)

MTR Spells – weeks 9-12
Meeting your Spirit Guide – an aid to help you interpret the messages in the ether - week 9
Basic Attracting – Engineering Your Basic Health spell – week 10
Basic Attracting – Engineering Your Basic Wealth spell – week 11
Basic Attracting – Engineering Your Basic Love spell – week 12

I'm stunned.

As I read, I can feel my cheeks blush. I hear no noise from this floor or the stairs but my heart is beating in my ears and I fumble with the page. I bolt for the kitchen to pick up my tea, scones and head for my room... *'What am I doing? Bea will be looking for this.'*

I put the tea and scones back down and run back to the copier. 'It's a copier you idiot!' I put the page back onto the glass and hit 'COPY'. Nothing. Oh shit! I have to calm down. There are no lights on so I push the 'ON' button. The copier begins to make all kinds of noise. My eyes widen. I tip toe to the stairs. Still no sounds from the second floor. The copier stops its racket and I push the 'copy' button again. Oh my God, it's working, but taking. So. Very. Long. Please be quicker. Please be quieter. Done.

I shove the page down the back of my pants. I grab my tea and scone plate and head to the stairs. I am one step up and realize I didn't turn off the copier.

"Crap." I say out loud. Too loud, then turn toward the copier again. 'TURN IT OFF', I scream to myself with no sound.

"Everything OK?" Bea says. I can hear her starting down the stairs.

"Oh yes, I may have spilled a bit of tea while climbing the stairs. All is well, I turned back for a napkin." I feel like both an idiot and a genius all at once. My breathing is ridiculous. I push the 'OFF' button and head through to the kitchen for a napkin. After one giant cleansing breath I steady my hands carrying the tea and scone plate.

Every step is a trial. My face is blushed. I pray Bea is back in her room otherwise she will see I am visibly shaken. I make it past their room and up to mine, put the scone dish on the floor so I can free a hand to open my door and the Cat rushes in upsetting the dish....

"Michael!" I say hushed, but as strong as I can. I can save most of the tea, but the scones have picked up some of the old Victorian carpet and probably some Cat's hair too. "Gross." I say throwing the scones into the trash.

I sit at the desk, head in hand, trying to calm down. I have a headache from the rush of adrenaline. "I would not make a good spy, Dammie." I admit to the Cat. "I did accomplish the mission, though." I say with a bit of pride as I pull the syllabus out from the back of my pants.

Shaking my head, eyes wide, I mutter breathlessly, "There IS a school." And then, "I gotta tell Brooke."

I can't dig my phone out from my purse fast enough. Brooke has already sent me a text...

'We've made reservations, It's Dress up! Chelsea's Mom says it's her treat. We'll pick you up by taxi at 7PM.'

I take a picture of the Syllabus, then text the picture to Brooke. As I head for the tub I can't wait for them to get this. Alternately, I realize, I could have just taken a picture with my phone, in the first place instead of all that crazy with the copier. 'I'm an idiot.' I mutter to myself as I run a bath.

Chapter 14

Much better than finding a dime.

After a long, bubble-filled, hot tub, full makeup, hair blown-dry, and curled, little black dress, including jewelry, heals, and even perfume, I still haven't heard anything from the Dorm. Brooke's phone must be dead.

It's just 7PM now, the doorbell rings. The taxi is waiting. This is going to be a wild ride. As I grab my purse, I fold up the syllabus and stick it in the side pouch. I don't want Bea and Beren to see it.

The 'Hackney' is a very large, very old, black cab. I wait for the driver, dressed in what looks to me like a tux, to open the door for me. "Wow! Beautiful." I say, as I climb in.

"Remise." Chelsea says, "Mom is going all out."

"Well, I have a surprise." I say, as I hand the syllabus to Kim. Her eyes get wide. "Bea and Beren just renovated the Library... I found it in the new copier." I turn to Brooke, "Brooke, I can't believe you didn't look at your phone. Didn't you see the picture message I sent?"

"No Way?" Kim says. "You made this up."

"Oh no." My hand up in pledge. "I swear, I found it in the copier."

"Holly Crap." Chelsea says, looking over her Mom's shoulder, and passes the page to Angel and Deidre, who start screaming.

"Mom, I got nothing from you. What is it?" Brooke says putting down her phone and snatching the syllabus from Angel. "NO! You made this up?"

"I did not. Look at it, this is realer than real. Not that I wouldn't, just for a joke, but THIS. IS. REAL." I swear. My hand up in pledge again.

"So, it's true!" Kim says breathless. "AND this means the school books have to be there too!"

"Yes, it does. But my Landlords are there too. I'll scan the library tonight when everyone is asleep." I say, thinking of a raid of the scones as an excuse to be in that part of the house so late, in case the landlords come searching.

"Oh, I think we should all go back to your place for a night cap." Kim says.

"Smashing!" Chelsea chimes in with her best English accent.

"I gotta see this place. How big is the library?" Kim asks.

"Just a small room. Nine by twelvish. I can do it when I get back." I'm getting nervous.

Brooke ignores my resistance. "No, Mom. We're all going in. This is crazy. And Frankly, I'm not positive I believe you."

"All-righty then. After dinner... drinks at my place." I concede, just as the cab comes to a stop. The cabby opens the passenger side door while the restaurant's doorman helps as well. I love this English style.

"Our table will be ready for us at 8, they're holding a cocktail table in the bar for us as well. I wanted to have a full-cocktail-hour." Kim says to me with a smirk. Then, looking at the girls, "I'm so glad we could all be together tonight for this. My company is picking up this tab."

"Even better." I say, following Kim to the lounge.

"This is cocktail hour, we're all having cocktails." Kim states emphatically as she gives her order. "I'll have a vodka martini, dirty with an extra olive."

There seems to be three waiters for just this table. I give my order as I assume the Alphabet Girls are attracting more servers and better service than usual. "I'll have a martini as well. Gin. Dry. Lime. No olives."

"Yes, I remember, you're a gin martini girl." From behind me, the deep voice of Chas.

I take a deep breath before I turn in my seat. "Chas." I don't know what else to say. I wish I had something. But no.

"I'm here with my son and a couple of his team-mates." Chas says loudly, hoping to get a reaction from the Alphabet Girls.

"Have you met the Girls? Brooke, my daughter, Angel, Deidre, Chelsea and Kim, Chelsea's Mom." I say, blushing. I want him to go away.

"Nice to meet you all." Chas says as he nods and focuses back on me. "I was about to track you down to ask you to lunch tomorrow. Will you have lunch with me?" Chas asks loudly while all eyes are still on us.

Now, I'm bright red and can actually feel my ears go hot. "Well, I'm really here just trying to see as much of your great country as I can, with the girls." I say, as I sweep my hand, referring to the troupe, but the movement comes out crazy awkward. I put my hand down on the table which comes off even more awkward, then on my lap not knowing what to do with it, now that it has embarrassed me, I want to cut it off. Anyone can tell, even from the next room, he makes me self-conscious. I hate that.

"Oh no, Joyce." Kim chimes in. Chas continues his focus on me as Kim continues loudly, "We were just going to hang around the dorm tomorrow, doing nothing in particular." Kim lies with a grin.

"Mom. Go." Brooke says, meaning; Stop this drama. You're embarrassing yourself. Just go.

I want to scream NO! But instead, I say, "I guess I'm free."

"Great." Chas says. By then his son and son's friends are talking to the Alphabet Girls and there is no one for me to talk to, except him. "What have you been up to so far? Maybe I can be of assistance. I could even be your guide."

Our drinks come, Chas raises his hand to the waiter. "This round's on me, Michael."

The fact that he refers to this waiter as Michael, but the Waitresses at the Cartoon Bar were Sweety, does not escape me. I'm shaking my head. He adds, "I'll have one of these as well, lime instead of olives. Take care of the boys." He nods into the crowd.

He looks back down at me, "Gin with lime sounds interesting."

He's standing too close. Positioned on this barstool, his chest is in my face, and again I can't think of a thing to say… Our table won't be ready for half an hour, at least. I want to escape to the ladies room.

Chas takes a sip of MY drink. "So really, what have you been up to?"

I need to refocus. I need to find the offense. Body language first. I decide to freak him out. "Well," I say as I reposition myself as far back on this barstool as I can, sit up straight, suck in my stomach, cross my legs and lean back, putting one elbow on the back of the chair. Change your focus, change your body language. Fake it until you make it. "I've come across a man in need. His whole family has been cursed and I have taken it, as a personal, solemn mission, to lift that curse for him, and for his family and all his family's generations to come." I pause. This sounds imbecilic, even to me. I look into his eyes to test for reaction. I muster more confidence, "Be careful Chas, you did say that the next time we met you were going to think before you react." Apparently, I have decided to put on my big girl panties and go on the offense. I smile, daring him to mock me. Just for effect, I pick up the martini, smiling a warning: This martini can easily double as a weapon, and I'm not afraid to use it, even here in a five star restaurant in front of my cohorts and yours.

"OK." He pauses, clearly surprised by my abrupt change in attitude.

I smirk and raise my eyebrows as I take a sip.

He continues slowly, "So, you've taken up a 'PERSONAL, solemn mission'." He pauses again, picking his words carefully. Staring alternately, deep into my eyes then down at the drink/weapon. "Why?" He asks finally.

"Because that is what us white witches do when we find innocents who have been victimized by evil witches." I say, still daring him to say something unkind, condescending or rude.

He pauses, looking up to the ceiling, trying to weigh his options.

I take another sip and realize the drink has become a comfortable barrier between us. I smile bigger than the Cheshire cat in Alice in Wonderland and chuckle.

"You are playing with me?" Chas says carefully.

"Oh no. There is, in fact, a man staying at my BNB who believes his family was cursed by a witch in the 1800's and..." I pause, lean forward, offering him another sip of my drink, "Further, he, one-hundred-percent, believes I am a witch, and further believes I am THE witch that can and will remove this three-hundred-year-old spell."

Chas takes the martini from me to take a sip, instead puts the drink on the table. Losing my barrier, I blush.

Just as I begin to feel I am losing control, Michael the waiter, comes with a fleet of waiters and drinks.

Chas leans in, "Can I order you another?"

"No, thank you. We can share." I say, trying to pull my confidence back into the room.

"Michael. I'm going to invite these lovely women to dine with us. Please find out if the poker room upstairs is free." Chas says very loudly, then turns to me. "Will you dine with us?"

"This night is not up to me. Kim is in charge of this outing." I choke a bit.

Kim apparently, has been paying attention, winks at me then turns to Chas, and says, "We would not dream of keeping the two of you apart."

"Thank you." Chas says, and immediately continues our conversation. "So, you have this man in your BNB who believes he is cursed, and he believes you are a witch..." Chas leans way in. I have no time to figure out what's going on. In my ear, he whispers, "What do you believe, Joyce?" His voice is deep. I can smell his musk, and the shoulder of his new dark blue suit is just an inch from my nose. As he rocks back, I notice his tie is deep, dark, blood-red. Instantly, I remember my dream and snap out of my hormone-charged internal dialogue.

"I know who I am, Coach." I bark, as I stiffen my back, remembering the bartender in my nightmare, with the coal-black eyes warning me to 'not come back until I know who I am and what I want'. The truth is, I don't know who I am or what I want. Right now, I want to run, but I also want to be alone with this man who makes my blood and hormones rage.

Chas offers me a sip of his drink, I want to slam his martini glass on the table and slice his throat with the broken stem for putting me through this agony.

I do take a sip and hold the glass between us, relieved that I have my barrier again.

Just then, the waiter enters to inform Chas, "Yes, we can have the poker room ready very quickly. Set for ten?"

I am in full flush. I have to keep up this brave pretense for the next, how long? I gulp the last of the gin, put the empty on the table and realize everyone is looking at me for a final answer. "Fine." I say to the waiter. "Yes, set for ten."

"Thank you." Chas is waiting patiently. I have nothing to say. Finally, solemnly he asks again, "So who are you, Joyce? Are you a witch?"

"That depends on your definition of Witch. For centuries, people have been accused of witchcraft who believe anything that is not approved by the church. But, yes, I am a witch, if your definition includes those who believe in the power of Love, feeling Love, the frequency of Love...understanding freewill and thankfulness. Yes."

"So you are a follower of LiFT?" Chas says simply.

"LiFT? You know about LiFT?" I'm shocked.

"Yes, many of the boys have..." Chas pauses trying to find the right words. He is obviously trying to be very careful, "...met... girls who follow the teachings of LiFT.foundation. The idea of frequency and power of attraction is not a philosophy, its physics. I'm sure you know more than most about that."

"I know more than most, why?" I ask.

"Well, I'm going to admit a bit of stalking on my part. I Googled you and then Googled your Dad. He was quite famous in his day, not just around the engineering department of ITT. Your Dad was 'Big Ed'. Right?"

"Yes. That was my Dad." I say, as I soften. I always do when thinking of my Dad.

"I saw the magazine covers and patent rights, many of his patents were the property of RCA, Link Radio, Warner Communications or ITT etc., but he did have a couple in his name. His 1950's design for the coaxial cable switch was revolutionary, used universally and still used today. Big Ed stories are still floating around the engineering department of ITT. And yes, you were right, I was just in nickers."

"Thank you. Yes, my Dad was quite a guy. He was Einstein meets Deepak Choprah. He was also a prolific writer of philosophy."

"I didn't find any books. What was the title?" Chas says.

"Oh, it was never published. A collection of his thoughts and poems. I have it. He titled it 'Spectrums'."

"'Spectrums', I see we have circled back to wave lengths, and frequency." Chas says as a team of waiters appear to seat us and carry our drinks. He leans in to whisper in my ear, "You are going to sit next to me, right? Please don't run away from me again."

I'm trying to get off this bar stool with five-inch heels, while shaking from just the nearness of this man. Chas offers me his arm. Ugh.

We're led through the kitchen and up a back staircase to a room no bigger than about twenty feet square, with one big round table in the middle and a bar in the corner. Apparently, we're getting our own bartender as well.

Brooke comes up behind me, "OK. This is cool, right?"

"Very."

"What can I get you all? Kim, you first." Chas says taking over as the host.

"Cabernet with dinner." Kim says, then turns to Chelsea who nods, "Make that two."

"Cabernet for me as well." I say, as Chas scoops up my hand, rests it on his arm to lead me to a seat.

"I want to be sure I know exactly where you'll be." Chas whispers in my ear.

Chapter 15

It's not about the frequency,
It's the messages riding ON the frequency.

Once we're all seated, Chas graciously starts a conversation for the entire table. "So, Joyce and I were just talking about frequencies. Radio waves and brain waves. Kim, you and Chelsea have been talking to Andrew, I wonder if you know he's an engineering major? I'm sure Andrew can recite some very cool facts about this subject."

Andrew, sitting between Kim and Chelsea, appears un-phased by Chas putting him on the spot. "Yes, aside from the obvious over-lap in frequency between radio waves and brainwaves, many brilliant scientists throughout the years have made the connection between thought and the laws of attraction. Tesla, Einstein..."

Kim interrupts, "And that Italian priest from the 1400's..."

"Mom!" Chelsea interrupts her mother. "Andrew, I'm sorry, please go on, what did Tesla say?"

Andrew, a bit confused as to why Chelsea was so abrupt, but noticing all the girls stifling a laugh, politely leaves the inside joke alone, and continues. "Tesla is famous for saying, 'If you want to find the secrets of the universe think in terms of energy, frequency and vibration.' ''

I quickly jump in to be sure Kim does not start up again, "Andrew you said, 'obvious over-lap'? What did you mean by that?"

"Well there are different brain wave frequencies, depending on your state of mind. When alert, your brain waves register at about 20 waves per second as you slide through meditation and into deep sleep, your brain waves can read as low as 1 wave per second. "

"Wait." Angel interrupts. "So, I have always heard meditation experts... all the books on meditation, say we need to RAISE our frequency, but you just said if we are alert and focused and trying to get to a meditative state, we are lowering our frequency. What am I missing?" Angel asks.

"You're not missing anything." Andrew, answers smiling, "Going from an alert state where your brain waves can get as high as 30Hz, to meditation state at 4 to 8Hz would be LOWERING your frequency or a decrease in frequency. Any other analysis is incorrect."

"I'm confused. All the books I've read say we need to Raise our frequency." Angel is still skeptical.

Andrew uses two cocktail napkins as reference. "Let's say these napkins are one Hertz long. A hertz is one second.

If 20 waves fit from the beginning of the napkin to the end, that's 20 Hz. Which happens only in an alert, waking state.

If only one wave fits in there, then that's 1Hz. Achievable only in deep sleep. Very deep sleep. Meditation is about 6 Hz.

You can see as you raise the frequency of the waves, you raise your awareness. That is: more awake and alert.

To lower the frequency of the waves, you are sliding into meditation and then deep sleep."

"So where is the overlap?" Chelsea brings us back to my question.

"Well, radio waves can be broadcast down to thirty hertz which overlaps high alert and focused."

Andrew removes his pen again from his inside jacket pocket, and begins to write on Chelsea's cocktail napkin.

"So, if we had the right equipment, we could hear a person's dreams?" Chelsea asks.

"If we had the right equipment, we could read minds in any state and project it as a movie, but that kind of equipment does not exist." Andrew looks up, "Not yet." Andrew smirks as he continues to write.

Kim leans over to me in a whisper, "Thank God for that."

"I'm pretty sure when he says 'any state', he is not including the state of intoxication." I whisper back.

"So when we feel Love," Chelsea says speaking to Andrew loudly, but looking at us, like a teacher with two unruly students, "or thankfulness, there's no difference in brain wave frequency?"

Andrew answers, "From what I know, your feelings of love or hate will not cause a frequency difference. The wave is just a vehicle to carry the information. Messages are attached to, or 'ride' on the frequency.

When you turn your radio dial to, let's say, channel 101.5 broadcasting frequency, you may hear opera and then, the next hour, hear a broadcast of Elvis. So, the frequency of the radio wave has not changed, only the information riding ON that wave." Andrew answers, as he turns the napkin around.

Hertz   .5HZ--------4Hz----------8Hz-----14Hz------30Hz

Brain Sleep---Meditation---Relaxed---Alert---HighlyAlert Waves

Earth   7.83Hz

The waiters are back, filling our table with appetizers and taking entre orders. The bartender joins in, filling our glasses.

Chas leans over to whisper, "So, what does the old Italian priest say, Joyce?"

I answer loudly for the whole table to hear, while looking at Deidra, because I know she can help if I stumble. "The Old Italian Priest asked, 'Why do we think love is a magician?', then answers himself, 'because the whole power of magic consists in love.' I can't remember the rest."

Deidra fills in, "The work of magic is the attraction of one thing by another."

"That was in the 1400's?" Asks Andrew.

"Yes. Mario Ficino, known as the father of natural magic. Cool right?" Deidra says.

"Yes, Deidra, very cool." Kim says, as I kick her under the table.

Chas is amused. He puts his arm on the back of my chair, and leans in to whisper, "I guess you're going to make me look that up."

I turn, lean in, to whisper in his ear, "I will never 'make' you do anything, Chas." I say, harshly, insulted that he has put me in a category of controlling women.

"All-righty. Good to know." Chas says, eyebrows up.

As I turn back, all eyes are on us. I may have said that a bit too loudly. I blush again. Not knowing what to say, I look down at the napkin on my lap.

Chas, knowing I want to flee, moves his hand from the back of my chair to my shoulder.

"Andrew, these women have been attending LiFT meditations. What can you tell us about the validity of this process?" Chas says, ending the awkward pause by turning attention away from us.

Andrew is happy to help, "Well, back in the early nineteen-hundreds, Einstein developed $E=mc2$ which was not initially designed to calculate how much mass will convert to how much energy, rather Einstein's equation states

MASS IS NOTHING BUT… ENERGY.

In other words this table…" Andrew knocks on the table and looks at Chelsea, "…and your nose, Chelsea, and Coach's wine are all just energy vibrating at different frequencies.

Most energy we can't see, like radio waves, micro waves, light waves, and brain waves. Everything in the universe is just energy vibrating at different frequencies, different wave lengths. Green has its own frequency. Your eyes are only instruments which can detect the difference between different light waves. It's your brain that says, 'GREEN'.

Your ears are just instruments which collect sound waves, but it's your brain that says, 'Elvis'. Yes. It's all very cool." Andrew says, "So, Tesla, who said, 'If you want to find the secrets of the universe, think in terms of energy, frequency and vibration', would not consider the LiFT method of meditation to be a philosophy, its physics.

Everyone's brain gives off, more correctly, **sends out** brain waves, animals too. Scientific evidence proves our bodies have equipment that will receive these vibrations. Some people have better equipment... better receivers. Just like some people can see more clearly, some hear more clearly, well some can sense... feel the messages, riding the brain-wave frequencies in the ether, more easily."

While everyone is focusing on Andrew, I turn to Chas and whisper, "I may have, said that a bit too loudly."

"You may have." Chas says with a chuckle, "Is it really that I irritate you," Chas moves closer, teasing, taunting, lowering his voice, "or do I just make you nervous?"

I can smell his breath, sweet red wine. I look up from his mouth, his eyes are focused on mine. I can barely think. I have been exposed and assaulted at the same time. "Irritation. ONE-hundred percent."

Chas lowers his voice a bit more, moves in, touching my ear with his lips... "ONE-hundred percent, Joyce?"

I want to slap him and scream, 'arrogant, ivy league prick'. I take a breath and gather my thoughts enough to go on an assault. "Do you know any of the waitresses at the Cartoon Bar?" I say, in a sickly sweet tone, pause, pierce my eye brows as if I'm to trying to recall... "What's her name?" I bait him.

"Ellen? Maggie? What did you hear? I have never...! Dear God, they're in their twenties! Is that why you're so irritated? You think I'm sleeping with Oxford students?"

I twist in my seat towards him even more. Leaning into his ear, "Oh No, Chas." I am sure to keep my voice hushed but harsh. "Apparently, even when you know the names of your waitresses you refer to them as Sweetie, but the male waiters in your life are called by their first name. THAT is just ONE example of what I see that irritates me." I pause, turn to take the last sip of HIS martini and check to see if we are too loud. The table conversation is going on without us. I turn back to him. Looking face on and straight in the eye, raising my eyebrows, "I'm wrong?"

Chas, trying to continue our semi-covert conversation, leans into my ear. I feel his breath. "I regret every moment of the way I behaved at the Cartoon. Please consider that was a very small sample of my behavior. I look forward to getting to know you better tomorrow, at lunch, and hope you give me a chance to prove that very small window of time at the Cartoon, was not, at all, representative of who I am." Chas says.

I flush and face forward to join the conversation. I have nothing more to say. I want to take this opportunity to cancel tomorrow's lunch, but I just can't say the words. I want to see him again. I want much more.

Angel is talking, "So, there are hundreds of messages all around us. It's amazing we're not overloaded." Angel says with a quick glance in my direction to tell me she has noticed my agitated conversation with the coach... and she's uncomfortable.

"Even the earth gives off its own frequency." Andrew is still the focus.

"The Earth?" Angel is riveted.

Andrew continues, "Yes. There is a layer of our atmosphere which is electromagnetic, which is continuous lightening. That lightening resonates with the body of the Earth, like a drumstick hitting a drum, which gives off a frequency averaging just under 8 Hz.

Angel leans forward, "Isn't that about the frequency of our brains when we are in meditation?"

"Yes, the averages are about the same. Our brains send out brain waves of anywhere from 5 to 8Hz while in meditation. The Earth's frequency of 8 Hz is just an average as well. You know, like beating a drum when the size of the drum doesn't change but the strength with which you beat it, and the spot you beat it, will change the tone a bit. A really cool fact is, the size of the wave length is roughly the circumference of the Earth. Since 2014 researchers have seen giant spikes. Some say the Earth is 'wakening' but really it's just chaotic solar activity which effects the lightening which, in turn, effects the drum beat."

"So, when we meditate we may be resonating with the Earth, not really with the entire universe. Interesting! But with all these 'messages' coming at us, not just brain waves but light waves and sound waves, how are we not overloaded?" Angel asks again.

"Great question, Angel." Andrew obviously enjoys playing teacher. "It's all about focus. I'm sure you didn't notice coach's shoes, but you probably can tell me, in detail, the shoes Chelsea is wearing, or Chelsea's Mom's shoes... because you choose your focus every moment."

"Actually, I didn't notice if your Coach is even wearing shoes," Angel giggles, "but I know Chelsea's shoes are the color of your Coach's tie, four inch plain pumps, her Mom has on similar shoes but in dark grey with a slightly lighter grey lace covering." Angel says, with a quick glance and smiles to Chelsea.

"It's all about focus." Andrew says. "ALL of conscious perception is all about conscious focus. If you practice, both bringing your brain waves into the meditation state and focusing on the messages around you, you may find you have tuned your 'equipment' to receive the messages in the ether. You may find that the messages you send are more easily received too. In LiFT the messages you're sending are that of Love, Freedom, and Thankfulness. I'm sure someone or something, or maybe everyone and everything, is picking that up and further, maybe more importantly... attracted to it."

"Cool." Angel says, "So, would you call any of this 'magic'?"

Andrew leans forward, "Many renowned scientists throughout history have compared the word magic to technology, or scientific principles. There's a quote from Dr. Ambrose 'Any scientific principles, no matter how primitive, are magic to those who don't understand it'. Dr. Gehm said something like, 'Any technology distinguishable from magic is insufficiently advanced'. In my opinion, as an engineer, LiFT is not magic, there is no such thing as magic, LiFT is applied advanced physics."

At that, the team of waiters enter with dinner.

"We have GOT to find those school books." Kim whispers in my ear.

"I was just thinking the same thing." I whisper back.

As dinner continues, the conversation turns to the Thomastown Witch's burning, the Mathews Family Curse, and finally, my Landlords.

The team of waiters are back, clearing dinner and taking orders for dessert. I see Brooke showing Coach's son, Chucky, the Syllabus.

"Hey Dad." Chucky says. "Look at this!"

As Chas takes the syllabus, Kim leans in past my shoulder, speaking directly to Chas. "I think we should all head over there to go through that library."

His eyes scan the syllabus, "Michael." Chas calls the waiter, "We'll take those desserts to go."

Chapter 16

The Curse has been cast
and Wicca will be served Karma tenfold.

As we invade my BNB, I'm thankful neither my landlords nor any other tenants seem to be here. While most of my troupe goes directly into the library, I head into the kitchen to begin the process of feeding ten people coffee, tea, and dessert.

"You're not interested in the library?" Chas follows me into the kitchen.

"There are enough, well-qualified detectives searching the library. My mission is to get the coffee and tea water on." I say, moving to the antique coffee grinder.

"Here, let me do that." Chas comes up behind me and takes over.

"Men." I say, ducking, and slip out of his arms.

"I'm trying to help you." Chas says as he finishes grinding the beans.

"You're trying to unnerve me."

"One is not exclusive of the other." I can hear the smirking in his voice.

"Haven't you gotten the memo that pulling a girls pigtails will only get you bad attention?" I ask.

"Yes, but bad attention is better than none." Chas says, as he sets the coffee to brew."

"Mom!" Brooke is calling from the library. "Chucky found a 'print history' in the copier."

"Dad, come check this out." Chucky says.

"What do you have?" Chas says, as we join the others in the library.

"There's two saved print jobs, Dad. One is just three-pages. The other is 130 pages. What would you like me to print out?"

I answer first. "I do not want to start a 130 page print job when anyone can walk in. Frankly, the worst thing that can happen is someone replenishes the paper and the rest of the job prints. Or we run out of ink…"

"We get the idea, Mom." Brooke interrupts me, "Chucky, just print the three pages. We'll get both paper and ink for this printer tomorrow."

Chucky pushes a couple buttons and the printer begins to print. We all wait in complete silence.

The first page is released and rests in the tray. All eyes are on me.

"OK. I'll get it, then." I say as I snatch the page. "It's the detail of a potions class. Let's go into the kitchen, where there's more light."

White Craft School of Natural Magic
Entered Apprentice
Prof S H VonAchen
MTR noon (kitchen) classes on recipes, elixirs, and perfumes – weeks 1-8

1. **WEEK 1 - 3 - Recipes for better living**
   a. Understanding your body – Required reading:
      i. You The Owners Manuel - by Dr. Oz
      ii. Eat to Live – Cookbook by Joel Fuhrman
      iii. The Green Pharmacy – James A Duke, Ph.D.
   b. Full annual battery of testing, blood tests, etc.
   c. Allergies and sensitivity testing
   d. Building your binder - Your Recipes for your healthy body
2. **WEEK 4 - Teas and other herbs**
   a. Required reading   Tea: Celebrations and Meditations
3. **WEEK 5 and 6 Aromatherapy**
   a. Required study www.soulvisiondesigns.nl
      i. History of Perfume
      ii. Distillation apparatus and variations
      iii. Building your binder – Your Perfumes Chapter
      iv. Choose the perfumes best for you - signature scent
         1. Fragrance wheel
      v. Human Pheromone
         1. How Pheromones induce a sexual response
      vi. Understand perfume scents and you
      vii. Making your Fragrance oils
      viii. Making your Water based Perfume
      ix. Making your (alcohol based) Cologne
      x. Hazards, warnings, and Guidelines
      xi. Vocabulary and Oils List with description
4. **WEEK 7 - Music – enhancing your loving mood with music.**
   a. Building your binder – Music for Your Loving Soul.
5. **WEEK 8 – Art – enhancing your loving thought with Art and Color.**
   a. Building your binder – Art for Your Loving Soul.

Essential Oils Steam Distillation

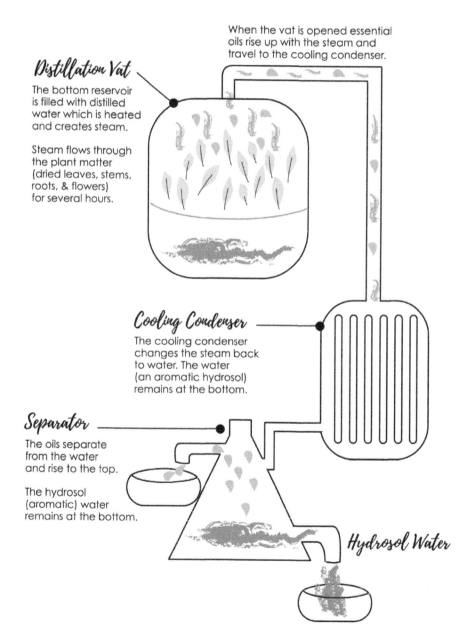

When the vat is opened essential oils rise up with the steam and travel to the cooling condenser.

Distillation Vat

The bottom reservoir is filled with distilled water which is heated and creates steam.

Steam flows through the plant matter (dried leaves, stems, roots, & flowers) for several hours.

Cooling Condenser

The cooling condenser changes the steam back to water. The water (an aromatic hydrosol) remains at the bottom.

Separator

The oils separate from the water and rise to the top.

The hydrosol (aromatic) water remains at the bottom.

Hydrosol Water

White Craft School
Entered Apprentice
Prof. S. H. VonAchen

Apprentice level – MTR noon (kitchen) classes on recipes, elixirs and perfumes – weeks 1-8

Welcome - The basic meditation of Love, Freedom, and Thankfulness is simple. This simple process is the best way to attract, from all the universe, people, things, and events that will bring you closer to your purpose: Your path will be clearer.

Everything else you will learn here, or anywhere, is just superfluous.

Yes. Everything else is superficial. All the rest you are about to learn are just tricks to enhance your **FEELINGS** of Love, Freedom, and Thankfulness with smell, taste, movement, art, and music.

Practice healthy living. Consistency will develop and strengthen your self-discipline. Consistently eating healthy, exercise, fresh air, and sunshine, but also ethical behavior, kindness, and generosity. These things will help you to send a clearer loving message on the frequency on which you are 'broadcasting'.

Through this class and all the classes in this school, you will learn to better understand:

1. Who you are. (We are all perfectly different).
2. What best, evokes the feelings of Love, Freedom and Thankfulness FOR YOU.
3. How to, more clearly, see the path where you can best serve humanity.

We are a collective. "Why are you unhappy? Because 99.9% of everything you do, is for yourself, and there isn't one." Wei Wu Wei.

You will be building a binder of personal tricks that work for you and your senses; Smells, tastes, movement, music, art and other visual stimulus.

I grew up, just one block from my town's railroad depot. Especially at night, I would hear the whistles blow and imagine traveling to far-off places, and having grand experiences. But, if you have had a tragic accident on a railroad or you have seen a tragic accident on a railroad, then the sound of that whistle will not evoke a sweet nostalgia and yearning for travel. Instead, that train whistle will bring back feelings of tragedy.

As you find just the right smells, sights, sounds, tastes, images, and even movement to evoke feelings of Love, Freedom, and Thankfulness, you will catalog this in your binder. Your life's mission is to find out who you are, so that, you can determine how best you can serve.

Let's begin.

"Sooo cool!" Angel breaks the silence.

"I guess this is all real, Joyce. I honestly thought we were all playing a game you created for us." Kim says, her disbelief not quite gone. "So, we're looking for school books." Then noticing the books above the sink, "All these books can be bought on Amazon. These aren't text books specific to this school, written by professors. In fact, above the sink is a copy of 'The Green Pharmacy'."

"I'm going into the library to look for these books, and what other books are there." Angel rises from the kitchen table.

"I found the website www.soulvisiondesigns.nl." Brooke says, not taking her eyes off her phone. "It's very cool. Anyone can take these courses."

As we serve coffee and tea, along with the desserts, the group's conversations swirl around individual experiences of classic items, sounds, and tastes which changed our perception from the 'norm'.

Deidre's story, is most memorable. She tells the story of her Aunt, who was home when her son tragically shot himself in his room. She was on the couch. She turned her head toward the shot that rang out to her left. Her Aunt says every time she turns her head to the left, she hears that shot. Our physical body, memories, and the feelings they summon are knotted together.

One of Chucky's friend's adds, "I used to be real heavy. I couldn't get enough pizza. Then, one day, I brought home a whole pizza pie, opened the box to find it filled with maggots. I haven't had a slice since. So, the 'knotting' of a thing, place, smell, or taste, knotted with a feeling, in my case, strong craving, can be changed."

I haven't said a word in an hour. I'm totally exhausted and frankly, I'm having a tough time figuring out what to make of all these crazy, convoluted new ideas swirling around. Thankfully, Chas stands to announce, it's time to go so I can rest. It's now passed

1:00 AM. I wonder, 'where are my landlords? Where are all the guests? Where is the Cat?'

I walk everyone to the door. The last in my parade is Kim who gives me a smirk and glances behind me. I turn to follow her gaze. Chas stands directly behind me, without his coat on.

"Out." I say simply, but sternly.

"Don't forget we have a lunch date." He says, as he puts on the coat he was holding (and hiding) behind his back... just to play with me.

"A very late lunch date." I say, thinking I really need another ten hours of sleep. "Two o'clock?"

"My pleasure." He says as he leans in for a kiss. I offer my cheek. He backs up trying to look indignant.

"Out. That faux indignant works for you?" I ask.

"Yes. Either that or my tortured pained look."

"Get out..." I try to say his name but it just doesn't come out. "Out!" I say too intensely as he moves quickly out the door.

Just before he vanishes says, "You look spectacular tonight. I look forward to our meeting later today at two. That's AM? One hour?" He pokes.

"Out!"

As soon as the door closes, I can't help but giggle. I don't regret deflecting that 'first kiss'. I'm way too tired and have to brush my teeth. A first kiss with this man must be... Spectacular.

I wonder... why I can't I even say his name?

I look up the three flights of stairs and know, if I sit, I'll sleep right there on the staircase. So, with the three pages printed from the copier crumbled in my hand, I climb. At the top of the first flight I notice the door to my landlords' room is open and guarded by the Cat.

"I have way too much integrity to rummage in someone else's bedroom while they're out." I lie to the Cat. "…and I'm quite sure I'm too tired to go in." I add, much more to the truth.

Waking briefly at 6:00 AM. I realize I don't remember climbing those last two flights, nor do I remember getting into my PJs. Apparently, I even found an extra heavy wool blanket to add to my bedding. The sun is not yet up. I think for a moment about brushing my teeth, using the toilet and taking aspirin, but instead, my eyes close, and off to dreamland I go again.

I'm walking down a cobblestone road toward a bar. The steady cadence of my clicking footsteps is calming. The words scribed above the front door read…

Bukowski Pub

'I puke on your feeble attempt at alcoholism.'

– Charles Bukowski

I pull on the huge, heavy, double-doors, which only give way enough to reveal they aren't locked. With this second attempt, I heave the doors, which gives them enough momentum to swing wide open, then pause. As I continue inside I smell the mold and rotting alcohol from centuries of spilled drinks. The light diminishes to darkness, as the doors boom loudly behind me, my peace jumps and looks for an escape from this new and sudden darkness. I'm totally blind as my eyes too slowly adjust to the dim lighting. I find myself back in that faintly lit bar. As my eyes adjust to the lack of light, the bartender slowly appears like out of a fog of darkness. His twirling, black, graphite eyes appear last. My mettle is melting.

"So, you're back. Do you know who you are?" growls the bartender.

"Yes." I say with loud, fake confidence, and continue to walk towards him. "I am Love and Truth. I'm Free and Thankful. I also know what I want. I look for purpose."

His grin grows. His crooked overbite is meant to be disarming, but his eyes twirl exposing a treacherous evil, inviting everyone to… indulge, let go, and ultimately, to destroy themselves in addiction which in turn will destroy everyone around them.

"It seems you haven't heard the news from the community at Thomastown."

"What news?" I ask as my peace hides in the darkest corner on top of a chair with a noose around its neck and is poised to jump.

"Hear for yourself." He points me to the back of the bar. "Some of the sweet residents of that community are in the back room. You'll find the fireplace particularly… inviting."

I hesitate only my first step. "Elizabeth?" I'm at a full run when I crash through the door to the back room and almost fall in. There, sits Patrice, sobbing in the arms of Ron, the stable keeper. My girls, Karen, Brooke, Olivia, and Olysah, are all in a pile, hugging and crying. Dozens of others I don't know are crying in the corners.

"Elizabeth?!" I demand this answer from Patrice.

"Last night." She chokes out.

I freeze. "This can't be true, Patrice. I didn't SEE it."

No one will speak. The only sounds are my girls sobbing, and the crackling of the fire. I turn to the blaze. "I see nothing." I try to focus on the fire dancing, trying to feel Elizabeth, and the cadence with which she lives, breathes, thinks… "I feel her. She's still alive!" I say as I try harder to communicate with her… Where are you, Elizabeth?

"No, Madame. I was there. Last night. Before sunset." A male voice from the corner breaks my concentration. "I knew her well. It was her. The Mathews' kept her guarded. We all tried to stop it."

"No. I feel her." I lie. All I feel is hate. Seething, heaving, undulating hate and the burning need for revenge.

"Madame." The young man steps out from the corner towards me. *"I'm sorry, I couldn't stop it. The Mathews are in charge of a great army. They control the lawyers and judges. They brought in a judge from Cork. He is a long-time friend of the Family."*

"How?" It was a question I knew the answer to, but no one would speak the devastating truth. There is complete silence now. Even the fireplace seems to have ceased crackling.

I whirl around to face Patrice. My look says 'this is all your fault'... her fault for allowing HER brutal husband and HER brutal son to whack away at my girls and me... physically and mentally, for ALL THOSE YEARS in London. I believe the effects on us all... have gotten us here.

"GET. UP. PATRICE." I'm enraged and instantly, I AM rage. Each breath is hot and deep, from the intensity of hate fueling my anger.

I spin to the girls demanding. "Get UP. Stand UP." My glance to the others in the room screams, 'This is your fault too.' They stand with feelings of guilt and bleeding sorrow...

But I am demanding their Revulsion.

I am demanding their Rage.

I. Am. Demanding REVENGE.

"I know but one spell to do harm. I'll improvise for these evil Mathews clan." I begin. *"From England bring a fenny snake. Bring into our great room to bake..."*

"NO!" Patrice drops to her knees, pulling on my skirt, shrieking again. "NO! Please."

"Get. Up. Patrice." I say, in a low growl. "We must be forever rid of these immoral, glutinous snakes! No one should ever feel the fear and frustration of leaders, who have no control over themselves, but abuse those over whom they DO have control. This is a moral outrage. RAGE with me, Patrice. We must take away their power. They wield not a sword but pay for sword wielders. They are not the law but pay for judges' verdicts. Their wealth is the power they abuse."

Patrice is slowly rising. "We will be punished... all of Wicca will be punished for this!"

"I. Don't. Care. We must stop them. We're their only obstacle."

Patrice, stands, with her head down, sobbing. "They're not the only evil in this world." She says warning softly, but signaling, she will give way to my demands.

"Yes, but THEY are the evil in front of us." I continue chanting, almost screaming,

"Eye of newt and tongue of thieves'

To throw to burn, we have none of these,

Just a frenzy of rage and ire

With these alone we conspire

FIRST: The family Mathews beguiled

Not one of them to raise a child.

SECOND curse on their golden health

To NEVER realize their family's wealth..."

Then with a voice that is quiet and low,

Seething in hate, a voice I do not know...

I hiss...

"Dearessst accuser of my Kind-Hearted Elizabeth.

Your guilt will grow 'til you KILL YOUR-SELF."

I hear the gasps in the room along with whimpering.

A black tempest appears immediately. The fireplace roars as the horrified but obedient occupants of that room, LED BY ME... repeat the curse.

Even when the swirling tempest is gone, the fire roars on. Its crackling is the only thing heard in the room until the sobbing begins again.

"You have gone too far." Patrice is wide-eyed and begins to shake.

As I look around, I realize...

This is the same scene as when I entered.

Nothing has changed FOR ME.

My Elizabeth the Kind-Hearted is still gone. Nothing we can do will change that. Nothing will put her in my arms. "Elizabeth." I call her. She'll have no effect on this Earth, ever again.

I have only memories. Memories of how she has filled the souls of those in deep despair.

My rage has melted to Love, with just the thought of her.

The door to this back room blows open with a bang, and there stands the Bartender. I look at his grin and realize He set this in motion. He set up the Mathews abuses. He serves the alcohol, tantalizing humanity with each of the seven sins...

...and now he's getting more powerful.

I'm horrified... I have led this community of white witches to step over to dark practices. HE has plotted this all along. My act of revenge has broken the first law of Wicca. He knew this would provoke an act of evil. These good people have professed to all and pledged themselves to do only good. To only act in Love and service.

Instantly, I understand, the enormity of our punishment is just the natural consequence of MY actions.

Losing our white, loving, Wicca Powers is exactly what He needs to grow more powerful.

...And now I realize, too late, I have fallen into his trap. The curse has been cast. Wicca will be served Karma ten-fold.

NOOOOO!

I yell myself awake.

I feel like someone smacked me in the head. Where is my aspirin?

I remember someone telling me, 'Revenge' is like taking poison, and expecting the other person to die'.

My phone dings. Brooke has sent me a text. "Wanna have dinner in Montpellier?"

I text back, "France?"

Brooke texts back. "The winter home of the Mathews family and the community started by Nostradamus. Yes, Mom. THAT Montpellier. Coach already booked us ALL on the 9:40 Chunnel! Whoop! Whoop! Hurry. We'll pick you up at eight. You only have an hour."

I text back, "I'll be ready."

Chapter 17

When the entire universe conspires with you...

As I arrive at the bottom of the stairs with my overnight bag, the doorbell rings and into the BNB floods all the Alphabet Girls, along with Andrew.

"Mom, is anyone up? Is anyone in the kitchen?" Brooke says in a hushed tone.

But no one waits for my reply. They have invaded the BNB like seasoned CIA agents.

"What's going on?" I ask Kim, who is now standing at the door with me.

"They've figured out they can 'print' that 130-page document onto a memory stick and open it onto one of their laptops, and can read it on the train." Kim says in a tone which suggests she's not sure if it's going to work.

"I forgot all about the document saved in the printer." I admit.

"Funny, that's all they can talk about." Kim says, "Check out the cool ride your boyfriend sent for us." Kim backs up to give me a clear view of the monster limo.

"Not my boyfriend, but speaking of him... Where is he?"

"Apparently, he has 'something to do today' and is taking the plane to meet us tomorrow morning." Kim answers, as the stampede carries us out the door and into the waiting cab.

"I have your bag, Mom." Brooke says, "Let's go!"

I'm thankful Chas in not coming. I know I look ragged from trying to keep up with these twenty-somethings. "I'm exhausted. I just want to sleep on the Chunnel." I say as I snuggle next to Brooke.

"Me too." Kim admits.

"Apparently, there is an old settlement of 'hippies' just north of Montpellier. There is an all-day wine tour through that region, which includes lunch. The Coach has booked us all on the tour tomorrow morning." Deidra is excited.

"Wine tour? Great. More alcohol." I mumble, then say louder as an announcement, "I'm taking an alcohol free day today ladies... gentleman."

"Go to sleep, Mom." Apparently, I'm humiliating Brooke, which puts a smile on my face. I snuggle closer to her, to be sure she feels me chuckle.

I wake only to scurry around at the London train station, where we are met by the rest of the boys.

I sleep again through the dark tunnel, under the English Channel, arriving in Paris two-and-a-half hours later.

Again, we have to hurry to catch the next train to Montpellier. I wonder if we can stop in Paris, for a couple days, on the way back. Unfortunately, all these kids have to get back to class on Monday. Brooke lets me know they opened the 130-page document. It's the 'Catholic Official Research and Commemorative Papers of Father Theobald Mathew', but resting is my priority right now. So, I manage to sit with Kim where, thankfully, we both sleep the entire way, from Paris to Montpellier.

The rooms at the beachfront hotel are lovely. Brooke and I have a couple hours to get ready to meet the rest, downstairs for dinner.

"Let's go out on the balcony. We have some time before we need to start getting ready." I say, as I sit in one of the over-stuffed balcony chairs. "Limo, two trains, tram, Uber... It's all a blur. I can't believe we're on the Mediterranean. It's beautiful..." Then I add with more thankfulness. "...and warm, thank God. The Oxford bitter cold was getting old."

"Mom, it's a 'blur', because you slept through it." Brooke says, with a chuckle and sits, staring straight ahead at the very calm, very blue, French Mediterranean. "Gotta love this weather, and the view."

"I hate the cold." I say.

"Me too." Brooke admits.

"Why did you pick Oxford?" I ask.

"I thought it would be an adventure." She pauses, looks at me and smirks, "In English."

"Brooke," I put my hand on hers and repeat a line from Winnie the Pooh, I have said to her often. "'As soon as I saw you, I knew an adventure was about to happen'."

Brooke slides her hand out from under mine, to put hers on top. "We both have a little Pooh in us, Mom." Brooke says, as she rises. "I get the shower first." Heartfelt words were never her comfort zone... Nor mine. She yells from inside, "Too bad we don't have time to stop in Paris on the way back. That would be a cool adventure."

Read my mind again.

Brooke and I arrive at dinner a bit early to find Chelsea and her Mom at the bar.

"Club soda for me." I order from the bartender.

"Joyce, what does this remind you of?" Kim asks.

"What? This bar?" I say, looking around.

"No, this whole escapade. The 'mystery'…" Kim says.

Chelsea cuts in, "My Mom has been saying this reminds her of… 'every episode of Scooby Doo'."

I almost spit out my club soda. I love this woman.

"I think the rest of the 'gang' is already seated at the table, Brooke. Let's leave Velma and Daphne here." Chelsea says, referencing Scooby Doo characters.

"I don't know why I'm so tired, I slept most of the way here." I say, as I get comfortable on a bar stool and lean both elbows onto the bar.

"Me too. I need a whole day, starting with a gym, sauna, massage… Too bad we were only in Paris to change trains." Kim seems to be day dreaming.

"Well, tonight I'm going to have a salad and water for dinner then go to bed early." I say, as I finish my club soda, and raise my right hand. "I'm taking the Father Theobald Mathews, total-abstinence-of-alcohol pledge."

"Ruh Roh, Joyce." Kim says, mimicking Scooby. "There's a wine tour tomorrow."

"One day at a time, Kim. One day at a time." I joke, knowing I'll be tasting wine tomorrow. "Let's eat."

At dinner, it's obvious the group has read the 'Father Theobald Mathews Commemorative Papers'.

"He was, like a rock star when he traveled to the US. The mayor of NYC shut down the whole of Manhattan. Hundreds-of-thousands of fans met him at the dock and took 'The Pledge'. Over those next two years, in the US, he gave 'The Pledge' to over seven-million people." Deidra sounds like she read and memorized the entire 130 pages of the 'Commemorative Papers'.

"Deidre, was there even seven million people IN the US in the 1850s?" I ask, because this whole thing sounds literally unbelievable, but THIS really can't be true.

Phones come out, and again Brooke is first to respond. "Over 23 million in the US census that year, Mom."

"So a third of the population of US, and that 23 million includes children, took this pledge and we are only hearing of this now? That's crazy." I say.

"There's a statue in Philadelphia and another in Boston to commemorate Father Mathews." Brooke says to counter.

Deidre adds, "There are dozens of statues of Father Mathews in Ireland, along with maybe one-hundred streets named after him. Thomastown has one, of course, but big cities like Cork, Limerick, and Dublin... are littered with Father Mathew's references."

"OK." I say. "He was a big deal. The US education powers-that-be have decided to exclude him from the history books. So, let's say these statistics are all true, how is it possible that a priest from some remote little fiefdom in the middle of Ireland, 'spread the word' so thoroughly; not just throughout all of Ireland and even throughout Europe but, throughout the entire world? No internet or TV. International news print was rare and traveled at a snail's pace. How did he become so popular, like a 'Rock Star', on the Entire East Coast of the US?" I ask.

"I don't know the answer to that." Deidre says. "Even though Father Mathews was a Catholic priest, the Catholic Church didn't take on this crusade. Eighteen-hundred's Irish history will tell you, it was not popular to be Catholic in Ireland around then.

At some point, the priest spent some time in debtor's prison, because he spent all his assets on those little coins, traveling and spreading the word. Queen Victoria paid his debts, pardoned him, and then gave him a small pension.

The potato famine was in full bloom then. For two years, all the potatoes in Ireland got a rot fungus. Ireland had only one export back then… potatoes. So, the people had no money or trade to buy food from other countries. The entire population of Ireland starved.

Out of Ireland's eight-million people, over one-million died and another one-million left Ireland, most of them went to America. I'm sure that helped spread the word." Deidre says. "His followers organized the Total Abstinence Society. Maybe that organization helped to spread the word."

"I still don't see how his quest could…" I'm at a loss for words.

"… have gone viral?" Angel cuts in.

"Yes, Angel. Perfect analogy. 'Gone Viral' World Wide?"

Angel is smirking, "If the universe takes on a campaign… well, the entire universe is a very powerful thing."

"Yes, Angel. I have agreed with you before on this. The entire universe is a very powerful thing." I realize, as soon as I said it, my tone was belittling. Instantly, I'm sorry.

Angel sits up. I have insulted her beliefs. She says in a tone that is stern but respectful, "Maybe the spell that nanny put on the Mathews, was not to 'never realize their wealth', but instead, she used her natural magic on Father Mathews, to stop the crisis of alcoholism. It's obvious the Mathews were deep into addictions many addictions, alcohol may not be the worst of them."

The table is silent. This conversation has turned from uncomfortable to enlightening.

"Angel, I'm sorry if I sounded offensive. I honestly… seriously, do believe in the power of the Universe… that is, the 'infinite' power of the universe. I believe, also, absolutely, in the power of Love.

Andrew cuts in. "It's hard to believe that anyone, who was wrongly accused of witchcraft and is about to be burned to death, would be interested in 'saving those who lead lives of multiple addictions.'"

"No." Brooke says staring at the middle of the table. "My sister, Liz… she would be grieving for the little girl that drown, and yes, also feel deeply sorry for the Mom and everyone else in that Castle.

I am impressed with Brooke. "I agree. I've been thinking of Liz too. Andrew, there are some people, it's rare, but there are some, who would feel empathetic for people around them… even those who are filled with evil." I pause and look at Angel. "What you just theorized, that the nanny was responsible for the unbelievable success of Father Mathews, is… Well it seems obvious now. What is it that Andrew said? There are three stages to a new belief? Andrew?"

"All truth passes through three stages. First, it is ridiculed. Second, it is violently opposed. Third, it is accepted as self-evident. That was Schopenhauer."

"Joyce, I think, more to Angel's revelation, is a quote by Gandhi," Kim leans in, speaking directly to Angel, "… 'First, they ignore you. Then, they ridicule you. Then, they fight you. Then, you win'."

"So why is Dan, the little leprechaun guy from my BNB, and his brother so sure they are 'cursed'?" I ask.

"Because," Angel says, obviously passionate about this. "…they lost all their wealth. Of course they're going to blame that on someone else. But, if you look at all the facts, it's clear they lost their wealth through guilt and Karma."

"Karma is a bitch." Kim says loudly, raising her glass of wine, (maybe her fourth), and we all 'toast' to Karma.

Remembering my dream from the other night, and the way I felt such horror, I add, "I'm positive the family of the nanny was crazy with grief and frustration. I'm sure the whole community knew the nanny didn't 'cast a sleeping spell'. I'm sure there was quite a large covert mutiny brewing against the Mathews BEFORE they burned the poor nanny. Maybe it was the nanny's family and community that put a 'curse' on them.

The First Earl had five sons and a daughter. Not one of them had children, the title died out and the mother of the drowned toddler, Lady what's-her-name jumped from the ballroom window and died."

"Lady Cherry Pennefather." Brooke helps me.

"'If you do no harm, do what you will,' is the first rule of magic." Kim reminds us.

"So, what would happen, if a whole bunch of really powerful, practiced witches, or maybe a better label is 'natural magicians', all decided to practice one big, badass curse?" I ask Kim directly, then to the whole table, "What is the worst that could happen?"

Angel is the first to theorize, "Then, all of their community of practicing witches would lose their powers. It's the natural law of Karma. The 'Bad' comes back to you ten-fold..." Angel hesitates. "Maybe the nanny's family did curse the Mathews but there was obviously a second curse by the nanny. Maybe we should call it a spell not a curse. She may not have chanted a spell exactly, but certainly the way in which the Mathews treated a sweet young girl, who did not put a sleeping spell on the drowned toddlers Mom. The burning of this sweet innocent girl to death, affected Father Mathews, inspiring him to lead the campaign of the total abstinence of alcohol."

Kim leans forward... "Someone look up; how old was this nanny compared to 'Father' Mathews... Were they lovers?"

Phones come out again, and again, Brooke is first to respond as Andrew writes down a timeline.

"1790 Father Mathews was Born.

1810, Interesting! Father Mathews was thrown out of seminary for smuggling in alcohol."

"1831 was the burning of the witch." I add.

Brooke continues, "1833 That Black Sheep Mathews guy died.

1837 the Thomastown Castle was sold by the Black sheep's sister, Elisha Mathew.

1840 Father Mathews starts the Total Abstinence Society.

1956 Father Mathews died."

"So, how old was the Nanny in relation to Father Mathews?" Kim asks again.

I answer, "From all my research I can't find anything about the nanny. The only mention of her is from Dan, the Leprechaun looking guy from my BNB. He described her as a young English girl."

Kim raises her eyebrows… "So, all of this is speculation with zero corroboration? This nanny story could just be a made-up excuse for why the Mathews lost their wealth."

I am a bit agitated. "We have the syllabus which confirms positively the school of natural magic is here in Montpellier."

Deidre is careful… "Well… Your BNB owner ran an 'artesian center' here and one of the Mathews was born, here in Montpellier. That is what we need to find here. Evidence of an actual school… NOT an invisible school, like in Oxford where a bunch of researchers meet in the back room of a bar once month… but instead, classes that are regularly scheduled all week, where students can get to morning, late morning, lunch in a 'kitchen' and evening, relatively close to each other."

Andrew says, also very careful not to insult or dampen our quest, "I have been searching Montpellier for 'natural magic', 'meditation' or 'schools' of any kind that fit the LiFT message. There's nothing. Maybe Coach found something."

"I hate to dampen this hunt even further, but the initials LiFT only work in English." Deidre says.

"Yes, and the Nanny came from an English community." I say.

"So, do we think, 'Father Mathews' and the nanny were having an affair?" Kim is drunk and will not let go.

"Mom!" Chelsea is a bit horrified.

"Sweetie, the nanny and 'Father' Mathews had to have some kind of relationship. They both lived at the castle." Kim says. She's drunk and now a bit arrogant. "The burning of the nanny happened in 1831. 'Father' Mathews was only 40, so even if the nanny was 16, that was totally acceptable back then. Kind-a gross, but back then, acceptable. Chelsea, when you were 16, I was only 40. So, that would be like your father and I marrying you off to one of our college friends. Totally gross. But, that was the way back then."

The thought of any of my girls, at 16, with a 41 year old is disturbing. "OK. I'm done eating. No dessert for me. I've lost my appetite completely. Let's get the check and get out of here." I say, ending the night.

"My Dad paid already." Chucky adds, speaking for the first time.

"Where is he?" I'm a bit stunned and immediately assessing my outfit, hair and lack of makeup.

"He's still in Oxford, but I have access to his credit card."

"Thank you, Chucky. Please, tell your Dad, thank you as well." I say.

"Mom, we're all going into town. It's a College town. We're going in to look for somewhere to have fun."

"OK. Be careful. Stay on the lookout for any rainbow girls." I say joking. "Hey, Kim, are there any secret handshakes they should know about?"

"Of course. But if I tell you, I'll have to kill you."

Kim is getting drunk and off her game. I give Brooke a hug and whisper, "I love you."

Brooke whispers back. "Get some sleep. You're lookin' tired. I'm starting to get worried about you." Then loudly, "Don't wait up."

I won't. I know I need my beauty sleep. The coach will be here in the morning.

Spectacular, massive, centuries-old buildings stand in the main square of Montpellier, attesting to the Freemason's craftsmanship of the sixteen, seventeen, and eighteen-hundreds. In contrast, the new efficient trollies are buzzing with tourists, students, and commuters.

I'm thankful for the warm beautiful morning and time to explore this square. We have arrived over an hour too early for the wine tour. Restaurants are open, their wait-staff is busy with patrons who are taking time to sit and drink this strong French coffee, and watch the street musicians.

"Hey, Mom. Check it out. McDonalds." Brooke points.

"McDonalds." Kim says with distaste as she comes up behind us with Chelsea. "That's a buzz-kill."

"Most of the big cities we visited have lots of the same stores. Victoria Secret, Tommy Hilfiger, Sub-way and yes, they all have McDonald's. It's sometimes indistinguishable where we are, London or New York. Only these smaller European cities still have entire regions of hundred-year-old buildings. Have you noticed, no one is carrying coffee?" Brooke says. "Europeans seem to make time for relaxing throughout their day."

"Well, when in Montpellier… Let's go get a table and coffee where we can watch the street band." I'm already moving toward one of the white tents covering the outside tables.

After we're settled, "Gee, you look nice today, Joyce." Kim pokes.

"Yea, my Mom was up at five." Brooke answers for me.

"I wanted to get in a quiet meditation." I defend.

"Speaking of Coach, where is he, Joyce?" Kim pokes again. "I thought he was supposed to arrive at the hotel this morning. Did you 'see' him while you were 'meditating'?"

"No. I did not 'see' him. I have no idea where he is. I know only that we are supposed to meet at the tourist building at the end of this plaza at 10 AM." I say, as I point to our left.

"May I join you?" Comes the deep voice of Chas, the coach.

Chapter 18

Your smile will light the way brightly.

Our guide for this wine tour is a tall, bearded, rustically-handsome, rogue-type. Lots of thick, floppy hair shows under his 'cap'. He looks like a Hollywood producer cast him, dressing him in an over-sized white shirt with blue ties halfway down his chest, keeping his shirt almost closed. All that's missing are the ruffles.

Kim comes up behind me. "Is that Russel Crowe? Wow."

"Double Wow. I'm going to go grab that front passenger seat before anyone else does." I whisper to Kim, while moving toward the guide, where he stands at the front of the bus. "I get a bit queasy in buses, may I sit in front with you?" I point to the front passenger door but don't take my eyes off his, which match the blue tie.

The guide says something, his voice is deep... the kind of voice movies and really great dreams are made of. Sadly, his thick, French accent is in need of subtitles. I have no idea what he's saying. He opens the front passenger door for me.

I guess that's a yes. "Merci!" I say with a big smile.

I purposefully don't look back. I don't want the Coach to think I snubbed him on purpose. The truth is, I do get motion sick, yes, but more to the truth, I could only imagine how uncomfortable it would be to take this ride, sitting next to that man who; either, would say something insulting and I would have nowhere to go, or worse yet, would say something nice and I would have nowhere to go.

Our guide explains, with the help of Deidre, he is from a very old Protestant community up in the hills. Apparently, the entire community, held onto their own regional 'language', switching to contemporary French only recently with his parents' generation. His name, Gerard, or something that sounds similar to that, (the pronunciation escaping me even with repeated tutoring from Deidre), means 'wood' in old regional Protestant.

Kim fakes a cough and choke to let me know... well... we are on the same page with that visual.

"You OK back there, Kim?"

"Oh yes. Quite OK..."

"Mom!" Chelsea has put a stop to whatever conversational path Kim (and I) may have been going down.

After a pause, Wood continues. We are in the Longa Duck region of French wine-making. (Which, later I find is actually spelled Languedoc). Apparently, the portion of the Mediterranean coast, beginning inside Spain, through all of Southern France and continuing east to the mountains of Italy, have the same climate, and therefore produce, the same or very similar tasting, grapes. The area we will be touring is the small Pic Saint-Loup district inside this very large Languedoc Region.

We round a corner and Wood points out the mountain, to our left, and how it looks like a 'Wolf'. I don't see it, but apparently the others do... or say they do. Pic Saint-Loup translates to 'Wolf Mountain'.

Wood takes us inside a winery where there are many different fermenting tanks. The newest is stainless but this winery is also using wood tanks that taper at the top and one very large cement 'tank' which is lined with something to keep the porous, acidic, cement from spoiling the wine.

Wood walks us into a room filled with wooden wine kegs. This region is known for the best Chardonnay. Something about the Monks organizing...

"I don't understand anything he's saying," Kim is whispering behind me. "But he is extraordinarily interesting."

"I'm riveted." I whisper back.

"Mom!" Chelsea and Brooke say together, in hushed whispers.

After tasting (and buying) this winery's production we move to the next winery.

As the group exits the bus at this new location we learn these grape vines are protected from fire by a massive 'bladder' filled with water, at least a half-a-football-field large. There are only three or four days of rain per month here in the Mediterranean but when it rains it's a down-pour of six to eight inches, flooding the vineyards, and everything else including the roads and towns. We learn there is a debate as to when and how to use these bladders in times of drought. Some say to trickle the water into the field of vines but others argue, since these vines are used-to rare watering but 'a real soaking' when the rains come, that is how to quench the thirst of these vines if need be. Release all the water at once.

As we all climb back into the bus, Wood gets on his phone to be sure lunch is ready.

Deidre, obviously understanding his conversation, asks Wood, "Are we having lunch at your house?"

"Yes." Wood answers "My Mom owns a compound... a retreat, just down the road."

"A retreat?" I say, too loudly.

"Yes. A quiet place people go to have solitude. I grew up there with my Mum and her Mum. They're both great cooks. They serve

Vegan for the most part," Then louder, looking in the rearview mirror, "but there will be a meat course."

The bus rocks through the deep pot holes in the entrance of the 'compound', then up a steep hill. We pass the house and take a hard-left turn into the back yard revealing this steep hill continues up another fifty-feet. The landscape is filled with... flowers, herbs, and produce, flourishing in developed terraces, raised-beds, stone steps, and even benches to rest, read.... Meditate. Strikingly picturesque.

Phones come out to take multiple pictures of this spectacular garden.

"Where do I book my stay?" I say, out loud.

Wood smiles, "They're booked-up months in advance."

"How many rooms do they have here?" I'm seriously contemplating a return for this, but our guide has moved away and over his shoulder, he says loudly, "Come on in. It's time for lunch."

I turn to find, what seems to me, to be, the natural 'front door'.

"Mom!" Brooke is at my side, pointing to the left. "A 'retreat' with a Rainbow flag."

"Well, there's a coincidence. Where's the Coach? He booked this."

"I asked the research department to find something that may lead us to the remnants of Nostradamus's meditation research society." Coach is directly behind me. "Having fun?"

And like that, I am back in his spell. "Yes. I am. Thank you." With Brooke still next to me, I put my hand on his arm, "Thank you for everything... the dinner last night, and the night before. The cab, train, hotel, this tour. I very much appreciate that you have signed on to this adventure." I want to kiss him on the cheek, but I don't.

"My pleasure." Coach says as he takes a tiny bow and laughs. "You're a unique woman, to take your curiosity this far. I do have an ulterior motive, though. Now you owe me a favor."

"Excuse me?" I say as I think, 'this man knows how to kill a buzz'.

"Yes, you owe me the pleasure of sitting next to you..." He adds, "...and Brooke."

Brooke answers, "Let's eat. It's after two o'clock!"

The entry door is a wooden work of art, almost square, eight-feet tall by seven-feet wide, and intricately carved with images of grapes on the vine. Coach pulls hard on the brass knob located in the middle of the door. We walk into a foyer which is only eight-feet deep with a back wall of solid glass exposing a large stone and cement patio, sunken pool, falling off into a deep green valley. Breathtaking.

The house is in an 'L' shape. To our right is a blood-red, arched-top door, with a round white plaque with red letters that say, 'Residence, Residenza, Residencia.' To our left are swinging doors, obviously an entrance to a bustling kitchen.

"I hear them." Brooke is referring to our troupe of loud, happy winos and moves toward the hallway which bypasses the kitchen.

"That's what happens with no food and five hours of drinking wine." I say as we follow her to find them in a very large, enclosed dining room. The décor looks more Spanish to me than French. Both the walls and fireplace are made of stucco and painted stark white. The art work is all Salvador Dali, Spanish style.

Our dining table is an odd size, with room for two at each end. Each setting has mismatched, colorful, stacked plates, and bowl. Of course, there are plenty of pairs of red and white wine bottles, open. Giant, glass water jugs rest on mats, all in the full-of-color, Spanish style. The white stucco is the perfect backdrop to the brightly colored art, wall hangings, table runners, rugs and even dark furniture. Perfect. I love contrast.

Our guide arrives at the dining room door carrying a giant tureen of soup and introduces his mother and grandmother, who are carrying boards of bread and butter along with wooden bowls of salad.

Deidre thanks the women, who are obviously relieved someone speaks French.

We're all a bit tipsy and very hungry. The bread, soup and salad disappear in minutes and the second course of beef stew with small potatoes take their place.

The Coach is at the head of the table with Brooke. I took the seat at the corner next to his.

I lean toward him, "Wine all day and now full bellies, our troupe is fading."

"Me too. I could take a nap. Where are those guest rooms?" He says as he leans in to put his arm around the back of my chair, stares in my eyes and raises his eyebrows.

"You're revolting." I say, backing up with distaste.

"Wow, I was just kidding."

"'I was just kidding' is a typical narcissistic excuse for bad behavior." I whisper critically.

Brooke says very slowly and in a whisper, looking down, "Mom?" Meaning, please don't make this uncomfortable.

My thoughts are not quiet. I am screaming inside my head, 'Why can't you be the man of my dreams?... A gentleman...

I need to change focus.

I push my chair out, freeing it from the Coach's arm. I head to the sideboard, in front of the wall of windows, to pour myself cucumber water. Outside is a seven-foot, white-washed, stucco wall. I'm guessing the driveway is on the other side. Between this building and the wall is a narrow, raised, stepping-stone path, slightly overgrown with ivy. I imagine what it would be like to live here and run the 'retreat'. I'd build a fire in the fireplace every night for my 'guests', serve hot tea, fresh fruit and cheeses. Place various French breads and butter on the side board. We would have deep conversations about love, truth, trust, freedom, and thankfulness.

The weekly parade of visitors will tell stories of their world-wide travels…

"Digestifs." Wood says, interrupting my thoughts, holding up two bottles of liquor. His Mom and Grand mom go to a cabinet to set out small aperitif glasses. He continues saying… something… no one understands. We all turn to Deidre to translate.

"Digestifs are liqueurs very high in alcohol content, each one at least 35%. The word 'Liqueur' comes from the Latin word liquifacere, which means "to dissolve". He's inviting us to have our after-dinner drinks in the living room, further down the hall to our left. The bathrooms are to our right, just before the kitchen."

The coach joins me in the hall as I wait for the bathroom to be free. "So I'm a narcissist now?"

"Typical narcissist. So now I expect you'll attack me. I'm sure you'll say now, I'm the one who has no sense of humor." I say. "Sorry. I divorced that guy. I don't need another."

"Mom?" comes the voice of Brooke from behind the bathroom door.

"Brooke?" I say as I roll my eyes. I have always tried, very hard not to insult her father in front of her.

"Yes, Mom. And Angel, Chelsea and Deidra." Apparently, this bathroom is large with multiple stalls. I realize I'm waiting in this hallway for no reason. Ugh.

"I apologize. I didn't know anyone could hear me." I say to Brooke and the coach. Ugh.

Coach leans into my ear. "How'd that taste?" …and walks away, leaving me blushing.

I can be an asshole sometimes.

I arrive in the enormous, cathedral-ceilinged, living room. These walls too are very-white stucco. The tile flooring is also starkly-white, making a perfect canvas to show off the deep rich colors of traditional Spanish-style art. Giant sliding windows give a slightly different view of the cement patio, sunken pool, and the breathtaking, plush-green valley below. Trying to hide, in the green valley, are a hand-full of little cabins, which must be where the 'guests' stay.

More fascinating, is the back wall, where another white, stucco fireplace is flanked by rows of bookcases. I walk closer to find the books are mostly on Yoga and Meditation.

"Deidre, ask Wood's Mom if there's one book that will best guide a beginner to…" I am at a loss for an adjective, "the correct meditation path." I say, unsatisfied that is what I mean.

Deidre translates the answer, while Wood's Mom pats her own chest, open handed, over her heart. "She says you must compile your own book. You are very singular from anyone else and therefore, you have your own path to find."

I'm reminded of the syllabus. Each class has instruction to add to a personal LiFT binder.

After Wood's Mom speaks again, Deidre translates, "She says your path may be difficult to find but when you get close, your smile will light the way brightly."

"Please tell her, 'that is great advice. I'll try to remember that'." I notice one shelf has a stack of brochures and remove one from the display, "Deidre, what is this? 'Fragonard'." I say loudly.

Deidre takes the brochure from my hand and walks to Wood's Mom. They have a short conversation and Deidre says to the group. "It is a brochure listing the major production sites of the French perfume industry. Her friend gives a four-day guided-tour of those sites. The highlight is an all-day stop of a working factory, dating from the eighteen-hundreds, where you can follow all the stages of perfume creation, in authentic, traditional surroundings.

There's another in the city of Grasse. A modern factory, surrounded by a garden of fragrant plants, which is dedicated to perfume and soap making.

The biggest is in Eze. It's an immense perfumery, soap and cosmetic factory equipped with the most modern laboratories and workshops."

"Deidre, ask her what her friend's name is and does she teach anywhere else?" I'm riveted. But we can see Wood's Mother is extremely uncomfortable and even my limited high school French can translate, 'I'm out'ta here,' and she disappears toward the kitchen.

"Where are these places?" I ask Wood.

"All of these cities are stops on a beautiful train ride along the French Mediterranean." Wood adds, "When we get back to the information center, they can give you the train schedule. You can also stop in Cannes, Nice, and Monaco if you'd like."

"Our plane leaves tonight." Brooke says.

"What?" I am surprised.

"We have class and the boys have practice early tomorrow morning. I thought the girls told you. We're leaving tonight." Brooke says.

The Coach is just as surprised that I am in the dark.

"I didn't know either." Kim adds looking directly at Chelsea.

"I know you hate planes. Go on the train to Paris. Stay for a couple days. We have classes, reports due. You know that, Mom. Come back to Oxford on Thursday night when our class week is over." Brooke says.

Chelsea agrees, speaking to Kim, "Go to Paris with Joyce. Stay at a spa."

I'm embarrassed. This was premeditated. Our children obviously want a break from us. The room goes awkwardly silent.

Coach moves toward me. "Your curiosity has uncovered a journey which seems to be presenting itself. You can go Paris in this particularly cold November or take a journey of self-discovery on a train ride through the French 'Riviera' along the beautiful Mediterranean... find smells that make you happy.

You have a syllabus which lists websites and the book list. You can 'study' or 'self-discover' as an online student." The Coach says overtly asking me... how dedicated are you to this cause? He has shown his dedication to this exploration by expending so much of his own time and money. I can hardly say no.

Kim reads my mind, "We'll get the train schedule online."

Wood opens one of the huge, double, sliding-glass doors while his Grandmother opens the other, and we're drawn outside onto the patio.

"Mom." Brooke interrupts my over-thinking.

There, next to a stone path... obviously the path to the cabins... Brooke points to three signs. Why. Do. We.

Brooke steps onto the path, I'm right behind her, trotting down the steps to reveal more signs. Think. Love. Is.

"No!" Wood shouts first then adds something in French, I have no idea what.

We stop and turn.

Deidre translates. "That's the path to the guest rooms. There are guests resting."

Brooke speaks to Deidre, "There are garden signs down here along the path that say, 'Why do we think love is a magician!'"

Deidre spins, and repeats to Wood, in French so his Grandmother will understand. "Why do we think love is a magician? Because the whole power of magic consists in love. The work of magic is the attraction of one thing to another by the affinity of nature."

Wood's Grandmother, gasps. She is visibly shaken as she dashes out of the room.

Wood speaks loudly, "We better get going so you all don't miss your plane."

"Well, I guess we struck a nerve. Jolly Good!" Coach seems pleased, then adds louder, "Let's get back on the bus, troupe."

Chapter 19

La Faculte de Medicine de Montpellier

The bus back to Montpellier is quiet. Lots of wine, then full bellies, will do that.

I break the silence. "The décor... the decorations in your Mom's house look more Spanish than French. Is she from Spain?"

"No. The house was remodeled and decorated almost 50 years ago by my grandfather. He passed when I was just a toddler. He was from Portugal. We still have property there. I've never been, but I'm told the land has a spectacular view of the sea."

A spectacular view of the sea is exactly how Bea and Beren described the land, in Portugal where Dan is staying. "In what town is this land located?" I say, as I pull out my phone to record the name.

Wood says something and we both laugh because he knows I have no idea what he just said. Unfortunately, our translator, Deidre is asleep, as are most of the occupants of this bus.

He spells it out for me, "A L J E Z U R. Have you heard of that?"

"No. I don't know much about Portugal."

"Aljezur, is the 'Land of the Knights Templar'."

This is literally, too much. My head is spinning. Do these people know my Oxford Landlords? Is Dan, (my leprechaun, BNB buddy) living on Wood's Grandmom's land? Or do I just have waaay too much time on my hands and want this crazy adventure to continue?

"Do you know Bea and Beren? They ran a Residential Artesian Center around here somewhere." I try.

"No. What's their last name?"

"I don't... I don't know." I'm just stabbing in the dark, then I remember the Wi-Fi name, 'Ferguson BNB'. "Ferguson." I say way too loud.

"No. I don't know any 'Fergusons'." Wood says, shaking his head no.

"Do you know a guy named Dan? He lives in Portugal."

"Do you have a last name for Dan?" Wood says, smirking. I assume Wood is used to incoherent passengers' questions on the way home from his wine tours.

"No." I'm tired of dead ends.

I wonder how long it'll be until I can get back to the BNB to ask more questions of my leprechaun-like friend, Dan and my landlords. What is Dan's last name? Where is Dan staying in Portugal? What, exactly, is the lineage from the 1st Earl of Llandaff to Dan? I'm too tired for more questions with no answers. All these dead ends are beyond tedious. 'This sucks,' I think to myself.

"Don't get too discouraged." The Coach is the only one awake and must have seen my frustration. He and his son are sharing the double seat directly behind the driver. "We found a syllabus, which is enough to start you, or anyone else for that matter, on a journey of practicing 'natural magic'. I think it's obvious we all have to take that journey alone, to discover who we are, discover the things that help us feel love, and ultimately help us to find the purpose that will bring us satisfaction.

I know coaching.... Coaching my son and his friends especially, makes me feel... like I'm doing something worthwhile.

The question that still remains for you is, 'are you willing to take the time necessary to find out who you are, and practice... feeling love, understanding true freedom, and get in a habit of finding thankfulness... with an end game of finding your purpose and ultimately, deep satisfaction?'"

I'm impressed and a bit embarrassed by the honesty of his words. I talk a good game... I say I'm passionate about finding deeper meaning to life... we all do. But am I willing to take the time necessary to practice?

When I don't answer, Coach continues, "Go with Kim on this part of your discovery. The scent of things, smell, is a big part of life experience. I'm quite sure you'll be filled with regret if you arrive back in US without taking this opportunity to travel through the 'French Riviera' discovering how different fragrances make you feel."

Wood interrupts. "Coach, this is your stop."

We're at the Montpellier Airport. "We can't come with you now. But we can join you in Ireland on Thursday night, late." Coach says with a big smile. "You and Kim go travel for the next four days, finding the smells that make you happy. I'll make sure the entire troupe is there in Thomastown on Thursday night. Deal?"

My mind is racing. 'Ireland?' I'm speechless except to say, "Thank you."

"The driver will take you all back to the hotel. The troupe is booked on the last flight tonight, out to London. I look forward to seeing you in just five days. We'll all put our heads together and remove that Mathew's Curse, which..." Coach quiets his voice even more, and says, with a hint of sarcasm, "If all your theories are correct, will lift all the bad karma that is hindering the efforts of all the natural magic practitioners." Coach pauses. "Did I identify all that correctly?"

"Yes. You did. You can be so… sweet, and then alternately, I want to slap you." I say, shaking my head then say with a smile, "Slap you hard." I'm trying to make a point.

"I'm a guy." Coach says, as he leans in to add quietly, "I can't wait for Thursday…" then raises his eyebrows, "…to smell you."

"Out." I say, softly.

I wake slowly to darkness and the muffled sound of Mediterranean waves. I roll over to check the time, it's only 6 o'clock but since I was in bed and asleep by 8 last night, I've already had ten hours sleep. I stretch slowly, wondering where the Coach lives. More to the truth I wonder, 'what does his bedroom look like' and 'is he still sleeping in it?' If the team really has practice this morning, then he probably is getting up around now.

My thoughts jump to New Jersey where my business, this time of year can be run by my employees efficiently for two, or maybe even three weeks. Unfortunately, February through October I can't leave for more than a couple days… and **he** gets 'heartfelt satisfaction', coaching in Oxford. Cruel reality creeps in to shatter my thoughts of a future with him.

"Bummer." I say, out loud, then add, "Buzz kill", as I throw back the covers and head to the bathroom.

While spitting toothpaste foam onto the mirror, and waving my toothbrush, heralding this new day and I say out loud, "The search continues."

It's been just over five years since my divorce. Even though the freedom has relieved my stress, anxiety, and frustration levels, the disappointments are painful. As I tell my wide-eyed friends, my stories of hopeful first-dates, I see hints of jealousy. Then a week later, while telling humorous tales of epic dates-gone-bad, they laugh, but their eyes are filled with pity.

I know I hang onto relationships way too long, hoping... one by one... that this will be my 'forever guy'. My next-door neighbor has correctly defined my problem as using my 'wishbone' instead of my 'backbone'.

While rummaging in my luggage for the printout of the LiFT phrases, I say out loud, "Where are you?", and realize I may be speaking directly to that forever-guy. As I open the giant slider to the balcony, I say again, louder "Where are you?" directed more correctly to... a guy, I probably don't yet know.

I spend the next hour on the balcony, bundled in one of the over-sized, over-stuffed chairs with a comfy blanket from the bed... trying to feel Love, feel Free, and list all the things, for which, I am thankful.

At some point, I lose myself, or more correctly, I lose my self-awareness. I stop using the LiFT phrases and simply sit, focusing only on the feeling of my breath streaming on the back of my throat, down into my lungs, then back out, mixing with... all the world.

"I Love you." I say out loud, imagining the message riding on my breath... mixing with... and becoming part of... this Mediterranean morning, then continuing to spread... to all the world.

On my breath in, I think 'I love you...' with no hesitation or premeditation I add, '...take care of yourself'. I'm not sure where that came from but my next thoughts are of the instructions we get before every plane ride. 'Put the oxygen mask on yourself first. You can't help anyone if you suffocate.'

I open my eyes. The sky is just beginning to lighten. As I review my list of things for which I feel thankful, I hear a faint knock. 'Is that my door?'

"Joyce. It's Kim. Are you awake? I have real coffee from downstairs."

"Coffee?" I say to Kim, standing in pajamas, "Coffee! Ah, the elixir of life."

"That instant, Nescafe crap should be outlawed." Kim says as we head for the balcony... once we're settled, she adds, "I brought my phone. Want me to book our train tickets?"

"Well, I haven't given up looking for that LiFT school. Wanna go for a tour of old town Montpellier today? We can leave tomorrow, stay in Canne, with a day trip to Grasse, which the brochure says is the Perfume capital of the world. Then onto Eze, and a daytrip to Monte Carlo, if we have time. Fly out of Monaco to Dublin on Thursday..."

Interrupting our plans is another knock on the door.

"Ruh Roe." Kim says as we both rise.

"Yes?" I say very loudly, after we arrive at the door. Whoever is on the other side is speaking French.

"Je ne parle pas Francais!" I say loudly. I won't open the door. Hopefully, he can understand my High School French, meaning 'I don't speak French'.

The male voice on the other side says something... again in French.

"Ne comprends pas." I say, 'I don't understand', again in High School French.

"Just open the door, Joyce!" Kim says, as she grabs the doorknob.

The waiter has a cart with a mouth-watering spread of cheeses, breads, an apple pie-ish thing, a giant hot coffee pot and a big, bright-white box... with a red bow.

"Thank you." Kim says to the waiter as he leaves without waiting for a tip.

"I hate not knowing if I should tip or not... "

Kim cuts me off, "For the love of God, open the box!"

"The card says, 'To help you on your new journey. Affections, Chas'."

The box contains a loose-leaf binder filled with dozens of sheet protectors and a book... "This is one of the books on the Syllabus reading list, 'YOU, the owner's manual. An insider's Guide to the Body That Will Make You Healthier and Younger.' By Michael F. Roizen, MD and Mehmet C. Oz, MD. Very Cool."

"Your Coach certainly knows how to woo a girl." Kim says.

"He's not 'my Coach', but yes, he does. Look at this. He's printed out the www.LiFT.foundation web site and put the pages into the first set of sheet protectors. I'm guessing this is his idea of a LiFT Binder."

All day Kim and I meander through the Old Town, Montpellier. My focus on 1550's Nostradamus, 1800's English school for young girls and even a possible LiFT meditation institute, is forgotten. Kim is attracted to anything shiny. So while she wanders in and out of jewelry stores, I look for clothing to bring back to my girls. We stroll slowly through the beautiful 'Garden of Plantes', stopping often to take dozens of pictures.

"I like the smells of ALL the flowering plants." I note, wondering what our upcoming three-day trip will reveal.

As we walk out of the garden, I read the sign on the iron-gate, which says the garden is the property of the University of Montpellier.

I grab Kim's arm, "Hey, I heard the expulsion document, from when Nostradamus was thrown out of the Montpellier Medical School, is displayed in the basement of the "Faculty De Medicine'." I point to a group of students at the bottom of this hill. "I'm going to ask those students where the Medical School is."

"Joyce!" Kim shouts, and points.

We are standing directly in front of a huge centuries-old building. Above the giant, arched, dark-blue door and a couple of carved-in-stone, ominous looking lions, are the words 'FACULTE DE MEDECINE'.

"Come on!" I say, changing direction.

Our mission is not as easy as I thought. The main building, built hundreds of years ago, has multiple additions with multiple 'basements'. Also, because this is all built on a steep hill, sometimes three stairwells down open to a courtyard. Hardly a basement. Refusing to give up, we begin searching the top floors where we stumble into a small 'library'. A dozen or so students are at desks with a librarian in the front.

"Do you speak English?" I ask her.

"No. No English." The librarian stammers.

I try to get my point across in words she may understand. "Nostradamus, expulsion document. Ou est-ce?" I ask, 'where is it'?

"Yes. Nostradamus." She goes to a reference rack, flips to a page and says, "Nostradamus, application."

"There is a display… somewhere in the basement." I say, but her face is blank. I pause with a deep breath. "Un momento." I say, and realize I just spoke Italian to this poor woman. I use my phone translation app.

English to French: Nostradamus expulsion document is on display where? Then show her my phone. 'Document d'explusion est expose ou?'

"No display." She says, but holds up one finger, meaning 'hold on', and turns to her computer.

Another staff member enters.

"Do you speak English?" I say.

"Yes."

"My research shows Nostradamus's expulsion document is on display 'in the basement' of the Faculte de Medicine." I say, so glad to finally be understood.

"Oh, no!" He says, with a bit of a smirk. "That document, if it still exists and we have it, would be in the archives, very well preserved and protected. No way would that be out, displayed to the public. No way."

With that, the non-English speaking librarian says, "Regaudez."

She shows us her computer screen which is the digital photo of the expulsion document.

"Yes!" I say probably too loud. I point to the signature at the bottom, "Signed by Guillaume Rondelet. So, where is it? Est expose ou?"

"No, no." They both say, interrupting each other.

"You're not going to get another answer from these two." Kim says, over my shoulder.

"OK. Thank you for your efforts. Merci." I say, shaking their hands. Then, whispering to Kim. "My research says it's on display in the basement."

"Yes, Joyce, you've said… several times now. So let's go find it."

I love this woman.

At a lower level, we find a room filled with sketches of plants. Nostradamus would love this. We move into the next room which has more glass display cases of flowering and fruited plant sketches.

"Joyce!" Kim points to a set of cement stairs, roped off at the top and curtained off at the bottom. "Let's go."

I look around to be sure no one sees us. "OK. Let me turn on my phone's video."

On the other side of the curtain are a bathroom and another set of stairs down. We follow the stairs to the left and left again, then another turn to the left. On the right, I see a lighted window which I'm sure this is the expulsion document. "Oh my Goodness! This has to be it!" But this display is an architect's building plan. I continue, and around the next corner, to the right is another display. "This is it!" Look the signature on the bottom! Guillaume! How cool is this?"

"Magnifique!" Kim says in her best French accent. "Another thing we have learned today is the Librarians need better training."

"Clearly." I say, watching my video.

"Our next mission… should you choose to accept… find a Café. Let's go get food and wine." Kim says.

"You've read my mind again, Kim." I say, putting down my phone. "Do you know how to post a video to YouTube?"

"Let's go fill me up with wine, then I'll give that YouTube a whirl."

Chapter 20

A fillet mignon by any other name
would smell as sweet.

I'm already awake when I receive a text from Kim. "J'ai la gueule de bois."

"?" I text back.

Kim replies immediately, "French to English: I am hung over."

I text back, "I love you. You know I do. But I will be on that train at 6:30AM... With or without you."

We did make that 6:30AM train. Booking first-class and reserving specific seats was a great idea. Kim sleeps most of the way while I read: YOU, The Owner's Manual. There is plenty of time on this four-and-a-half-hour train ride to wonder about 'natural magic'. Is there a 'certain affinity of nature', that, with practice, will attract people and things? Is karma just natures response to guilt? Was there really a nanny burned in 1831? ...but most of my time is spent wondering about Coach. I don't see a path where we can be together. My business is like a ball and chain. One-hundred-percent of my clients are within twenty miles of my office. Financially, I can't just up and leave. While his son and his passions are all in Oxford. I have to refocus.

As I guessed, our tour through Grasse reveals little about my 'favorite' smells or those that bring any impressions of Love or feelings of Love. I LIKE all the flowering smells, but Love? No.

What I do learn is, I don't like anything with a 'smoked' smell or anything 'musk-y'. Both Kim and I find Patchouli to smell like rotting moss and mud, mixed with warm poop. The guide describes this oil as having a 'strong, slightly sweet, intoxicating scent'. He goes on to say this oil may smell a bit like Marijuana, and is the favorite of many 'hippie' types. But Kim and I agree, the smell reminds us of steamy, morning, dog-poop… and the giggling escalates to rambunctious kidding, along with a couple laugh-snorts.

I find that even though I did like all the flower smells from the gardens, I do not like any of the perfumes. Each one is either too sweet, too musky or too powdery, and all of them are… Just. Too. Much.

In the end, I have a headache.

Kim asks, "So do you feel Love, Freedom or Thankfulness now more than before we took this tour?

"In fact, I do" I say. "I am extremely thankful, I do not work in this building! My vote is to leave this tour now."

Kim has had enough as well. "Let's get back to Cannes, find a café to eat and drink until our train leaves for Nice."

"Perfect." I say. "All this stink is getting me nauseous. I need food."

We arrive in Nice very late in the evening. Too late, too tipsy and, (we're told by the taxi driver), smelling too much like a perfume factory, to go out on the town. I fall into bed. Kim booked us at the Hyatt. Not until morning do I find we are in the top-floor, Grande-suite, center-room, over-looking the Mediterranean.

"Holy crap, Kim. This is spectacular!" Out through giant columns I can see a 'promenade' filled with bikers, runners, and couples romantically strolling. Down below, inside the columns, is the Hyatt pool and a restaurant beginning to bustle with patrons in business suits. Most spectacular, from this top-floor balcony, is the calm seas of the French Mediterranean. One lone sailboat catches my attention. "How do I get on that sailboat?" I mumble to myself, as I set my phone to take a panoramic picture of this utopia.

A knock on the door sends my imagination flying. "Coach?" I whisper to Kim.

Whispering back, Kim says, "It must be! Don't worry, I'll find somewhere to go, to leave the two of you alone." When her hand is on the doorknob, she adds,"...or it's the coffee I ordered." ...and opens the door... to a waiter.

"Bitch." I say, blushing. "The view from this balcony got the best of me. Frankly, I was just thinking, when Coach and I get married, I'm going to insist on our honeymoon be spent right here."

"Now marriage? Good for you."

"Yes.... And our honeymoon... In Nice, in this Hyatt, in this room, next November." I say as Kim hands me coffee. "I'm not sure I want coffee, it may break the romance buzz I got going."

"I think it'll take way more than a couple cups of coffee to shake that romance buzz, you and the coach 'got going'." After a slight pause, Kim looks at me... "So, how did you meet Coach?"

"The girls and I were at a bar, he was there with his team." I answer, still a bit in a daze.

"He always shows up, at the right place and the right time." Kim says, pausing to get my full attention. "Very coincidental." Pausing, to try again. "Unnaturally so."

"You think he's stalking me, or having me followed? For what purpose?"

"I'm just pointing out, or asking you, 'who does this?' Have you EVER heard of someone who pays for almost a dozen people to travel thousands of miles for one wine tour, that **happens** to include lunch at a meditation center, that **happens** to display the phrase 'why do we think love is a magician'?" Kim is serious.

"He said he had his research department try to find something that might be the remnants of a Nostradamus meditation center." I pause to consider other options. "Do you think he had Wood and his family plant those signs, like a game for me to play?"

"No. I'm saying... maybe he knows more than you think. Maybe he's part of the LiFT cult."

"So, he's a male witch now?" I say pretending to laugh it off, but...

"I didn't say 'witch' exactly, or warlock, but... student of white magic, natural magic... I think he knows way more about the LiFT Foundation than he's letting on." Kim says, without a smirk.

"You're serious?" I say, while my mind is racing, "How could he have known I was going to the bar where we first met?" Then answer myself. "Brooke did tell me we were going there in front of my landlords, Bea and Beren."

"Ohhhh. You're talking about Bea. Bea, the chick we think is the 'Grande Poobah of LiFT? All of this is literally unbelievable." Kim is solemnly serious. "You've said that yourself. Frankly, Chelsea and I began following you because we were having fun watching you play this cool game. But now, I'm beginning to wonder if this is real." Kim pauses, "When we got off the train, I found this." She flicks a euro dime onto the coffee tray. "And then when we got out of the cab at the Hotel, I found this." Kim flicks another dime onto the tray.

"More dimes." I say, because I don't know what else to say.

"I'm just pointing out the obvious here. I haven't decided if he is after you, after an answer to these riddles or something else. Maybe he thinks you can take away the curse. Maybe he thinks that's a good thing, or maybe he thinks it's not."

After a long pause where we're both trying to figure out this ridiculous puzzle which is getting more and more unbelievable,

Kim says, "I'm going in for a shower. I'm really asking you to keep your eyes open. He may just be mentally unstable." Kim pauses to change the subject. "The fresh air from this balcony is making me realize… we smell like a whole lot of perfume. Our entire room smells."

"Agreed. Perfume is not for me. Did you book the train to Eze? My vote would be to skip EZE and 'discover' Nice. Let's stay another night here."

"Perfect. You read my mind. This beautiful day should not be wasted on a train. Certainly not on yet another perfume tour."

Kim and I wonder east along the 'promenade' which stretches along the Mediterranean, up a hill and around to view the marina basin. While Kim climbs the handful of staircases to a castle above, I sit to people-watch. There's a particular group of much older bathers. Obviously friends, all very fit, laughing and swimming. I wonder if they know LiFT.

We walk back west where we stop often for the surprisingly-talented musicians, playing every fifty-feet or so.

"It's afternoon. Let's find food and wine." Kim says, grabbing my sleeve to pull me down a ramp which leads to 'beach-side' dining.

The Nice 'beach' has no sand, but instead is filled with fist-sized, smooth stones which roll in-and-out in the small waves with a 'clack-clack-clack'. We learn later that many people record this clacking sound to sleep and/or to meditate. These tables are on top of a thick carpet to make it easy to walk. Without the carpet the stones are unstable and slippery.

Kim points to a couple, holding hands, trying to gracefully, (and failing), to get into the water without taking each other down.

I shake my head and giggle a bit. "This beach is full of unstable bathers which turns out to be a people-watchers delight."

Kim looks at me surprised. "Schadenfreude!"

"What?" I say, adding. "Did you sneeze? Should I say, God Bless you?"

"Google it." Kim says, calling for the check. "Let's go shopping!"

For the next few hours we walk the old district of Nice, stopping to look at shiny things for Kim and clothing for my daughters. This adventure has been way longer than what I packed for, "Kim, I'm heading into the lingerie store."

"And I'm going to help you pick out a tiny-little nighty for your first night with the coach."

"Kim, I really just need more underwear."

"Yea, me too." Kim says sarcastically, then adds, "Seriously, you should get something for the coach... for all he's done."

"You think I should get him Pajamas? Really?" I say, a bit disgusted.

"No, sweetie. You should buy You a tiny-little nighty, for You to wear... For him."

After a painful hour in a store, whose name I cannot pronounce, it's time for happy hour. The agonizing realization, from trying on tiny-little nighties, that I am far from the body I had in my twenties, is less painful after two red wines and only a tender throb after three.

"I need to eat." I say, after Kim orders a fourth round.

Kim calls the Hyatt to make reservations for dinner. "I think you should picture text that tiny-little nighty to coach."

"Oh yea. Great idea." I say sarcastically. "You're hilarious." I say stressing the 'L' in hilarious way too much. Then add "You're an inzs-tigator." Slurring on purpose for comic effect.

"Yes, people have said." Kim says, proudly.

"How about I just picture message him the bag with the name of the store? Let him look it up. Let him guessss. Imaaaaagine." I say, as I take out my phone, prop the bag up on the table and click. 'DARJEELING'. We both begin to giggle.

As my phone makes the whooshing sound of a text going out, Kim grabs my sleeve, "Holy shit, Joyce. Did you really just send that to him?"

"Yessz." I say, slurring more than a bit.

"I'm guessing he will be here by morning." Kim warns me.

"And we…" I say, as I hold up my fourth red wine, triumphantly, "…will be gone. Bloody brilliant!" I say way too loud and trying to imitate coach's accent.

"Good show!" Kim toasts with me, also trying to add an accent.

"Jolly Good! I'm ready for the knacker's yard." I add, almost tipping over as I put the Darjeeling bag back on the ground.

"Don't get too tired we still have to get dressed for dinner. I think we should start with champagne."

"Holy Crap, Kim!" I say as I spot… next to the shopping bag… a euro dime.

The posh Hyatt five-star restaurant has wait-staff trained well enough to politely ignore the fact that we are sozzled. Our main course arrives and I breathe a deep nose-full of the sizzling steak.

"The LiFT school should have more than just flowers in that nose-iology class. This steak smells amazing." I say.

"Nose-iology? I believe 'olfactory' is the term they used in the perfume tour." Kim says.

"Wait," I take another deep breath. "Yup smells the same, no matter what you call it, just like in Romeo and Juliet, a fillet mignon by any other name would smell as sweet."

"But that's a good point." Kim says. "What do you think your nose-iology chapter will contain? If you list all the smells you like, it'll be literally thousands of items."

"I don't know. I probably should have gone onto the website to check out what's taught there. We certainly got nothing from the tour." I say.

"Not true." Kim says wielding her champagne flute. "We got headaches. So we learned things we don't like."

Our meal goes down quickly. Unfortunately, the dessert sits on the table untouched.

"Those two forks are teasing us to partake... in berries and chocolate cake. See what I did there? Rhyming? We need to come up with a spell to lift the Thomastown curse. Remind me to do that on the plane tomorrow." I say, in drunkin' disjunctive-ness.

"Those two forks say to me, the wait-staff thinks we're Gay." Kim says.

I turn to one of the team of wait-staff who seem to be hovering, "Can you rap that up to go?"

"We can have it sent to your room, Mam." The waiter says politely.

"O.K." I say, a bit bewildered.

After the waiter leaves, Kim says, feigning horror, "You did not seriously ask for a doggie bag in a five-star restaurant?"

"What? We're ready to go. It's early-ish. We may want some chocolate, later." I say, snickering.

"Oh dear God. I'm not quite ready to call it a night. Let's move this party to the bar." Kim says.

"No one is in the bar." I say. "I can see it from here. Literally. Not. One. Person. Look around. There are only two tables of people, besides us, in this dining room. It's eight-o'clock. Shouldn't the Hyatt be busier?"

"This is off season. Our rooms were a steal. A room like ours in-season would be thousands per night." Kim says.

"This is the time of year when the Mathews were here. For the Irish winter. So for people who live up north... This is 'in season', like all the New Jersey 'snow birds' who leave the New Jersey snowy winter for Florida." I say.

"Well, this is definitely off-season for Nice." Kim says.

"Maybe Coach and I can get a 'winter rental' for our honeymoon." I say, smirking.

Kim looks just above my head. Her eyes get wide "Hi, Coach. What are you doing here?"

My face flushes red with blood, then instantly drains. I feel faint and think of the circus game, 'hit the lever with the mallet... the weight goes up, hits the bell then goes down'. I still feel faint when I turn my head, apparently too quickly, and things start to darken, my equilibrium fails me and I can't stop my progress to the floor.

I come-to with Kim's face in mine. "I'm so sorry." She says, "There is no Chas here. I was just kidding you. I really am so sorry. Can you get up? Take your heels off, it'll be easier to steady yourself."

"No coach?" I ask, bewildered.

"No coach." Kim says. "Hey, did I mention I'm sorry?"

After I get up, a waiter hands me my shoes and Kim and I walk, unassisted, to the elevator.

When the elevator doors close, "Bitch." I say, looking straight ahead.

Chapter 21

What are they going to do, shoot us?

"Hey, wake up, sleepy head." Kim is standing over me, rubbing my shoulder.

Unmoving and eyes still closed, I say, "Please find me some aspirin."

"O.K." Kim says. "That whole fainting thing, last night, was really all my fault. So, to make it up to you, the Hyatt has a lovely, full-service spa. I booked us for… steam room, massage, facial, nails, hair, includes lunch… you'll feel and look fantastic by the time we board the plane later."

"Plane? Today? Ugh. I hate you."

"As well, you should." Kim says dismissively, as she hands me aspirin and water. "We fly into Dublin then the Airlink bus to Houston Station where we take a train to Limerick Junction. Then, finally, a taxi to our BNB."

"Sounds like… 'It's a long way to Tipperary.'" I say, with my eyes still closed.

"Yes, well, hopefully your sense of humor will return soon." Kim says, as I show her my middle finger. She continues un-phased. "I've been coordinating with the Alpha Girls. There's only one BNB in Tipperary that's responding to online requests. We're all booked."

"Be careful, there are two Thomastowns and Tipperary is a County, as well as a small town. Please find out, for certain, how close this BNB is to the Thomastown Castle ruins?"

"Four miles. Our Alpha Girls are on this." Kim says, obviously re-naming the four.

"Good job." I say with a thumbs up, then opening one eye, "I drank too much yesterday. Not your fault. Please call room service for oatmeal. That always settles my stomach."

"Sure. Hey, you should have seen the maitre d's face when you fell off the chair..."

With my eyes still closed, I hold up my middle finger. "Too soon, Kim. Way too soon. And..." I open one eye. "What happens in Nice, stays in Nice... agreed?"

"Got it. Yes, our daughters would be so proud." Kim says sarcastically, handing me a cold wash cloth, "Do you remember what you were saying just before you crashed and burned?"

"Yes, I was talking about a months-long honeymoon with Coach. But the reality of it all is, I still own an un-movable business in New Jersey, at least ten years away from the financial ability to 'retire'... and he coaches in Oxford, England."

"His son won't be attending Oxford forever..." Kim replies, trying to be positive. "Have you asked your coach how long his son is planning on doing this Oxford thing?"

"How would you suggest I ask? 'Hey, I want to marry you and spend the entire winter in Nice, wrapped in your arms with my face planted in that giant hairy chest of yours. How long will your son be in the way of our bliss?' Is that what you're suggesting?" I say.

"Obviously, Joyce, you need to find a way to make that a bit more covert."

Our Tip-town inn-keeper, Gerry Casey, is an Irish-sized, unassuming, old man, with a thick Irish brogue, whose very pretty wife runs the Tip-town flower shop next door. Kim and I are booked in separate rooms. Mine is big enough only for my full sized bed. I'm very thankful I have my own bathroom, although the shower stall is not big enough for most grown men. The single, small, casement-window opens to a view of the garages.

"Kim, this is a bit different than the Hyatt." I say loudly.

Kim comes into my room. "Wow, I think your room is smaller than mine."

"Come look at this shower." I say, as I step aside to let Kim see into the bathroom.

"Don't drop the soap, you'll have to open the door to bend down to get it." Kim says as she slides the shower door open. "No showering with Coach in there."

"No. Coach. Jokes!" I say harshly, but whispering while looking out into the hall. "He could pop up any minute."

"Chelsea's been texting me. They're still more than an hour away." Kim says, laughing. "Gerry, our innkeeper, says the best place to drink is right next door. Let's go. Have you ever had Guinness beer in Ireland? It's different than the Guinness in US, they say it's the water in Dublin where it's bottled. The frothy, foam top tastes like whipped cream!"

"As appetizing as that sounds, I'm tired and going to crash. I want to get an early start tomorrow, but first, I'm going downstairs to talk to Gerry. Thomastown Castle is only four miles away. I want to know the best way to get there tomorrow, first thing in the morning."

Gerry could not be more accommodating. Although he had never heard of the Thomastown Castle, (which was concerning), he makes the effort to bring out a local map, (confirming the ruins are four miles away) and calls a cab service to schedule an early-morning pick up.

As I study the map, Gerry comes over to the table, "My wife called the local Councilman, Michael Fitzgerald. Here is his number." Gerry says, placing a tray of tea and scones in front of us. "Michael is traveling now, on the campaign trail, but he says you can call him any time and you should talk to the historian at the library. She lives in a house on the land that used to be property of the Thomastown Castle. Her name is MaryAlice and he'll try to find her home phone number. In any case, you can find her working at the library any afternoon. I'm sure the owner of the pub in Thomastown will know a thing or two as well. The Pub is located across the street from the Castle. The pub and restaurant over there don't open until 1 o'clock tomorrow afternoon, though."

"Gerry, thank you so much, for everything. Please tell your wife I said thank you as well. Breakfast? What is first-thing in the morning for you?" I say, wanting to get a fresh start, as soon as possible.

"Breakfast, every morning 7 until 11."

I look at Kim. "7AM then?"

"Ugh. I don't think we need to begin our day with a 7AM breakfast."

"You owe me… and that's showered, and ready to go at 7AM."

"Yea, yea. OK. I'll be here. But you have to come to the Pub now. Just one Guinness while we wait up for the gang."

"I'm heading to bed." I say, definitively. "I'm not going to wait up for them. I need my sleep. Sorry, Kim." I say, as I fold up the local map, grab another scone and start upstairs. The truth is, even though the Hyatt steam-room helped and my hair and nails needed the attention, I don't want Brooke or the Coach, to see me feeling this run-down."

In my room, I sit alone on my bed and open the binder from Coach.

"Who am I?" I say out loud.

I understand, and one hundred-percent believe, in the power of Love... I understand we all have freedom of will and I understand the need to focus on that which we are thankful. But who am I, unique from everyone else?

While looking back on my life, trying to determine my strengths, I find myself swimming... more to the truth, drowning, in my weaknesses. Ugh. Each time I refocus on strengths and begin to write, my 'worst' floods in and I am drowning again. It's not long before I climb under the covers... where sleep falls gently... and even though the invasion of my 'troupe' into this BNB could not have been a quiet one, I sleep right through until the alarm sounds.

It's a beautiful morning. Lots of peaceful sleep will do that. I knock on Kim's door and hear a grunt, which is way more than I thought I would get. Life is good and I bounce down the staircase with my map.

"Good Morning, Gerry!" I say with a big grin.

"Yes, Miss, would you like eggs, blood pudding and bangers this morning?" Gerry looks tired.

"If you have porridge and fruit, I'd love that."

"Oh yes. Yes we have some of that. And coffee, Miss?" Gerry says, already moving toward the kitchen.

"Yes. Thank you. Strong coffee."

"Strong coffee for me too, Gerry." Kim is dragging herself into the dining room.

"You don't look ready. Have you taken a shower?" I scold.

"Good morning, ladies." It's Coach. He's wearing a big, cream-colored, cable sweater over a button-down blue shirt.

I think to myself 'His chest is as big as Wyoming' and wonder if I remembered to put on my eye liner.

"I was told you wanted a very early start, although I don't think you're going to get many of the gang to tag along." Coach comes to sit at our table, and Kim moves over to give him the seat opposite me.

Kim drapes herself over the table and says, "Joyce, I love you. You know I do. But please release me from bondage so I can go back to sleep? I'm sure Coach will be enough company for a first reconnaissance to the Castle."

"Oh, for the love of God, stop the drama. Go back to bed." I say, then pointing to the door. "Out."

"Wow. That was way easier than we expected, wasn't it, Coach?" Kim says, as she slaps him on the shoulder and skips out of the dining room.

"We neither 'expected' nor 'planned' anything. She's just a trouble maker, you know that right?" Coach says, rolling his eyes.

I choose to ignore the shenanigans because I'm grateful to have a willing adventurer, and I'm quite sure not one of our twenty-somethings will be ready before noon.

"Let's just eat and get out'ta here." I say leaning in, catching a whiff of his fresh, out of the shower smell.

Coach leans in too, and looks straight into my eyes. "So, are you going to show me the item you bought in Nice?"

I retreat. Straighten. I forgot I drunk picture-messaged him. "Kim. She's just a trouble maker. You know that right?" I say, repeating exactly, his early assessment of Kim.

"Did you buy anything from Darjeeling or no?"

"Yes." I admit.

"So, my question is, are you going to show me the item you bought?" Coach says, still leaning in.

"Here's Gerry with our coffee." I say, using this as a diversion.

As soon as Gerry leaves, Coach leans in again, "Do you have it on now?"

"No! It's a nighty." Instantly, I'm sorry I divulged my purchase of intimate apparel.

Coach leans back, "So." Pausing for effect. "You bought a French little naughty, nighty-gown…" pause again, "and thought of me?"

"Kim is a trouble maker, filling the world with shenanigans. And, for the love of God, it's NOT a **naughty, nighty-gown.**" I say avoiding the question.

"What color is this tiny-little-nighty-gown?" He tries to lean closer but Gerry is back with breakfast.

"It's a giant tent-like-thing, flannel, buttons, a high-necked collar." I lie, while visualizing the dark blue, lace, and silk lingerie.

Coach waits for Gerry to leave. "So, are you going to show me this Mo-mar-the-tent making thing?"

"Let's eat and get out'ta here… and for future reference, he's Omar the tentmaker not Momar."

"Oh my Goodness, there it is! That's it! That's got'ta be it. I didn't think we'd be able to see it from the road." I say. The cabby looks in the rearview at me wildly poking at my phone, trying to pull up my camera app to get a picture.

"I'll pull over in the parking lot of the Thomastown Pub and Restaurant, but they're closed and not opening until 1PM." Once stopped, he turns to face us. Actually, to face Coach, "I'm not comfortable leaving you out here with nowhere to go. Those ruins are on private property. You could get yourself shot if you're not careful."

"What would you suggest?" Coach says as he puts his hand on mine, requesting I let him handle this and find a bit of patients.

"There's a town, just a couple kilometers up the road, the breakfast place is open there."

"I think that's a lovely idea. Thank you for your concern." Coach is patting my hand now.

"So you'll be available to drive us back here in an hour or two?" I say, not real happy but I do see the problem.

On the short ride to Golden, I notice, navigating this very narrow road, lined with either ditches or stone walls, there is zero room for error. Walking back the two miles is not an option.

"We've already had breakfast, Chas." I say as the cabby lets us out at the café.

While Coach is paying the cabby, "Yes, but having coffee here will give you time to write an anti-curse spell, dear." Coach says loudly, for the cabby's benefit.

After the cab leaves, I say, "So, our cabby now thinks I'm a crazy person."

"Not at all, dear. Why would you say that?" Coach is chuckling.

"You Know most people don't believe in this hocus pocus thing. I'm honestly not sure I do either. And stop calling me 'dear'. It sounds like we're married." I say, as coach holds the café door open for me and waves me in. But there is very little room between the doorway and him.

As I pass him, I put my hand on his chest, pause and say, "Thank you," while we are nose to nose.

I smell his fresh, out-of-the-shower scent again and wonder what he smells on me, what he feels, and what are his thoughts about me... about us?

"Table for two," He says and points, "by the window, please. Just two coffees will be lovely."

I'm flustered to the point of being debilitated. I don't know where to put my hands. Did I bring my purse out of the taxi? I look down to where it hangs at my hip from the long strap over my head and shoulder. I touch it to be sure. Should I leave my sunglasses on, this table is sunny, but I won't be in direct sunlight…? My sneakers are squeaking, they must have just mopped the floor. My sneakers and my thoughts both sound like idiots. I try to sit, wondering if everyone in this café is looking at me. Awkwardly, I try to slide into my seat without pulling it out first and have to bounce around to sit full onto the seat. I want to kill him for doing this to me. In fact, I want to do way more.

I need to find something to keep my focus away from him. I'll grab a pen from my purse and try to rhyme some sentences together on this placemat. But my attempt to get into my purse is a Giant Fail. My purse seems to be trapped between my lap and the underside of the table, which means I'll have to struggle with this chair AGIAN to back out farther.

I close my eyes and take a breath.

"Would you like a pen?"

I open my eyes. He is offering me his pen with a smirk.

Now, I may actually kill him. Oh God, he's been studying me and now he can read my mind… I'm screaming in my head, 'Fuck You'!

With the calmest voice I can steady, I politely take the pen and say, "Thank you." I hate him for being able to do this to me, and I hate myself for being so weak.

I need to escape to the bathroom where I can pull myself together in private, but I'll 'squeak' again, and no doubt, trip. Fall. Fall onto someone's table, knocking over food and…

"I'll be right back." Coach says, interrupting my breakdown.

In the time Coach is away, I gathered myself, release my purse from around my neck, and begin the process of rhyming an anti-curse spell, which is just as futile and ridiculous as it sounds.

As he slides back into his seat, Chas says, "I was surprised to hear you say you're not sure you believe in this, your words, not mine, 'hocus pocus thing'."

"I'm not sure. I need to investigate more. Then maybe I'll believe. Maybe not. I'll admit there are a lot of coincidences going on." I say, and lean in. "What do you believe? Why are you so interested?" I ask.

"Honestly," he pauses, obviously trying to pick his words carefully, "I see a woman of Math and Science." Pause again. "You understand probability and the fact that nature's laws don't bend. And yet, you're seeing something that makes you curious enough to…" He pause and looks out the window. "…take all this time to investigate." And adds. "I don't know anyone else who would go to this extreme." He looks back at me. "Through your eyes I'm seeing these… 'Coincidences' too. I like following you… watching you." He leans forward, elbows on the table, "I'd like to watch you in that tiny-little naughty nighty. What color did you say it was?"

I roll my eyes. I will not respond to this obvious attempt to change the subject. I do realize I started it by sending that suggestive picture-text. So instead, I say, "Let's get out'ta here. I need to get to the castle ruins. I don't care if it's private property. Really, what are they going to do? I'm sure no-one will shoot us. Please call the cabby?" I say, impatiently.

Coach pulls out his phone. "Bad luck, no signal here." He says, then adds as he rises, "Yes, I'll ask to use the Café phone, Dear."

"My name is Joyce." I gather my items, crumple up the placemat containing my half-hearted attempt at an anti-curse spell and head out the door.

As I wait for him outside I wonder, is he a male witch? I contemplate telling him, 'Kim thinks you're a wizard or warlock' just to see his reaction. But that may not end well. Also that would betray Kim's confidence, and a promise of 'what is discussed in Nice, stays in Nice'.

"No answer." He says, joining me outside.

"Let's go." I'm already walking toward Thomastown.

"I knew this was coming. OK, let's go. If these cars don't kill us, a shotgun may."

"Thank you. I do appreciate this." I say.

"I live to service you, Joyce" Coach says with a slight bow, waving me to walk first, through this single file two mile journey.

"I believe the phrase is 'serve me', not 'service me', Coach." I say, as I pass him to take the lead.

"Oh, please explain to me the difference, Joyce."

I'm glad he can't see me smirking,

Chapter 22

Snakes, gophers and cows, oh my!

"Please walk ahead of me, so I can keep my eye on you." Coach says, showing me his Alpha male. I chuckle.

The two mile road from Golden to Thomastown is dangerously narrow for vehicles, but for pedestrians, could easily be deadly. The fact that the traffic travels opposite than that of US is just another level of confusion and therefore, an additional hazard for me.

"Hey! There's a statue! Got'ta be Father Mathews. Let's go!" I say, as I let a car pass and step out of the grass onto the road.

Coach grabs my sleeve and pulls me back. With horns honking, we both trip and land in a wet grassy ditch.

"There were three vehicles in that particular parade, dear." He says calmly, looking into my eyes deeply. Dangerously.

"My name is Joyce, not 'Dear'." I say too loudly, avoiding his stare and rolling up, onto my feet. I extend my hand to help him get up and think to myself, 'Who's the Alpha now?' but say, "Thank you, Chas." In the prettiest, fake voice I can muster.

"Joyce." Coach begins by submitting to my request to call me by my name. "These are real roads, with real vehicles, that can really kill us." He says, hands on my shoulders, right in my face.

His submission, obviously, decisively over.

Then more to himself. "I may be earning my pass into heaven today but I don't want to actually GO there today."

"Sorry. Really." I say, sticking my face in his with a sincere apology, while putting my hand on his chest to keep distance between us. "I appreciate your help. I appreciate all that you've done." We are so close to a first kiss, but I'm nervous... terrified, so instead... I turn away, "Now let's look both ways, cross the street and check out that Father Mathews Statue." I say, as I realize I was just inches from being completely... out of control.

After Chas helps me take pictures of the statue, while I avoid his eye contact, we move again down the road.

By the time we're safely in the parking lot of the Thomastown Pub and restaurant I am laser-focused on the castle ruins.

Between us and the castle there are rows of cow pastures, stretching from the road half-mile up a gently sloping hill, to a thick thorny hedge row and electrified fencing.

Chas follows me down the road where I hop onto the stone wall directly opposite the castle. There are no cows in this particular pasture, but I can see herds being moved between pastures by farmers on both sides.

My father's parents owned a farm in upper New York State. I used to accompany my 'Cousin' Burton around the pasture and in the barn and never felt the cows to be a threat.

"Have you ever drank milk squirted right out of an utter?" I ask Coach.

"I have not."

"When I stayed at my Grandparent's Farm, every morning there was a big pitcher of fresh milk, warm out the cow, for our cereal." I look to find him taking a camera out of his backpack. "You brought a camera!"

"Of course." Coach says as he sets it on the wall to steady, pushes a couple buttons and a long range lens scopes out.

"Cool." I say. "Thank you, Chas. I do realize, without you I may be in an Irish hospital right now... or worse."

"My pleasure." He says with a deep, calm voice and a slight bow. Then straightening, puts both hands on the wall next to my thigh and says, "What are you afraid of?"

I blush. This wall I'm sitting on is about chest high, so he is looking up at me. I don't know what to say. All this honesty is so uncomfortable. I want to run but I have no excuse to 'go' anywhere. We are at our destination. Unpleasantly, I have nothing to say... more to the truth, nothing to say out loud.

"You seem to be a woman, always..." he pauses. "...always **needing** to be 'in control'." He pauses again. "Have you ever been uncontrollably 'in love'?"

I look away to think about each of my relationships; with my High School boyfriend, College boyfriends, Ex-husband, even dating after the divorce. No. I always chose men where I had no problem walking away. This long silence is becoming absurd. I'm hoping he'll break the quiet, but no. And now, I find myself almost in tears. Then just as he begins to move away, I find courage. "No." I say, simply. Honestly.

Chas moves back toward me and puts his hand on mine, "I'm sorry."

His pity hurts. I feel tears begin to burn and, well up, but I'm not going to let them fall down my cheeks. I blink them away, refocusing. This silence is painful. I have no idea what to say to such empathy... honesty. He's again, patiently waiting for me to say something.

Again, I find truth, and apparently in this truth, I find a bit of courage. "I seem to be attracted to men who cheat, or men who selfishly push me or pull me in directions I know will not be good for me in the long run. These men were all **my** choices, and therefore, the fact that all these relationships went bad are **my** fault.

To answer your question completely, I believe I have the capacity to 'love uncontrollably', but no one, with whom I have been attracted, deserved that from me." I pause, and look to him, "You?"

"I will be carful to never push or pull you... unless it's to avoid oncoming traffic." He says, trying to lighten up the conversation.

"No. I mean, have you ever been 'uncontrollably in love'?" I ask.

"Yes. My wife. We were high school sweet-hearts."

"So, the divorce must have been heart breaking?" I ask, very quietly.

"There was no divorce." He pauses.

I jump in. "You're not divorced?" My voice is filled with accusation and disgust.

"She passed away. Cancer."

I'm an asshole. I am an asshole. Dear God, I AM an asshole. "I'm so sorry. I didn't know." Why am I such an asshole? And like that, I want to kiss him. I'm no longer afraid. But it's not a passionate, 'please take my clothes off as fast as you can', kinda kiss, but a 'you poor thing, please let me hold you all night', kiss. Unfortunately, I'm up here... sitting, up here, on this stone wall and he's standing... Way too awkward.

"So, I'm going to change the subject." Coach says.

Thankfully.

"When I go hunting with my buddies, and we think we're going on someone's property, we just knock on doors and ask the property owner's permission. Com'on. I see cars in that drive up the road a bit. Let's go knock on a couple doors." He says as he packs up, and straps his backpack on, "Let me help you down from there."

I blush and can't bring myself to say yes. "I'm almost down." I say, because I can't say 'no' directly either, but I do turn to give him a hug, my head down. "I'm sorry." I say, as I release him and walk on up the road ahead of him… tears welling in my eyes again… but this time for him.

We walk up to the neighbor's property in silence. I stop at the street, while he continues up to the door. I say, "I hope he doesn't answer the door with a shot gun."

Coach knocks on the door and looks back at me, shaking his head. "You're gon'na get me killed." The door opens. "Good morning. My friend and I are doing research for a book on the Thomastown Castle. Can we walk through your property to the ruins?"

A book? I think to myself, 'good story'.

The guy comes out of the screen door with a dog on a leash. Chas takes a step back. Maybe these people really will shoot trespassers.

"There's a gate," he points, "toward the pub. You can go through there. You may have to fight through thorny brush and over a stream, but you can walk up through there OK." He says, and as he's shutting the door. "Be careful of the cows. They don't take kindly to visitors."

The metal gate is not locked, so we easily pass through into a beautiful pasture steaming with butterflies, padded with high grass, and spotted with white and yellow wild flowers. I take out my phone to take a video.

"Do you think there's snakes in this grass?" I ask, as I double-step to catch up. Chas has a thoughtful, steady, cadence to his walk. I have to continue at a quick-step to keep up with the decisive stride of his long legs. I can imagine him in hunter's camouflage gear and a rifle over his shoulder. What would he do if I tackle him to the ground right here? I look to our right to see if the neighbor has come out into his back yard to keep an eye on us.

"Just watch your step, there may be gopher holes. I wouldn't want you to turn an ankle." Chas says, continuing up this pasture. Steadily.

I'm not sure if my breathing deepens because I am getting winded with this climb or imagining him... his measured, rhythmic tempo... Steady, stable pace. Fixed, firm cadence...

"Be careful! This is an electric fence." Chas says, interrupting my thoughts, fishing out a plastic water bottle from his right leg pocket and holding the fence up for me to duck under.

"Hold on! That one's electrified as well."

I stop just in front of a second wire fence.

He pauses again, to lift the wire with the plastic bottle. "What's distracting you? Isn't this what you want?"

I stop, turn towards him, and stomp my foot, "Snakes and gopher holes!" I lie. Directly ahead there seems to be a hole in the thorny hedge row. "Let's go!"

"I'm going to check out the fence down here. Maybe there's a better way." He takes off to the right.

I clear some dead brush out of the already semi-wide opening and crawl into the thorny tunnel, up a three foot berm, then down to find another electrified fence. Coach arrives on the other side to lift the wire for me to easily get under and...

There's the castle!

The structure still has only some of its outside walls but the huge towers still stand. All of it is mostly covered in ivy.

One giant tree, taller than the towers, comes alive with birds squawking, filling the sky like a black cloud, circling the ruins.

To our left is a small structure. "That must have been their church."

Everything is so overwhelming. I gravitate to the very small church building first.

"Joyce, you have to see this." Chas is taking pictures of the cow pasture behind us. There's a maze of foundations. "What do you think that is?"

"I have no clue. Looks like a Labyrinth." I put my hand on his bicep. "Please take pictures, we'll figure it all out later. Let's get to the Castle."

"I'm uncomfortable with you going inside the ruins. All this rubble did not grow here. It all fell from what once were the walls. We walk around the far side first, he's in the lead then quickly comes back. "This way is where all the cows are. Let's go back the other way first." Chas takes my elbow to guide me back.

"Where do you think the main entrance was, and the servant quarters?" I ask, as Chas keeps taking pictures, now of this north east side.

"I don't know. But I'm thinkin' we better get out'ta here as soon as possible."

"I feel an uneasiness too. The birds seem to be going crazy, like a really loud alarm. I'm going inside, to try to meditate, see if I can 'see' anything." I say, as I very slowly, pick a spot to enter and decide to sit very close to this hole in the wall, in case anything happens.

Instead of the birds calming they seem to be getting louder. I take out my camera. "If there are spirits here, they are well protected by the birds and cows." I say to the video, then add, "Almost two hundred years, is a very long time to be alone with just a bunch of birds and cows."

I close my eyes and try to find calm through the birds screaming.

"Oh crap!" Chas yells.

"What? Are you OK?" I open my eyes and lean in to look out the hole I came through.

"I stepped in a cow pie."

I lean back with a chuckle, and try again, to calm.

I hear Chas's camera clicking and open my eyes to watch Chas, thirty feet in front of me, walking into the castle, unsteadily through the rubble.

"They're looking in here... at me." He says, not taking his eyes off forward.

"Who?" I say, faking horror, knowing the answer.

"The cows. This one has a two-foot-long spit drool. I got a picture of it. They want us, Joyce. We have to get out of here." Chas says, in dead seriousness.

"Chas, the cows do not 'want us', sweetie. They're harmless. I walked in the fields with them all the time at my grand-parents farm." I say, but I do feel the distress of the castle. The birds are getting even louder, when I'm pretty sure they should be settling down by now.

I close my eyes again.

"Shoo." Chas says as he waves his arms, "Shoo, Shoo."

"What the fuck are you doing?" I say in a harsh whisper. "You know you're just taunting them, like a toreador. All you're missing is the red cape."

"It works when I hunt. Thank God these cows can't come in here." He says.

"What do you mean, 'can't come in here'? There are cow pies everywhere in here. Of course, they can... and have, come in here!" I am now speaking way louder than a hushed whisper to be heard over the squawking birds which are not only getting louder but seem to be diving, swooping farther inside this castle ruins.

"We have to go. Right. Now! They're coming!" Chas is holding out his hand to me but looking straight ahead to his four footed adversaries.

"I'm ducking out this way." I scream as I bolt through the whole in the wall.

"Let's go around back where I came through." Chas says, and holds out his hand for mine.

I grab onto his hand and we run to the corner of the castle... and see... a wall of cows.

We stop together. "NO!" I whisper. "Along the fence, the other way. We need to find where I came through."

We are both jogging now, along the thorny hedge row, alternately looking back at the castle holes, to see if the cows are coming through, and at the hedge row so we don't miss the spot I came in.

"They don't seem to be following." Chas says.

"Here! This is where I came in!" I say.

Chas reaches into his pants leg pocket to pull out the plastic water bottle and lift the electric fence wire for me to crawl under. I scramble up the berm but my sweatshirt gets snagged on a thorn at the end of a branch, and I stop to unhook myself.

"Joyce, hold this up. I can't get under." Chas's voice is steady, but urgent.

I turn, he's handing me a stick, about three feet long, but as I hold up the wire I get a steady pulse of electricity.

"I'm getting shocked!" I say, as I look up and twenty or more cows are walking around the corner of the castle, obviously very interested.

"I can't get under without your help."

"Hand me your backpack." I say, while still trying to get unhooked from the thorny bushes.

Chas quickly takes off his pack and throws it passed me, through the hedge opening and out the other end.

"Joyce, get out of the way. I'm coming through." Chas says.

I feel the ground rumble first. As Chas bends down to try to fit under the wire, I'm horrified to see this herd is in FULL STAMPADE RIGHT TOWARD US!

I turn and scramble out of the brush, taking the end of a long branch that's hooked to my sweatshirt, with me. Then I feel it release. "Watch out!" I scream to Chas as I look back.

But Chas is still on the wrong side of the electrified wire. There are at least thirty cows in full stampede, now just yards away. I see one cow 'buck' like a bronco and another running, head down, almost to the ground, snorting.

Apparently, Chas never made it 'under' the wire. He jumps up and steps one very long leg… tippy toed, over… gingerly trying to avoid the electric shock… but even on tip toes… can't avoid contact.

"Ouch!" I scream for him.

Chas finally gets one foot solidly on my side of the wire and in one motion jumps through the hedge, over the berm.

"Let's GO!" I scream and we run. "They're coming!"

Almost immediately, Chas begins to slow. "OK. We're safe. They know the fence is electrified. They've learned."

"Yea, the first row of cows will stop, but the next twenty cows behind will push them through and break that wire."

"No, Joyce. Look. They've stopped." Chas slows the pace as I spin to assess the hole in the hedge row. Yes. They have been stopped.

We both bend over, hands on knees, trying to catch our breath.

My hand and especially wrist are tingling. "The electricity came right through that three foot stick!" I say, as I massage my right hand.

"Yes, and right through my pants." Chas says, with no emotion.

I stand up straight. Stop my breathing, for dramatic effect, look at him and we both burst into laughter so hard we fall into this pasture.

"You owe me big time." Chas is laughing.

"Dark blue, lace, and silk accents." I say simply, and roll over to face him.

This pasture… filled with cow pies, snakes and gophers…

Our breath… sticky with running, and humid with coffee…

is the perfect place… for the perfect first kiss.

Chapter 23

The untold will unfold

"So... he has to STEP OVER the electrified fence..." I am screaming the story, to be heard over the laughter of the entire troupe, the bartender and some half-dozen patrons of the Thomastown Pub, all listening intently.

Coach is trying to keep a straight face, feigning humiliation, which makes the story so much funnier. "Apparently, you enjoy the fact that I am the butt of your jokes."

Kim breaks in, "Yes! Schadenfreude is strong with this one." She points to me but looks down the table at the troupe, "Google it."

"It's not your BUTT that is the joke, Coach." I say, loudly, igniting a thunder of laughter, again.

"I can't wait 'til this story dies out." Coach says, shaking and hanging his head.

"Oh NO, Coach. I'll be 95 years old, rockin' on my retirement porch, STILL tellin' this story." I say, loudly.

Under the table, Chas puts his hand on my leg. I look deep into his eyes and touch my lips. Our secret is screaming in my head. I notice, his cream-colored cable sweater is much more than grass stained. Embedded pieces of blades and smudges of yellow wild flowers are betraying our secret.

Brooke holds up her phone so everyone can see the YouTube video of 'Schadenfreude', and the place is roaring in laughter again.

Coach's son Chucky, who rarely speaks, says, "Dad, 95 years from now the Oxford Athletic Department will still be telling this story."

"Do you know anyone man enough to tell the Oxford Athletic Department, Chucky?" Chas teases.

"Dad, this story has already posted in the *Oxford Spokesman*, online."

The troupe explodes in laughter again as Coach pretends to take an arrow to the chest.

Life is good. I sit back to take in the scene. Everyone seems to be either talking or laughing, and many times doing both at once. All is well. Yes, life is good.

I notice, hanging on the wall of this Thomastown Pub, a huge, three-feet tall by almost two-feet wide 'Notice of sale.' From my seat, I can see it's the June 15th, 1837, Auction of the Thomastown Castle and property. I get up to look at it in detail.

Brooke and Angel join me at the notice.

"Auctioned 1837! If the nanny was burned in 1831, it didn't take long for the Mathews to lose all their wealth." Brooke says.

"Coach, look at this." I call him. "This notice says there were 'three walled gardens', so those 'foundations', or what we thought were 'foundations' are really what's left of the garden walls."

"Where the toddler drown." Angel adds somberly.

"Yes, Angel." I say, putting my arm over her shoulder.

"Coach brought a camera and has pictures of the ruins of those garden walls." I say, then call to Chas again, "Can you show us the pictures you took?"

"Wait. Mom!" Brook is looking at a third 'notice'. "This says 'when Francis, the 2nd Earl of Llandaff, (that must be the black sheep), died in 1833 the castle was inherited by his sister, Lady Elisha Matthew, and when she died in 1841, the Castle passed, by inheritance, to a cousin, Viscomte De Chabot. So if the castle passed from Elisha to DeChabot, in 1841, then the Castle never sold in this foreclosure sale, dated 1837."

"Good catch, Brooke." I say. "Which makes sense because, if the castle was sold at public auction, then my leprechaun friend, Dan would not be an 'heir', and therefore, not be destined to any curse."

"Here, I set it up for you." Coach says, holding out his camera.

I sit in my seat next to Chas, while Brooke and Angel look over my shoulders.

"Here is a picture of a church, or maybe it's the official entrance to the castle. These are the walls of the gardens. Here's the tree that unleashed, literally thousands of birds that all went insane. You'd think once disturbed they would settle down but instead, the squawking escalated. It's not a peaceful place up there."

Brooke points to the one picture, Coach took of the castle with me in it. "Oh my Goodness, Mom. The castle is huge."

"I know. The pictures don't do the place justice without someone in the frame to give it scale."

"What is this giant purple ray of light?" Angel says. "You may have captured a picture of a spirit."

We all move in closer to the camera.

"Maybe there's other pictures like that." Angel says.

As we click through, we do find three pictures with a purple ray of light, seeming to come from the ground, reaching all the way to the sky. After several reviews, I notice all the pictures with the purple ray of light were of the east-north-east corner of the ruins.

"Coach. Look at this. Did your camera ever take a picture with a purple streak before?" I ask, handing the camera to him.

Coach takes his time searching through his camera's pictures, then looks up to simply say, "Nope." Then raises his hand to get the bartender's attention. "Set us all up for one more round, then please message the restaurant next door. We'll need a table for ten."

For the next three hours our troupe continues with cheerful conversation, laughing, and playing absurd videos from YouTube.

After dinner, we all saunter down the road, single file, to sit on the stone wall opposite the Thomastown Castle ruins. This pasture is now filled with cows. Walking the half-mile through to the castle is not an option.

The sun is setting, and one by one, we all feel the reverence of the unholy Castle, and drop into silence.

"I didn't get a chance to think of an anti-curse spell. Anyone got anything?" I say, breaking the silence.

Angel breaks the very long pause. "I feel so sorry for everyone involved with this Castle's history. Starting with the First Earl of Llandaff. He was obviously very successful. Gaining power and titles while keeping all his lands profitable, here and in Wales. He must have been heartbroken, knowing his children were rogues, and to top it off, even with five sons, he had no heirs."

I interrupt to correct her. "Actually, he did have an heir. The first son, born in Paris. The one who went to fight in the war in India. That first son had sons, and they had sons. I think my BNB leprechaun guy, Dan's Uncle, would be the tenth Earl of Llandaff if the Black sheep hadn't 'stolen' his inheritance and title."

Angel continues. "I feel sorry for his children too. They were all without ethics, giving in to the excesses of drinking, gambling, drugs, and even bribing judges. No one in this community could get justice from this generation of Mathews' thieving and bad behavior. In that time of famine and other hardships, they could have done great things for the community. Instead they took everyone down, including themselves."

I try to summarize and focus our troupe. "First, we can all agree that the nanny **may have** put a spell on Father Mathews. But even if the nanny was not a 'witch', we're certain that her death was the catalyst to inspire the Father to become a truly great man, who did great deeds, and obviously elevated the 'Mathews' name to one of the most famous and respected in Ireland.

Second, there may have been a curse that my BNB leprechaun buddy, Dan, and his brother, believe has been put on them and still to this day, carries through to their heirs." I stop. I don't know where to go from here.

Angel continues. "If there was a curse, and not just karma riding on the Mathews' guilty feelings... then this curse was from the nanny's family and community. They had to be wildly angry."

I interrupt. "Even though the entire community was probably involved, I'm sure the nanny's Mom was the catalyst. Yes, the entire community was probably frustrated for many, many years by all the unfair and hurtful decadence-gone-wild going on at this Castle, but the Mom had to be the angriest." Angel continues. "So, maybe we don't have to convince an entire community to release their very powerful, very effective, successful spell. Maybe we can plead to the nanny's mom, or whoever it was that facilitated the curse."

Coach says simply, "The Alpha."

"Yes!" I say, loudly as everyone in our troupe leans in to be sure they actually heard the Coach chime in. "Well, our first priority is to be sure we preserve the good works of the nanny and father Mathews.

Then, we need to convince the 'Alpha' that led the curse of the Mathews, to release them for three reasons:

First: It's been almost two-hundred years. The black sheep, all his younger brothers, and sister did not have children. There is no one left to punish.

The people that are being hurt now have nothing to do with the shenanigans going on at the castle back then. In fact, these relatives, my BNB pals, are the descendants of the real heir, who suffered from the black sheep decadence-gone-wild too. And third, and maybe most importantly, the natural magic community has suffered and is suffering under the nature laws of Karma."

Angel is determined. "To begin, let's feel Love, Freedom, and Thankfulness." Then a little louder, "To all that remain in these Thomastown ruins, we send our Love."

"If I were the nanny's Mom," I say loudly, "I'd want everyone to know how amazing she was. I'd want everyone to know her death was the catalyst for the already famous Father Mathews. I'd want everyone in the world to know, that even wrongly accused, found guilty against the laws of Ireland, sentenced to be burned, SHE wanted nothing but to cure the addictions."

Brooke adds to my theory. "If we have this story right, both the injustice of her death and her kind-hearted LIFE was the catalyst for Father Mathew's campaign."

"Which brings us to a really important point. No one has verified this nanny story." Kim points out.

"Yes, tomorrow afternoon, I'll be going to the library to see the librarian-slash-historian to see if I can verify this nanny story." I assure, Kim.

I hear clicking, and Coach has his camera out again.

Brooke, "Mom, there are other cool things to see in Ireland. We want to go see the Cliffs of Moher and go to Dublin to take the Guinness tour and still make the last plane out on Sunday night."

"OK." I say, a bit unnerved. "I'm going to stay to talk to the librarian tomorrow, but then I'll meet up with you in Dublin for the

Guinness tour. All is well, Brooke. But for now, the sun is setting. Does anyone have a couple of rhyming words for the castle?"

After a long pause Chucky says, with a beat. "Addi-tion-ally, we send our love un-condi-tion-ally."

"Good job!" Coach leans over speaking directly to Chucky, then leans back, speaking to me, "I guess we're rapping this spell."

"We send blessings of joy and love, to the ruins we see above." I say, "OK even I think that's lame."

"Mom! No." Brooke yells.

"OK. So how about, 'How now brown cow. We're here now with the cows, shoutin' it out. But the birds in your clouds are just too loud." I say, trying to find a rhyme, then look at Coach. "I was trying to get in the cow thing."

Coach sits up straighter and covers his injured manhood.

I burst out laughing.

"For the love of God, Mom. Please stop." Brooke is horrified.

"I'm hoping my son can save this." Chas says, then to his son. "Hey Chucky, got anything?"

While Andrew 'raspberries' the beat, Chucky is ready.

"The ones who controlled the gold

Are way passed old, man, they're souls are cold

Let the untold, unfold

As foretold, your curse took a toll, ten-fold." Chucky says

We all erupt in applause and cheers.

"I have one." Andrew says. "The Father Mathews we admire was inspired.

By the girl in the fire on the spire.

She is where he acquired his desire

She conspired with nature so father sire would go higher."

We erupt in applause and praises again.

"I have one, but it's not a rap." Kim says, with a reverence I have not seen before. "She is the beacon we should all follow

We have grown in desires that are dangerously hollow

Through her story we must learn to humbly live

To all of humanity, is where we should give."

"Mom, I don't think you're getting the point." Chelsea, scolds her Mom.

"Well, I love it." I say, as I begin applauding.

"I think that's exactly the point." Coach says, and begins to clap too. "It's getting dark and cold. Anyone else?"

"I have another one." Chucky says raising his hand.

"When this loving bell is tolled

When her pure truth is sold.

When the untold, unfolds

Then behold - magic will again rock and roll."

Again applause and cheers erupt.

"I believe your son may be brilliant." I say to Chas.

"I knew that already." Chas says, then loudly to everyone, "Let's go. I need a shower." Then in my ear as he rolls off the wall in my direction, "Wanna join me?"

Be still and peace to your kind-hearted soul,
For here-in your untold will unfold.
A beacon for us all to follow
A map to shed values that are hollow
A second prayer, I beg you pray.
Forgive the Mathews curse away.
For all of Wicca, a price has paid.

Chapter 24

Truth is the other side of Love

"Mom, we're leaving really early, on the first train tomorrow." Brooke says, as we all get out of two old taxis in front of our BNB.

"Right now, I have to take a shower, sweetie. Why don't you grab us a pot of tea and two scones from Gerry, our new landlord, and come up to my room? I'll be out of the shower by then. We'll sit and talk." Then add, "Decaf, please."

While we sit on my bed in the coziest BNB room ever, Brooke and I talk about her studies, her professors, her goals, and all her options once she graduates.

"You're OK staying here by yourself, right?" Brooke says.

"I'm just staying here until after I talk to this historian tomorrow. Then, I'm taking the next train to Dublin. I'll be there when you all arrive." I say, "I seem to have spent my vacation chasing this mystery instead of visiting with you. Are **you** OK with this?"

"You're just being you." She laughs a bit, then adds. "Not one of these people will ever forget this adventure."

"We both have a little Pooh in us, Brooke." I say, with all the love in the world and beyond.

My phone dings. "It's Kim. She texts 'Good luck at the library, See you in Dublin.' Then asks, 'Is Coach staying here with you or going to the cliffs?'"

I text back. "Thank you and I don't know about Coach. I haven't seen him."

"Looks like you made a friend, Mom." Brooke says with a broad smile.

"I love Chelsea's Mom." I say.

"Chelsea and I knew you guys would be good friends if you ever met, but I'm talking about the Coach."

"Coach? He lives in Oxford. We live in New Jersey. I'm not getting involved in a long distance thing." I say, while thinking about that pasture and wonder where he is now. Probably in bed. It's well past midnight.

"Well, I think he's a fan." Brooke says, as she rolls onto her side and closes her eyes.

I close my eyes too, hoping I dream of Coach in a cream-colored cable wool sweater, pastures of butterflies and wildflowers. I'm glad Brooke insulated me tonight from another encounter with him. I know all this flirting and teasing has no future and I don't want it to go too far.

As I drift into sleep, I think of how it felt to kiss him. Actually, he, most definitely, kissed me. I correct myself as I chuckle a bit and adjust my pillow. I can feel his arms pulling me closer into that cable sweater that smelled... musky. Not like the musky smells on the perfume tour, that always turned my stomach, but the sweaty musk that comes with a man... a man desperate for a kiss... for my kiss... and more. His breath smelled a bit like the coffee we had hours before, but sweet. Wet. I remember, my hands, exploring under his sweater. My hands revealing a bit of desperation too... I blush and roll onto my side and away from... these feelings which can only end with him, breaking my heart.

I refocus on feeling love for humanity, and humanity loving me back. I feel my blessings of freewill and start counting all that I am thankful for, which sends me into a peaceful, deep sleep.

I wake very slowly, vaguely remembering Brooke's alarm going off hours before and a kiss good bye. Brooke and the rest of the troupe must be long gone.

The BNB is quiet. The clock says, ten-fifteen. If I hurry, I can still catch breakfast with Gerry. As I'm brushing my teeth I wonder if Coach is here. I doubt it, but I take the time for some make-up and even use the curling iron.

"Good morning, Gerry!" I'm feeling good.

"Eggs, Bangers, and Blood pudding, Mam?" Gerry says as he rises.

"I think I will. I should eat one Irish breakfast while here in Ireland. Is anyone else still here from my troupe?" I ask.

"No, Mam."

Bummer. The chance I'd spend an entire day, and maybe tonight in Dublin, with Coach was slim, but apparently, I was hoping. I do have to get home, back to work, and even though I know there's no future for Coach and me... I still would like to have one more day... and night with him.

"We'll always have Thomastown." I murmur to myself, as I raise my coffee cup.

"What's that, Mam?" Gerry's coming out of the kitchen with my breakfast.

"Just talking to myself, Gerry."

The little cakes of blood pudding were beyond delicious, that is, until I looked up the recipe; which begins with four cups of fresh pig's blood and two cups of finely diced pig's fat. And now, I feel a bit ill.

After I pack up, it's time to head to the library, which happily is just a couple blocks away. Tipperary Library, The Excel.

"Hello. I'm looking for Mary Alice."

"I'm Mary Alice." She says, with an intelligent smile and a very easy way about her.

"I'm staying at the BNB in town, doing some research on the Thomastown Castle. Gerry says you're the expert." I say.

"I'm not sure I'm the expert, but I live just in front of the ruins." She says.

"I've heard there were some Shenanigans going on there in the 1800's. I also heard a story about a nanny?" I ask.

"Oh yes. There is a crazy history of that castle. There was a nanny accused of witchcraft, found guilty by a judge, a friend of the Mathew's family. She was burned, right there at the castle. You may want to check out the book, *Land and Violence* by: Dr. Des Marnane.

But my mind is racing. The story I heard from Dan is true! Confirmed! I can't focus. "Please write that down. Which book?" I say, shaking my head. Wow. "So, the little girl who drown?"

"Yes. That little Mathew's toddler drown in one of the very fancy fountains. The nanny was accused of putting a sleeping-spell on the Mum. Witchcraft. They brought the judge up from Cork to find her guilty and burned her to death, right there on the Thomastown property. There's a lot of sad history there. That, not being the least of it. I live on property that was part of the Thomastown Castle estate." She says, as she hands me the note and points to the other side of the building. "The librarian will help you."

In a daze, I hand the note to the librarian who disappears into the back but comes out with nothing. "Let's see if someone checked it out." He says, passing me to sit at his computer. "No. It must be here." Then, he rises and starts searching the racks next to his desk."

I put my coat and bags down at the nearby table and help him search. We both move a little further into the library. The sign above this rack says, 'Historical, non-fiction." There are mostly books on the history of the Tipperary County towns, Cashel, Golden. I let out a laugh to find books on cows.

I pull out my phone, search online, 'Land and Violence by: Dr. Des Marnane'. I find it easily, download it, and email it to myself.

I go farther into the stacks to find the librarian. "It's fine." I whisper, "I found it online."

"Oh. Good job. But, it should be here." He says, and continues to look through the racks.

Just as I'm leaving, at the very end of this rack, I spot an old, hand-bound book.

Interesting.

I slide it out enough to read the title. "Personal Diary of..." is stamped in gold on the front. The name is too worn to be legible.

I carefully open the cover to find none of the pages are still 'bound' to the spine. I hold the book gingerly and turn to the first hand written page.

If you do no harm, do what you will.

I almost drop the book. I look up. The librarian has now moved on to another rack, still looking for '*Land and Violence*'.

My hands start to shake. My breath is difficult to control. I know I need to find my seat. The intense disbelief brings tears.

"This is impossible," I whisper to myself. I begin walking toward the table and chair in a daze. I look for a copier. With no copier in sight, I go to the front desk to ask. No one's around. Is this guy the only one working over here?

"Knock, knock." I say, as loudly as I should in a library. I'm holding this treasure to my chest with both arms. My eyes go huge as I'm struck with the idea of taking this home. I don't want to steal it, but I do want to spend lots of time with this book. In this instant – I can just… Walk. Out… with this book.

I could own this book. No one knows I have it. They obviously lose books all the time.

I would take really good care of it, I rationalize. Certainly, **they** are not taking care of it. This should be in an environmentally controlled 'archive' alongside the Nostradamus expulsion document.

This is a book that, no one knows who, held with her own hands. I turn and walk to the table to retrieve my coat, scarf, hat, and gloves. I'm shaking and drop my scarf. While picking up the scarf I drop a glove. My face is bright red and my breath is out of control. I can hear only my pulse pounding in my ears. If the librarian is around I won't be able to hear. I swivel my head back and forth looking for any potential witnesses. I realize how guilty I look, but I keep moving quickly for the door. I catch myself just before breaking into a run. 'Calm down! Walk', I say to myself. I count. This will surely help me walk slower. One, Two, Three… My winter coat is not covering the book but I'm afraid to adjust the coat while trying to escape. Five. Six. I'm so close to the door now, I'm not going to look around.

If I had the word GUILTY in a word balloon above my head, I would not look more guilty than in that moment.

"Mam?" I hear through the blood pounding in my ears. "Did you find it? 'Land and Violence', I mean?"

I stop and turn to find MaryAlice, the Historian, walking toward me.

"The librarian couldn't find it, but I found it online and downloaded it. Thank you."

"You can't remove any of the books without a library card, but I'm sure Gerry or his wife, will be happy to check this out for you." She says as she points to the book in my arms. "You can keep it up to a week."

"I'm leaving later today." I say. "Do you have a copier?"

"No, Mam. Not one that works."

"Do you have some paper?" I ask.

"Of course. As much as you need."

I return to my table, and prepare myself, for an entire afternoon trying to decipher the handwriting of a woman studying witchcraft from the eighteen-hundreds.

PAGE 1

If you do no harm, do what you will.

Page 2

Spells are dangerous things.

Always use your powers for good and not evil.

Page 3

Rule One – Anything is possible in Love.

> God is Love.

> The universe was created in love.

> It's all about intent.

> Your spell must be born in Love.

Rule Two – Feel the love. Feel the intent of the spell. Those feelings will reverberate throughout the universe and the entire universe will conspire to bring the spell to fruition.

Why do we think love is a magician? Because the whole power of magic consists of love! The work of magic is the attraction of one thing by another. - Ficino.

Love yourself, love the people in your life, love all of humanity, love boldly with generosity, and love freely.

Understand Freedom, Feel Free until you **are** freedom.

Be thankful. Feel thankful until you **are** thankfulness.

Rule Three - Every line of a spell must be in the positive

The universe will not "hear" or "feel" the negative word.

EXAMPLE: I will not drop the glass. Close your eyes. What do you see?

Most people will see me dropping the glass first and understand it didn't happen, second.

The universe feels what you see... the glass dropping.

Replace with "the glass is safe in my hand".

Rule Four – Start with a blank page.

Wake early, well rested, before everyone else starts their rushing around, noisy day.

Drink a small glass of room temperature water.

Think of all the people you Love. Think of just your breath in and out.

Imagine love is riding on that breath. Each breath Out. Then when you're ready, each breathe IN.

Sit, find calm. Eyes closed.

You may burn enough incense or cedar, so no other smell will enter while you're chanting.

Better to engulf the room with a smell that reminds you of the person or thing relating to the spell.

Feel Love, feel the love you have for the person or thing then feel the spell taking effect.

Let nothing interrupt.

DO NOT starve yourself. You can't both love yourself and starve yourself.

DO NOT alter your mind with pills, elixirs, smoke or drink. You must be able to see the world as it is.

You may feel you're more creative after a bit of smoke or drink but you'll never be more creative than purely how the universe has created you. You need to see the world exactly how it is.

PROTECT YOUR SLEEP! Sleep is important. Wake up at the same time every morning, after 'enough' sleep. Love your sleep. Protect your sleep and the sleep of the people around you.

Rule Five – keep the spell alive. Reminder items

Set up, in your home, a reminder of what you've created. A little vase with beautiful flowers to remind you of the types of people and things you want to come into your life.

Also create a reminder bracelet.

Rule six – Don't tell the universe how to solve the problem.

Let the universe be the maker of creative solutions. Have faith. Have faith in LOVE.

If you want someone to get well, do not ask for a doctor. Ask for health.

If you want the house to be cooler, don't ask for a wind, ask for the house to be cooler.

If you want a couple to have a baby, don't ask for a pregnancy. Ask for a happy healthy family

If you want more money to support your humble living, do not ask for a gambling win, ask for a small pension that will support your healthy living, healthy life of service. The universe will figure out where that pension will come from.

Rule Seven - To create more feeling, DRAW what you want.

If you want to live by the water, draw all the things that make you feel happy.

Spend time with your picture. Draw details and Color the picture

Add words, symbols and diagrams.

Words have power. The spoken word has more power.

Add the sun for warmth, add red heart shapes for love.

Add friends and family to enjoy your success

Make sure all the people you draw have big red hearts in their chest.

Friends and family can be holding hands.

Add more hearts in the air.

Love is what will bring the spell's intention

Take your time, focus on nothing but the love in your design.

Rule Eight – You CAN NOT bring selfishness into a place of Love and Truth.

Don't ask to be more beautiful. You can't be thankful and want more beauty.

Don't ask for more wealth. You can't be thankful and want more jewels.

Certainly, you can ask for a plentiful table of fresh, healthy food to share.

Certainly, you can ask for safety and security.

Certainly, you can ask for a warm place to sleep safely.

Certainly, you can ask for strength to do that which you know is good for you in the long term.

Don't ask for more love. You are just admitting that you're not loving yourself and those around you.

> A good first spell is to ask for guidance. Lead me to be Love's tools… while leading others to me in need of my special talents and gifts.
>
> Another good first spell is to ask for safety. Lead me toward Love's safe arms. Safe and Secure.
>
> Your first spell should be to ask for a sign that you're doing this all right. Don't tell the universe what that sign will be. You may notice that odd things are set up in your path in threes. Or, you may notice that birds act outside their nature while you walk by. You may notice that water is spilled while you are around. Multiple people will tell you the same thing using the same phrase. Some signs are so, very clear. Some are not. All of this depends on how well you connect in Love, Truth, Freedom, and Thankfulness.

Last step: Spells are dangerous

Be careful what you ask for!

Take a fresh look at your words and design.

Is this born of love? Do you feel love enough?

Do you feel free? Do you feel free enough?

Do you feel thankful? Are you truly thankful enough?

Is it selfless?

Is it all TRUE? Truth is just Love turned inside out. Can you see the truth?

Truth is on the other side of love.

If you harm none, do what you will.

The first time you evoke a spell, you'll need a dozen good women who see the truth above all. Women of water are best at this.

The time and date of your birth have no bearing on whether anyone is 'of the water', 'fire', 'wind' or 'Earth'. NO ONE is one-hundred percent any of those. We must all find our own talents and gifts. This is our 'nature'.

This leads into our next lesson: Know the truth first. Find the truth of your spell. Your intent is what is most important.

Knowing - the Truth Spell:

The other side of Love is Truth. Be sure you want to see. A witch, who is 'Of the Water' is helpful. A bowl of water, while holding it very still, will show you a reflection of the now.

Knowing - the Future Spell:

After truth of the present is accomplished, time forward with wind. A witch born 'with wind' is helpful. Lighting a row of candles, one at a time, each candle signifying a period of time. One candle per month or one candle per year will go forward. Blowing out candles will go back in time.

Love spells

There are no spells to make one specific individual fall in love with another specific person. You can however create the feeling of love in a man, but he will choose whose favor will attract him.

You can create a feeling of love in a woman but she is free to feel the path she must walk, and with whom.

A witch born of fire, and another born of air, is necessary.

Use embers of coal for a woman and add chips of wood to create flames, for a man. While chanting, drop water onto a hot skillet, watch and listen to the water sizzle into air, signifying the dissipation of any resistance a man might have to love freely and with abandon; concerns of his loss of freedom will change to understanding through his need for a loving family.

For a woman, the feeling of aloneness dries up; all that is left is hot passion and a place to cook and feed her family with warm love and caring meals. Add to the skillet butter and eggs.

Beware: Bringing a woman of air and a man of fire together may be a disservice to them and all the people around them.

Attracting wealth – spell;

You cannot differentiate between giving or receiving wealth.

Be sure that the give and receive are equal.

The GIVE should NEVER be a sacrifice.

Be sure that whatever you are ready to receive you are also ready to release

There are movements:

of giving an outstretched dominant (usually the right) hand

of receiving outstretched, non-dominant (usually left) hand

A witch of the air will chant with each inhale and then exhale.

A witch of the water will chant at the ocean's edge, feeling the waves and tide.

A witch of the earth will chant, barefoot, to the ever-changing waxing and waning, but unchanging moon.

A witch of the fire must understand that the fire both needs and takes our air and in turn, gives heat. If a witch of fire is chanting a give and receive spell, no witch of air must be near.

The chants should loosely be structured around the concepts of give and receive:

I give of myself, my talents, and gifts while searching for purpose.

I receive a modest income to sustain my humble living, to free my time to be dedicated to serve.

Special witches

Witches born 'of fire' that are particularly "bright" are said to be "of the sun". They are the best teachers.

This has nothing to do with the day you were born!

Witches born 'of water' who seem to also have an early ability of vision, are said to be "of the still water". They will see the present and see the real intent of the people around them. They are amused by those who lie. For they see the lie so clearly, they see the truth, and finally, they see the faulty yearnings.

Witches born 'of air' are the most volatile although they are the best leaders. The mood of air will greatly effect water and fire. Those born of air, if they can contain their emotions, can be ultimately the best creators of spells. They are referred to as "of the craft". They alone, will set the emotion, the tempo, the cadence with which the spell plays out.

Witches born 'of earth' who seem particularly introspect are said to be "of the body". These are the most powerful of all witches. When chanting with Air, Fire, and Water, they can summon and control the power of the all the elements and with practice, the entire universe. Air, Fire, and Water are too volatile. It is the calm of the earth that gives confidence to the power of Love to create and, evoke, bringing to fruition the intension of the spell with the best and most creative solutions. Witches of the body cannot be effected by the other elements. Only other witches of the Earth can bring change to another witch 'of the body'.

All women have the power if intention. Some more than others. Powerful witches have both a strong natural power and have been practicing with guidance from a witch born of the sun.

Warlocks have no power of their own. They can magnify power, change direction and increase intensity **but craft no power of their own**. Warlocks need a powerful, experienced witch from whom they can draw power.

Some Warlocks know they have power over people and events but have no idea their power comes from the women in their life. Their mother, wife, sister, or, on a rare occasion a daughter is the force he is using.

Male witches are not Warlocks. Male witches have powers just like witches. Male witches are very uncommon. Some call them Wizards. I have only met three male witches. One called himself a Wizard. He was a fun-loving, jolly elf-like character who loved a good party. The other was a Professor of Theology in a Catholic University. The other was a scary, dark force who reminded me of a dragon. He had bad breath that he could not mask and a sharp tongue. He was born under the sign of fire, but somehow he could master over both fire and ice. I know only that the forces of spring could dampen his hold on his intentions. He seduced young virgins as a matter of entertainment. He prayed on braggarts to watch them fall in shame. He changed his name as he moved from town to town. I know for sure he stayed at the Inn of Thomastown under the name Drake MacDiamond.

Chapter 25

Behold. Magic will again rock and roll.

On the train to Dublin, I'm captivated by this Diary.

I think about the book of Nostradamus' Elixirs from the 1500's and how, hundreds of years later, we know most of his recipes for medicines are definitely harmful. With research, science has come a long way, discovering which medicines will help, and which medicines will hurt. Most may help short-term but can easily ruin your life in addiction.

I know that a vitamin A deficiency will cause many serious problems, not the least of which is infertility. Taking a 'recommended' amount will cure you. I also know if you take too much vitamin A you can go blind. So the research on how much vitamin A to take each day is crucial to good health.

Similarly, this Diary of 'rules' and 'spells'… may be helpful, but also may be harmful. It's the syllabus I found in the copier, with its hundreds of years of research, I trust to follow.

I put away the Diary and move on to '*Land and Violence*', where Des Marnane examines the relationship between landlords and tenants in the 1800's. Apparently, Ireland's pastures and farmlands were owed by landlords who leased these pastures and farmlands to tenants who lived on, and worked these lands. Most of these leases were very long term.

A few Landlords received substantial loans, based on the rental income generated by these leases. These debts can out-weigh the value of the property and buildings. In addition to the pressure of the landlord's insolvency, there was a lot of tension and violence throughout Irish history because of the stresses of the 1800's; the great flood and the potato famine, to name just two, which incited fear and frustration that ultimately led to violence.

Then, I get to the paragraph that begins, "During this period, the surest way to have oneself certainly threatened, probably attacked, and possibly killed was to fall under the category of so-called "stranger". I spit out my tea. "...A person was likely to be deemed a 'stranger' if he dared to have unfairly gained access to either land or position." When I see Coach, I'll have to thank him again for taking me the safe way up to the castle.

Once I arrive at the hotel, I order dinner in. I want to spend more time with these books and my LiFT binder. I text the Alpha Girls, 'Please email me the 130 page document of Father Mathews'. Their email with attachment was immediate. Gotta love those twenty-somethings.

At some point around midnight, I'm fully immersed in Thomastown history and slowly fall into a Thomastown slumber.

I wake to full sun. I'm late. The alarm was set, but my phone is off. Dead.

I'm already in the shower when my phone is charged enough to register texts. I hear the text messages rolling in. Ugh!

The last text from Brooke. "MOM! Where are you? Hotel? Dead? CALL me!"

I text back. "Sorry. My alarm disabled, phone was dead. I'll meet you all at Guinness Tour. When?"

"MOM! We were about to check hospitals. You have to keep your phone charged!"

"When are you guys going to Guinness tour?" I ignore her motherly warnings.

"We're walking into lunch now. We'll be at the Guinness Storehouse for the tour in three hours. Then Plane. What flight are you on?"

Shit. I forgot to book a flight out. I have to pack and eat too. The hotel breakfast is closed by now. I probably passed by check out time too... Ugh!

I have received texts from my office as well. They're all wondering if I'll be in the office tomorrow. I read the list of clients who want to book appointments for my 'first day back'. I feel the pressure from all sides.

At the end of a deep breath, with eyes closed. "I love you." I say out loud, and take the time to find peace.

Now, fully composed, I call the front desk for an extended check out and decide to have a peaceful brunch. I'll ask the front desk for a name of a really cool restaurant. "I'm free to relax." I say out loud and decide to take my time getting ready with full makeup, curling iron, and jewelry too. "Thank you." I chant over and over for, calm, for Brooke, for a seat on a plane same day, for this crazy adventure, for my new friends...

Timing is everything. As I get out of the cab at the Guinness Storehouse, my troupe is on line to get in, directly in front of me.

"Mom, where have you been?" Brooke says.

"You look well rested, Joyce." Coach says, holding out his hand to help me over the ropes, to join the troupe.

As I take Coach's hand I look straight into his eyes with a smile... and ignore Brooke.

Once inside we begin with a walking tour which demonstrates the process of making beer. Guinness is made from only four ingredients, Hops, Barley, Yeast, and the most important ingredient, water from the hills of Dublin. Even though the Brewery is located on the banks of the River Liffey, the water used to brew Guinness is from the Wicklow Mountains, not far south of the brewery. Reportedly magical.

We all shuffle through the Guinness Store, and finally, belly up to a bar where we learn the proper way to pour a Guinness. Which is to fill the glass most of the way, then let it sit for a time, (a long time) while the foamy part rises to the top, only then top off the glass. Yes, the foam tastes a lot like whipped cream. We learn also how to draw a 'shamrock' design in the foam with the nozzle. Then finally, we get to pour our own beer and try our hand at creating the shamrock design in the foam. It's not easy.

After we find great seating (miraculously, room for us all) in the top floor observatory, which looks out on the entire city of Dublin, we decide that Chucky had the most accurate shamrock design.

Coach has not left my side since I stepped out of the cab.

As I show him my two middle fingers on my right hand, I complain loudly, so everyone can hear, "If I tap on these knuckles they tingle."

He sits up straighter, moves his hands between his legs, and fakes a blush. "Yes, Joyce. Me too."

We all laugh, and begin another afternoon of happy joyful conversation. I tell them about the diary.

"Brooke, I'm going to have to go soon." I say putting my arm around her shoulders.

"Yeah. I was thinking about that. It's kind of a waste for you to fly to Oxford for just one or two days, then fly back to the US. I can always bring your bag from the Oxford BNB, home with me. I'm only here one more week."

"I'm glad you offered because while I was at brunch I booked a flight back to Newark. Actually, I have to get to the airport soon, and first, I have to pick up my bag from the hotel baggage room." I add, "I love you."

"I love you back."

We hug a long, loving mom-and-daughter hug. "When you get my bag from the BNB, please find out where Dan lives and get his email address." I add, "That email address is important."

"Got it." Brooke says simply.

"OK troupe, our luggage is back at the hotel and we need to get to the airport. Let's get moving." Coach says.

We all begin to gather our coats and bags, when Chucky says, "Here's another euro-dime, Dad."

Kim says. "Joyce, we've all been finding dimes. Both yesterday and today."

"Brooke and Kim have been telling us about your incredible dime story." Coach says, as Chucky tosses the euro-dime he found onto the table.

"I have one as well." Andrew tosses another dime onto the table.

"I found an American dime as we were getting out of the cab, right here in front of the Guinness Storehouse." Angel says.

"I told them I found two euro-dimes in Nice, then you found one." Kim says.

"Has anyone found a nickel, penny, quarter, or any coins other than dimes?" I ask.

After a pause, I say, "I'm really not sure what that means. If it's a 'sign' I certainly don't know what the 'sign' is trying to say. I do know, that the probability of finding all these dimes in this limited time, is astronomical, to the point of being impossible. Certainly, especially as a student of Math and Science, I've come to this conclusion; there are forces in the universe, that I once thought impossible, to be possible."

"Well maybe, **that** is the message, then." Coach says loudly, then glances at Chucky who is grinning oddly.

Do they have a secret? Do they know more about this LiFT foundation then they're letting on?

I decide not to go down that uncomfortable conversational path, especially now, when I need to catch a taxi. "Let's Go." I say, instead.

On the way out, Kim whispers to me, "Did you catch that glance between Coach and his son?"

"I did, indeed. Do you think they planted those dimes?" I whisper back.

"No. I was there. Chelsea and I have been talking about that, but the circumstances just could not have been set up." Kim says.

"From what I can tell, our flights are just half-an-hour apart and at the same terminal. We'll see you there." Coach says to me, instead of good bye.

The troupe is already at the terminal bar when I arrive. The coach's back is to me. I come up behind him, very close to his ear, and say loudly, "Moo!"

The coach spits out a bit of Guinness and the troupe is again, laughing and talking over each other in jovial conversation.

"I've been thinking about what you said about your older daughter, Elizabeth." Coach says. "It's hard to believe anyone would hold onto their love and grace while wrongfully accused of any crime, much less murder and awaiting a fiery death." He pauses.

"We dubbed my Liz, 'Elizabeth the Kind Hearted'," I say, loudly, with some fan-fare, "when she was just two years old.

"I can assure you, Liz is one of those people who sees the best in everyone." Brooke says to the entire troupe. "She really sees none of the bad in anyone. I can tell you an hour's worth of stories enumerating her total blindness to the bad in people, but we don't have time." Brooke stands and raises her glass. "To my sister, Elizabeth, the Kind Hearted."

"To Elizabeth the Kind Hearted." We all stand and toast.

"I have to meet this girl." Coach says.

"Me too." Chucky agrees.

Kim and I catch each other's eyes. "We all should meet up next summer on Long Beach Island." Kim says with a smirk.

"We should be settling in by Mid-August." Chucky says.

We all get very quiet. During the pause we hear the second call to board my flight.

"Settling in where?" I ask, standing to get to my gate.

"I was accepted to Princeton for my graduate studies. I start in the fall. My Dad's moving too." Chucky says, obviously bewildered why his Dad didn't tell me this little tidbit of information.

We hear the announcement again as I turn to Coach. "New Jersey?" I ask simply.

"Yes." Coach says. He's standing now and takes a slight bow while looking directly into my eyes.

"Mom, you're going to miss your plane." Brooke says, as she pulls up the handle extension of my carryon and begins to move to my gate. "Let's go."

"O.K. Well good bye to you all." I say, "I'll see all you Alpha Girls this summer, yes?"

"Will the book be done by then?" Chucky asks, with total seriousness.

I stop. "Book?"

"Mom! There's no more line at your gate to board." Brooke is impatient.

"Yes." Chucky says, walking towards me. "I'll walk you to the gate." Then adds in rhythm.

"When this loving bell is tolled,

When her pure truth is sold.

When the untold, unfolds,

Then behold - magic will again rock and roll.

It means, when you write her book…"

I don't remember much of the plane ride or the car-ride home. In-fact I unpacked, and got ready for bed in a daze too.

The next day, I got a text from Brooke. 'I went to your BNB. There's still no guests. Didn't they say the rooms would be filed at some point these last two weeks? I emailed you Dan's Email address. He lives in Portugal, ALJEZUR.'

Chapter 26

Spoiler Alert!
Don't read this last chapter first. Really.

Really, don't read this chapter first.

In summary, I found that you don't get what you want, what you need or what you pray for. You receive who you 'are'. You 'are' what you consistently feel. You feel the thoughts on which you focus. So, use your free-will to focus on the people, sights, movement, smells, and sounds that inspire you to feel Love. Enumerate that which you are Thankful. Be Joyful, until those feeling become a habit. Your smile will light the way brightly.

Understand you are free. Whether you believe God gave us freedom-of-will or not, we can all agree that we possess free-will. With developed self-discipline, freedom is a blessing. Feeding your addictions will surely make your freedom a curse. Make a habit of doing the right thing so your self-discipline doesn't have to work so hard.

Discover your talents and gifts. Use these talents and gifts for good and not evil. Find projects where you love **both** the journey as well as the result. In that journey you'll find your purpose, and you will be deeply and truthfully satisfied.

This syllabus, which has been developed over the last 300 years, is simply an aid; tricks to help you fill your thoughts with love, freedom, and thankfulness.

Consistency wins this challenge. Write down your talents and gifts. Write down blessings for which you are thankful. Review and revise these lists constantly, consistently. When you go out into the world, change your internal dialogue to 'I love you' to all those you meet, and again, 'I love you' to yourself. Take care of yourself.

You'll attract unlimited health, unlimited financial wealth, and a troupe of loving characters which will surround your loving soul, ultimately, that will help you to find your path to serve, enabling you to live the rest of your days glowing with love and satisfied with every moment...

I learn too, the very real warning to be careful what you ask for and how you ask.

Whatever you believe to be true in this story, understand the thirty months of finding dimes was very real. I have the testimonies of many witnesses who were there, standing next to me while I lived through the impossible. Not an improbability, but in fact, statistically impossible. At the end of those thirty months, I had to admit and said out loud, "Yes, there are forces at work here that do not follow the natural laws of probability." At that moment, the dimes stopped showing up.

Was I attracted to them or were they attracted to me, or both? Did they manifest from the atoms around me? I don't know. All I know is that for thirty months, immediately after I read 'The Secret', I began finding dimes. No pennies, nickels or quarters. Dimes. Averaging twenty per month.

The wide spectrum of love that lives in the ether around you, is in you… lives through you and as you. Love yourself, take care of yourself.

I believe I didn't find this fantastic, bizarre, unbelievable but true story. It found me. The 'secrets' passed through me.

My Dad would say, I'm only the conduit through which this spark has passed.

We all are.

To Daddy, on Father's Day
June, 1981. (I was 22 years old)

Today I creep down to think in the dark
And there in the corner I notice a spark.

I remember a crystal, just one solitaire
Which must be reflecting a light from somewhere.

But there is no light in this room or this house
No streetlights or moonbeams could glow through those
clouds.

And yet this lone crystal has found from somewhere
A smidgen of light to reflect through the air.

I thinking back to my Dad, who has said through my life
He saw in me sparkles and moonbeams so bright.

Again, I reflect on the light that I see
And believe in my heart that the light comes from me.

So thanks to my Dad and all that he gives
For that light in my life is a reflection of his.

By: Your loving daughter, and three boxes of tissues.

The Curse of the Thomastown Castle.

One of my editors said, "'The Secret' convinced us we COULD invoke the powers of attraction, this book instructs us how."

My best friend said, "If DiVinci Code and Eat Pray Love had a baby… this would be it."

1735, by law, witchcraft was deemed no longer a crime that could be punished

1785 by law, it was deemed a crime to accuse someone of being a witch

THIS was in 1831

This family was so powerful, they owned many judges. So they brought one of their friend/judges up from Cork… and in 1831, not only was this poor sweet Nanny accused and found guilty but burned to DEATH!

Further, my BNB friend says the Nanny cursed his family, "to never realize their wealth'.

I found that was not the case, there is a twist ending to that.

My research shows this family hired this Nanny while they were in their winter home in the south of France. I went there. To Montpellier. Where I found. (This is where it gets even weirder)

Turns out the University of Montpellier… is where Nostradamus got kicked out of medical school. He went to study with a guy named Cezar to study meditation. Ultimately, Cezar's plantation and all his books were burned, Cezar was jailed and Nostradamus went back to Montpelier to research, and this is a quote from book only recently translated into English, (YES I know, it is just ridiculously unbelievable. But I have cited books from experts, pictures, videos, quotes from people who were there with me during this journey…)

His mission was to research all matters of meditation dealing in the 'realms of medicine and magic'. Incredibly, this school is still operating, NO I could not find the school, but I did stumble on the school's website and found a syllabus, now focusing on meditation and the keys to awaken the natural laws of attraction.

ww.LiFT.foundation

In summary, I found that you don't get what you **want**, what you **need** or what you **pray for**. You receive who you 'are'. You 'are' what you consistently feel. You feel the thoughts on which you focus. So, use your free-will to focus on the people, sights, movement, smells, and sounds that inspire you to feel Love. Enumerate that which you are Thankful. Be Joyful, until those feeling become a habit. Consistency wins the battle.

Go to the website to get more info. It's totally FREE. There's NOTHING for sale.

I hope you read and enjoy my book. Even though some of the names of the people I met have been changed, and the four years of my research and travel have been condensed to three weeks where I'm running around Europe with a troop of Oxford graduate students, The historical FACTS are 100% true. One of my friends said it's as if the "DIVINCI CODE met EAT PRAY LOVE

I'm not a writer, or English major, I've never written a book before… I'm a CPA with a 35 year practice. I **believe** I didn't find this fantastic, bizarre, unbelievable but true story. The story found me.

My Dad would say, I'm only the conduit through which this spark has passed. The Curse of the Thomastown Castle, I hope you enjoy it.

About the Author

Burgess Bartlett

Yes, I understand, this story is literally unbelievable. I've posted on YouTube and JayBirdPartners.com, (the publisher's website), pictures and videos of my journey and even testimonials from those who have witnessed these incredibly implausible events.

Some of you will still choose not to believe, but for those who see truth and follow… your life will never be the same.

If enough of you follow, the world will never be the same.

I'm not a writer. I'm an accountant with a thriving practice, who came upon an incredible, compelling story. I see clearly now, I didn't find this story, this story found me. I'm merely a conduit of Love, Truth, Freedom and Thankfulness.

We all are.

Joyce and her daughter, Elizabeth 'the Kind-Hearted', work together in their accounting practice in south Jersey, while her youngest daughter, 'Brooke', (shown here) continues graduate studies in California near San Francisco.